COULTER MEN BOOK 2

ELIZABETH SECKMAN

This is a work of fiction. Names, characters, places, and incidents are products of the author's imagination or are used fictitiously and are not to be construed as real. Any resemblance to actual events, locations, organizations, or person, living or dead, is entirely coincidental.

World Castle Publishing, LLC
Pensacola, Florida

Copyright © Elizabeth Seckman 2012
ISBN: 9781938961663
First Edition World Castle Publishing, LLC December 15, 2012
http://www.worldcastlepublishing.com

Cover: Karen Fuller
Editor: Eric Johnston

Dedication

To Dixie

Thanks for the encouragement, the advice, and the inspiration.

Acknowledgements

Seeing my words in print is fun and exciting, but it would never be possible without the support of some awesome people.

Thanks to my husband and my boys...I am grateful for your tolerance of my really long "just a minutes". To my mother, Caroline Hartman, for just being the best mom a girl could ask for. To my other sister, Lisa, for being a good sport and thickening my hide. To my brother, Dennis, for always being a good man. (Still grateful to you too, Cathy!) My nieces, Kari and Stacey, I'd be crushed without you ladies helping with the heavy lifting.

A special thanks to the people of New Martinsville and my church, there is no better place to live...even if there isn't an ocean. And to my hometown of Middlebourne...more like a family gathering than a place on a map.

A thousand thanks to Celeste for her prayers and input. Thanks again to my beta readers who read the rough stuff...Sandy, Sonya, Kari, and Cathy. Special thanks to Donna, the best volunteer editor a writer could find.

And of course, continued gratitude to Karen Fuller of World Castle, book publisher and dream maker. And a special thanks to Eric Johnston, editor, for putting the polish on the words.

And for my favorite people on earth...readers! Thank you from the bottom of my heart. Without you, the work is pointless. I'd love to hear from you. You can find me on Facebook at Elizabeth Seckman, Author; on my blog, "Use Your Words..." (eseckman.blogspot.com); or email me at eseckman@ymail.com.

Blessings,
Elizabeth

Chapter 1

Craig Coulter drifted through his party with one thought: he should have kept the damn fish. Moved by a rare moment of humanity, he had looked into its unblinking eyes and felt pity on the finned beast. Hooked and vulnerable, its life resting in the palm of his hand, he gave the creature a toss and watched it swim away. Now, as he looked around at the revelers in his yard, he couldn't help but think fresh trout and cold beer would have been a much deserved consolation for the intrusion.

He felt duped. He simply wanted to be alone, preferring to click off another year on his life calendar in the company of no one. Why was that so hard for people to comprehend? Knowing his requests for solitude would be ignored, he had thought he had outsmarted them all with careful planning and ruthless execution. His answering machine caught all the calls from his family, he called off work, and he headed to the mountains before daybreak to avoid well-intentioned friends. When night fell, he came home assuming he could fall into bed alone, but someone had a different idea.

And he knew exactly who. It didn't take Craig long to find him hiding in the shadows where the tiki torches and bonfire couldn't cast a glow. Ron Stiles was closer to Craig than family ever could be, but no one would ever mistake them for brothers. Craig was tall, dark haired, and white. Ron was short, bald, and black. As Craig approached, Ron grinned and held his arms out like he deserved a hug. Craig scowled.

1

"Hey, Ron," Craig said through clenched teeth and a snarl of a smile. "What the hell's going on, *buddy*?"

Ron's eyes danced with mischief, and his natural smile broadened. He wrapped an arm around Craig. "Look here, man, you're my boy. Have been since we were what, sixteen? And it's your birthday, and I know you're getting old…but you're not so damned old that you need to be as grumpy as you are. What the hell, man? Fishing all day for your big 3-0? I figure you can do that when you turn freakin' ninety or something. For now, you party."

"I don't feel like a party. Thought I was pretty clear on that."

Ron shrugged. "Yeah, well, I didn't listen. Besides, I have to save you. This, um, relationship dry spell is eating at your soul, and, you know I love ya, but," Ron rolled his eyes, "*all* your bitching is getting old. I just wanted to get you out and get you mingling. That's all."

"I don't bitch."

"The hell you don't!" Ron laughed and looked to the sky. "My God, *you* are like hanging out with my gramps. Get you some diabetes and start yanking your drawers on up to your freaking man boobs and you two'd be twins. And I love ya man, but you need a change of pace. And for God's sake, you got to quit blaming yourself and…."

"Shut up, Ron. You're in deep enough shit. I told you no party. I explicitly said no party, no anything." Craig looked around his yard, cringed as people moved in and out of his house. He rubbed the back of his neck and wondered when this stopped being fun.

Ron touched his heart with his hand. "See what I'm talking about? Telling me, your best bud, to shut up? Come on man, who saved you when you first arrived at Trent Academy? The commandant would've had you doing push-ups till your arms fell off if I hadn't taught you to survive, and you know it." He leaned closer to Craig. "You know man, you never knew when to just ease up and go along. It's up to me to guide you, and since *I* have a better feel for your *emotional* state than you do… tonight… you are going to enjoy some entertainment." Ron shoved a six pack in his hands then turned him toward the crowd. "Now get out of here. No more bitchin', start livin'."

Ron gave him a push. Craig turned to argue, but Ron stuck his fingers in his ears like a child and repeated, "stop bitching," till Craig shook his head and huffed, "You're a dick, Stiles," and then stormed off.

"Happy Birthday, buddy," Ron called.

Craig flipped him off over his shoulder and kept walking.

"I love you too, man," Ron yelled.

Craig rolled his eyes and clutched the six-pack. A couple of years ago, he would have loved the opportunity to drink too much, dance too close, then end the evening with a girl whose name he'd likely not remember in the morning; but not anymore. He supposed it was maturity. He opened a beer and decided the problem might be that he was simply bored. There was nothing new to this scene to spark his interest.

The fire dancing across the logs offered him more entertainment than anything. He stood mesmerized by the flicker until a timber crackled, snapped, and broke in two. It sent a spray of fire to the heavens then settled back down into the bon fire. The lowered flames cleared his view to the other side. A woman stood across from him. There was nothing special about her that would normally catch his eye, but catch it, she did. She was pretty, not drop-dead gorgeous, but cute. Perfect little button nose, petite body, with rounded curves that couldn't be hidden by the baggy jeans she was wearing. Her chin-length chestnut hair looked soft, so soft his fingers itched to touch it and find out for himself. Same with her lips, they looked smooth and supple, perfect for….

Whoa, he thought with a shake to his head. Maybe the drought was dehydrating his brain. Maybe his friend was right. Maybe he should take the opportunity to break his fast. He looked around his party. He scanned each of the ladies there and trusted his years of experience to accurately locate the ones who would likely warm his bed with the least amount of effort.

Then his eyes returned to her.

She would never be easy pickings and since he refused to lie or make false promises, she would probably never be the kind of girl he could bed, but still he couldn't stop staring. He was boldly fascinated.

And she never noticed. She evidently wasn't looking for company, because she never looked around. She stood in that crowd of people all alone, hands stuffed in her sweatshirt pocket. He wondered if she too was dragged here against her will. He was about to brave the other side of the fire when she pulled her phone out of her pocket and spoke into it, covering her open ear with her hand to block the party noise. She closed her eyes for just a moment and then shook her head. She snapped the phone shut and then returned to her original position... head bent, shoulders slumped, hands hidden. She chewed on her cheek. A tear fell. She wiped it away quickly. She looked across the party, took a single step back, turned, and walked away.

He followed, sticking to the shadows.

She sat on his porch. Her phone buzzed again. She sighed hard, but answered. He felt bad for eavesdropping, but not bad enough to stop. Besides, who ever confused him with a gentleman?

"No. You're lying." She leaned against his porch pole. "Please, tell me you and Meggie are pranking me." She covered her eyes with her hand. "Oh, this is so much worse than bad." She removed her hand. "Can you make sure Mom and Dad don't see?" She leaned forward. "Why would she call and tell them? Oh, dear God... I think I may vomit." She listened a minute, then shook her head. "Hell no. I don't want to come home... especially not now...no I don't want to talk to... hi, Mom." Long silence. "Joanie just thinks she's funny." Her hand twisted in her hair. "I'll talk to her." Head nod. "I can take it down as soon as I get off here...I know her password." Silence. "Why would I want to come home now of all times? I don't care if it offends him or not...I did just talk to him...It was just a joke. No big deal...I'm not under stress. Please, it's nothing. I just want to enjoy my vacation." She closed her eyes and rubbed her forehead. "Mom...Mom...please stop crying." Her voice was quiet, soothing. "Mom. Listen. Everything will be fine. I'm fine. I feel fine." She took a deep breath, said her love yous, and hung up the phone. She was doing something on her phone when it rang again, and again, and again. She responded to each call with the same response, "You know Joanie. She thinks she's a riot." Then she would hang up, then answer, and repeat. Her voice was becoming more strained and brittle with each call. He could feel her frustration, and without thinking, he stepped out of the shadows and ordered, "Just turn off the damn phone."

She looked up at him with the biggest, most vulnerable eyes he'd ever seen. They looked as rich as melted chocolate, and he guessed they were the windows for something far sweeter. "But," she managed.

He sat beside her on the porch. "It's driving you crazy. Just shut it off."

She looked at her phone. It lit up and buzzed in her hand. She looked at him like a deer trapped in a car's head lights. He took the phone from her and killed the power.

She stared at her now quiet phone, "Thanks."

"You're welcome." He pulled a bottle out of the carrier. "Beer?"

"Sure…I guess."

Craig opened it before handing it to her. He held his up for a toast. "Here's to ignoring problems for a peaceful life."

She clinked bottles and laughed a little. "Is that your motto, or just tired of hearing me whine on the phone?"

"You weren't whining, but yes, I have made avoidance an art form. I am the master." He drank his beer and grinned at her. His voice was rich, like a roughened purr, and she suspected he had just a hint of a southern drawl. He reached out with his empty hand. "Craig Coulter, you are?"

"My name?" she said barely above a whisper. Her heart sped up when her small, cold hand touched the large, warm one of the gorgeous man across from her. His face was shadowed from the dusk to dawn light that glowed behind him, but she had seen him earlier tonight. He stood a head taller and burned several degrees hotter than most men. He had black hair and a firm square jaw. His

5

features were perfect, yet rugged enough not to qualify as pretty. She couldn't help but remember his body was firm, athletic. The man neared perfection. The realization made her blush deepen as she reluctantly pulled her hand back and squeaked, "Mollie. My name's Mollie."

"You from around here, Mollie?"

Mollie shook her head no. She suddenly couldn't think of words. She'd already forgotten his name. No, she didn't, she thought. It was Craig. Craig something. Craig the lumberjack with his big brawny arms and... she took a long drink. She was getting warm. She looked at Craig. He was a fully developed man, one that was way out of her league.

"So, where are you from?" he asked, evidently unaware of the pain she was under trying to think in his presence.

"Pittsburgh. In Pennsylvania."

Craig laughed. It was a low rumble. "I'm aware."

Mollie shook her head. "I'm sorry, it's been a *really* long night."

"I heard." He drained his beer and dropped it back into the carton. "So, how did you wind up in Windham, Montana? Not exactly a vacation resort."

"That's a long story."

"Entertain me," he said smoothly as he opened another beer.

Mollie blushed. "Well, we were touring Custer Park, and we got a flat tire. This state trooper helped us fix it, and he invited us to this party, and we came."

"That's not a long story." Craig looked at his beer. "I'm not even one drink in."

"I guess it's not...I'm sorry." Mollie blushed.

"You're quite beautiful when you're flustered. Anyone ever tell you that?"

Mollie laughed. "No. Never."

"Well, you are."

Mollie rolled her eyes.

"You saying I'm lying?"

"I didn't say anything."

6

"You rolled your eyes."

"Well." Mollie picked at her beer label. "That's just because I know better. But it's nice of you to feel sorry for me."

"Why would I feel sorry for you?"

"Because you overheard my phone calls."

"You were fighting with your mom. What else is new?"

"I wasn't fighting with my mom," Mollie explained. "She was just worried about me."

"Oh. Well, for the record, pretty lady, I could only hear your end of the phone conversation, and I heard nothing that made me think you needed my pity."

"Oh." Mollie bit her lip. "I guess I should say thank you then."

They drank in silence a moment. Then Craig said, "I know it's none of my damned business, and you can tell me so, but what the hell was all that about? And why does a beautiful woman at a party look like her dog died?"

Mollie looked out across the people laughing and having fun. "I guess pouting on a porch does make me look like a real ass."

"I didn't say that."

Mollie blinked back tears. Craig frowned. He looked off into the night at the moths dancing in the light. He said gently, "This is my house. House rules are if you cry, you are obligated to tell me why."

Mollie laughed a little. "You really want to know?"

Craig nodded. "I really want to know."

"Okay." Mollie thought a minute, then started her tale with, "I have a friend who is totally moronic, childish, inconsiderate, thoughtless, and," Mollie paused a moment before adding, "feel free to add in any other word that means lame, stupid, ignorant, callous, rude, crude... well, I think you get my point."

"Sounds like the bitch pissed you off."

"She is. And I am."

"So, what did she do?"

Mollie took a drink. "Joanie, that's my friend, has a blog. She calls it Horn Dogs and...."

"What's a blog?"

7

"Kind of like an online diary on the internet. One that's open to the whole world."

"I see, and this blog pertains to you...."

"In that Joanie blogged about my needing to heal over the summer from the heart ache of my break up, henceforth this road trip. Then she goes on to add that I'm still just too moody, so she is going for plan B... and that is...oh, lord, Joanie...I could just kill her." Mollie took a drink. She lowered her voice to a whisper. "Joanie wrote that I needed to, you know, hook up with some guy...that she and Jack, my blond friend with that guy you called Ron...." She pointed toward the fire.

"Trouble making Ron."

"So anyhow, my friends, Jack and Joanie, worked out this arrangement that they would fix me up with some guy tonight...which makes me mad, cause I hate hook-ups...but to make it absolutely horrible... Joanie blogs it...she actually blogged that I need to get laid!"

"Now the story gets better." Craig laughed. "Now I have to wonder, who's the lucky guy?"

"Could be anyone." Mollie waved her hand across the crowd.

Craig shook his head. "Might want to have your friends check. He might have died in a car wreck on the way over, cause that's the only thing I can imagine that would stop a guy from a sure thing with you."

Mollie gasped. "I'm not a sure thing. I never agreed to this. I never even knew what was going on until my little sisters called to read me her post. Oh Lord. Trust me, had I known, I would never have come here."

"So you came, but you didn't know you were here for a date until just now?"

"Exactly. *All* of my family in P.A. heard the news before I did. Oh, mark my words, when I get hold of those two at the hotel tonight? They're going to get it. I have half a mind to fly home and leave the both of them." Mollie sighed and stuck out her lower lip. "Honestly, I totally don't want to be home right now either. This all just stinks." Mollie took another swallow. "Joanie actually wrote that the cop who fixed our flat, what's his name?"

"Mitch," Craig answered.

"Yeah, Mitch. She wrote that the cop promised her that he had a friend who could seduce a nun, and Joanie thought that was just great because *my problem* stemmed from a lack of variety in my life…and oh, what did she write, that I needed to trade boys for men…a good mind blowing, well you know, that was the balm my broken heart needed…and Mitch's friend would be eager too because it's his birthday. Sooo, Mr. Birthday, Mr. Don Juan himself, gets laid, I get such great sex that I forget *all* about my problems, and everybody wins."

"And that's on the internet?"

"Well, it was until five minutes ago when I deleted it."

"Too bad, would've made an interesting read."

"Trust me. Enough people read it." Mollie drank her beer. "Including my mother."

"Ouch."

"Yeah. Ouch." Mollie picked at the label. "And to make it all worse…my fiancé, well my ex-fiancé, called me and was kind enough to point out that he didn't think he should be blamed for all my troubles, and that it's not his fault I'm a frigid little bitch. I mean, my gosh, of all the things Joanie wrote about, the only thing he gave a damn about was the fact that his prowess was threatened?"

Craig laughed. "He didn't worry about you meeting Mr. Don Juan?"

Mollie paused, and then said, "No, he didn't, and I guess he was right not to be concerned." Mollie sighed. "I don't see anyone lining up to take a crack at the ice queen. Maybe Justin is right. There probably *is* something wrong with me." Her eyes glistened with unshed tears. She bit her lip and willed them to go away.

Craig looked at her, then up at the stars and said with a sigh. "I suppose I would have to agree."

Mollie let out a wide-eyed gasp. She couldn't believe he just said that to her face. She expected him to think it, but expected

9

propriety to stop him from saying it. She didn't know how to respond to such honesty. Her mouth hung open, but no sounds came out.

Craig looked back at her and shifted his body closer. He took her by the chin and turned her face to his. He moved her hair away from her ear and leaned in so close she could feel the heat of his body. "You definitely have a problem." His lips were warm against her ear as his whisper sent electric current down her spine. "Your problem is… you *haven't* been with the right man." A puff of warm breath made the skin on the back of her neck tingle." His voice dipped low and husky, "Tell me, Mollie, when he kisses you, does he do this?" His hand wound its way into her hair, tugged gently, and tipped her head back until she was looking up at him. "Does he touch this very tender spot right here?" His finger trailed lightly across her throat. She closed her eyes and licked her lips. His lips returned to her ear. "Does he remember to tell you how beautiful you are?"

Mollie shook her head no.

"That's a shame." His lips descended toward hers, and then stopped, barely brushing them. "You are definitely beautiful."

Mollie swallowed. "Thanks," she whispered.

His hand cupped her chin. Strong fingers stroked against the pulse that now hammered in her throat. His kiss was sweet, gentle.

Mollie's first thought was to pull away from him. She didn't even know this man. But she didn't…couldn't. It felt too…right.

He lifted his head and smiled down at her. His thumb brushed against her bottom lip.

"I…I…don't normally…."

"Enjoy a kiss so much?"

"No. I…."

"…talk too much."

Molly didn't know what to say. Her voice lost, he pulled her close again, but this time his kiss wasn't gentle. His hand moved down her sweatshirt, pressing against her hot flesh. She gasped when she felt the warmth of his hands on her skin. Her body jerked as she gasped.

Craig winked down at her and smiled. "Can't blame a guy for trying, Mollie. It is my birthday."

Chapter 2

It took Mollie a full minute before her mind put his words together, but when she did; she took a suck of air and was up and off the porch in a second. Her body trembled. Her mind reeled from a night of constant injustice. She sputtered, got out a couple of incoherent phrases, and then abandoned the attempt at making a reasonable statement. She chose to flee instead.

Craig stood and stepped in front of her. "Please Mollie, I shouldn't have told you that…well at least not like that."

"Why do people think it's fun to make me look like an idiot?"

"I wasn't trying to do that. I swear to you, I never knew any of this until you just told me that story. You have to admit, it is ironic."

"Ironic?" she stammered. "That's how you see this? It's more like pathetic. What did they promise you? Did they say I was some kind of whore? Is that what you think? Well, start walking creep, 'cause it ain't happening."

"I swear. I didn't know," Craig professed.

Mollie snorted and crossed her arms over her chest. "Yeah right. Prick. Men are all pricks."

Craig reached out and took Mollie by the arm.

"Let go!" she demanded.

He ignored her protests, pulling her along with him to the bon fire where he looked for Mitch, but he found no sign of him. He headed for Ron instead. Mollie dragged her heels, but she couldn't stop him from bringing her along. "Ron." Craig's voice was harsh, clipped. Ron's head snapped at the sound, and he gave his friend his full attention. "What do you know about this?"

Ron's eyes were big as saucers. "I don't…buddy…you're going to have to give me more info."

"What did you and Mitch cook up?" He gave Mollie's arm a jerk and pulled her forward.

Mollie's friend, Jack, grabbed hold of Mollie's free arm and pulled. "Let go of her, you goon. Damned Neanderthal."

Craig let go. Mollie stood next to her friend and glared at Craig.

"You weren't in on this with Mitch to hook her and me up?"

"I have no idea what you're talkin' bout man. I've never seen her before in my life."

"Where the hell is Mitch?" Craig asked.

They looked around. He was nowhere to be seen; neither was Joanie.

Jack put an arm around Mollie and frowned. "I told Joanie to forget it. She still tried to set you up?"

"She blogged it. She blogged she was going to get me laid with…with…him." Mollie pointed to Craig.

"Look, I told you. No one ever told me anything about this," Craig said.

"Yeah right," Mollie spat. "Then why did you follow me?"

Craig looked at the people staring and shook his head. He grabbed Mollie again and pulled her forward until his face was nearly nose to nose with hers. "I already told you. I thought you were pretty."

"So all of this was just a coincidence? Out of all the girls here, you just happened to pick me? No one told you to come and talk to me?"

Jack cleared her throat. "I actually threatened Joanie with bodily harm if she fixed you up with this pig."

"Excuse me?" Craig turned to Jack. "What the hell? What have I ever done to you?"

Jack sneered. "I did my research."

Mollie blushed. "So, you really didn't come over and talk to me out of pity?"

"NO. I did NOT."

"Oh."

"Since then I've been called a pig, a Neanderthal, ah hell, what else?"

"She started with goon," someone close by offered with a grin.

Mollie's blush deepened. She stepped toward Craig and said quietly, "I'm sorry."

"You should be. I didn't deserve any of this. I saw you across the fire, and I wanted to meet you…."

"Really?" Ron said, his voice too cheerful.

"Stick to your guns, Mollie!" Jack insisted.

Mollie shook her head. She reached out and took Craig by the hand and walked him away from the crowd. Jack started to follow, but Mollie held up her hand. "Back, Jack." Jack hesitated, but in the end, she stayed where she was.

Mollie stopped walking when they were far enough away not to be heard by everyone. "I really am sorry. I was a bit mean."

"Yes, you were," Craig answered like a petulant child.

Mollie laughed. "All right then…I'm sorry. I should never have assumed the worst of you, though given my history with men, the worst is to be expected."

"I could say the same about women."

"Really? I'm really, truly sorry. I made all kinds of assumptions, and I don't even know you….and I'm sorry about whatever woman broke your heart. I understand…"

Craig coughed as if choking on laughter. "Stop. Stop. Please, Mollie, don't feel sorry for me. I'm lying to you. I've never been hurt by a woman, and I've definitely never had a broken heart."

"For real? Not ever; not even once?"

Craig shook his head. "Never."

"You're teasing."

"Not at all." He tucked his hands in his pockets. "You see, I've found that women think every encounter leads to love. Men don't."

Mollie's eyebrow raised. "That's rather sexist."

Craig winked at her. "Ah, ah Mollie…you already called me a prick on my birthday. Don't make it worse."

15

Mollie's mouth dropped. Craig gently pushed her chin till her mouth closed. "I'm only saying men aren't always looking to fall in love; women are. Would you have sex with me tonight just because it seemed like the thing to do at the time, even if you knew it would lead nowhere? Would you have sex with me with absolutely no intention of calling me in the morning?"

"No," Mollie answered.

"Go ask the people to give a show of hands of how many of them would take the offer of no strings sex. I bet the guys outnumber the girls…hell, I doubt you'd get a single female to raise her hand."

"Ha! You're wrong! My friend Jack would. So there went your stereotypes down the toilet."

"A rare exception. If she really means it."

"Oh, she means it."

"Is she straight?"

"Of course. What a question!"

Craig shrugged. "Well she evidently thinks like a guy… and her name is Jack."

Mollie laughed. She'd never really thought of Jack being a guy's name. "It's really Polly, but she just isn't a Polly."

"So, why Jack?"

"Because she's leveled more wood than a lumberjack."

Craig said nothing. Mollie gasped. "I didn't just say that, did I?"

"You did." Craig smiled.

"I can't believe I told you that! You're a bad influence. I can't believe I said that."

Craig touched her cheek. "You're blushing aren't you?"

"Why of course I am. Nobody knows why we call her Jack, and by leveled; I don't necessarily mean in a sexual way. I mean she has brought them to their knees…you know leveled them."

Craig chuckled. "Better stop, Mollie. You're digging deeper."

Mollie thought of her words. "Oh, lord, you're right."

Craig wrapped an arm over her shoulder. "You're the best present I could've gotten tonight. I never thought when I first pulled

16

in, saw all the trespassers on my property, that I'd find a single damned thing to be happy about. Thank you. You're a breath of fresh air."

Mollie pressed cool hands against flaming cheeks. "I suppose it was the least I could do after attacking you."

"You're right. That is the least you could do." He touched his hand to his heart. "I'm still rather hurt. I think you should agree to go out with me. I think I deserve at least that much from you."

Mollie hesitated. Was it proper? Things were barely over with Justin…sort of. She liked Craig, was intrigued by the thought of an actual date with him…and she couldn't deny that was the best kiss she'd ever had or even dreamed of having. However, he was still a stranger, and she was still possibly, technically in some sort of screwed up situation. Wasn't it smarter to end one relationship before starting another? *Relationship*? She shook her head. Craig was right, she was assuming every date must lead somewhere else. Couldn't she just go out with a guy because he was fun and nothing more?

You can't turn me down on my birthday."

"True; and it is just a date…."

"Don't sound so enthused. You've already thought the worst of me. Now, you're hesitating to take my offer like you're debating between going out with me or making a dental appointment. That's enough to make an old man feel like he's being put out to pasture."

"Old man? You're crazy. You don't look old."

"There must be some reason why you don't want to go out with me."

"Oh, no." She grabbed the hand that hung loosely from her shoulder. "It's me…I just didn't know…I just, well you caught me by surprise and…."

He put a finger on her lips and grinned, "Shh Mollie, don't worry about it. I'm just teasing you. I know why you hesitate."

"Really, you do?"

"You're in the middle of shit with some guy. I understand. I think you're interesting, and I'd like get to know you better. It's no big deal. So, if it causes you problems, forget it."

17

"No it's not that, completely. I'm also not sure how long Joanie and Jack planned to stay in Windham before moving on, but considering Joanie is lucky if I let her live, and it's Jack's car...I suppose staying around here is doable." She smiled and rocked on her heels with excitement. "I'd love to go out with you, Mr. Coulter. As a matter of fact, let me give you my number." Mollie dug through her purse for a scrap of paper. "And to be perfectly honest, I just never dreamed you'd be interested."

"Then you evidently don't look in too many mirrors."

Mollie felt herself blush again. She bit her lips to stop the compliment from making her grin from one ear to the other. She pulled out a pen. "Pen, no paper. May I write it on your hand?"

"Of course." He moved his arm from her shoulder and held out his hand.

She cupped his hand in hers and wrote her number with shaking hands. She hoped he thought it was the cold that caused her to tremble. Would he know it was the warmth of his hand and her desire to not let it go that made her heart race and her body shiver?

She was relieved when he asked, "You cold? We could go inside."

Mollie didn't have time to answer before Ron and his friends came toward him carrying a big cake and singing happy birthday. They came like a swarm and dragged him to the fire. He looked back at Mollie. She waved good-bye and smiled as he was closed in by the crowd.

Jack emerged from that crowd. She looked concerned. "Molls, people are calling me asking if you're all right? What's going on?"

"It's that blog of Joanie's."

"What a twit. I should bust her lip for this."

"Let it go, Jackie...it's over and done."

Jack didn't look convinced. She looked back at the crowd. A stripper popped out of the cake. Jack rolled her eyes and said with a sigh, "I'm bored. I'd rather be sleeping. Mind walking back to the hotel with me?"

Mollie thought about Craig, then decided he was busy. Besides, he had her number. If he wanted to call her, he would. She agreed, and they walked off into the darkness, down the road that lead to the one story cinder block building that was their hotel. Mollie stopped in the gravel parking lot and looked around. "Joanie took your car. Where do you think she went?"

"Hell if I know." Jack looked around. "Her and that Mitch guy are kind of weird…I mean who meets some stranger and goes all bonkers like that? I mean it's bad enough that we drove two hours out of our way for this little shit hole."

Mollie grinned as she unlocked the door. "I'm kind of enjoying it."

"Seriously? Why?" Jack asked.

Mollie stepped into the room and lay down on the bed. She giggled. "Craig asked me out on a date."

Jack sat on the bed next to her. "You've got to be kidding me, right? Mollie, this guy is a creep. Joanie really was going to set you up, but I ran a background check on him, and he's not the kind of guy your parents would approve of."

"You did what?" Mollie laughed, not at all shocked by her friend's overprotected response.

"I ran a background check. You can get anything over the internet."

"I understand that, but why?"

"Because at first the idea of hooking you up with someone other than Justin was so appealing. And I figured any guy that wasn't the fantabulous Mr. Bell was acceptable, but then I had to be rational. Your parents expect that of me, you know? So, I checked him out. His juvenile record is sealed. You know what that means, right?"

"You two have something in common?"

"No," Jack moaned, "mine aren't sealed. It means there is something there that needs to be hidden; something bad. I also found a Facebook page that is dedicated to him, called 'I Hate Craig Coulter.' And it has over four hundred friends. That's a lot of hate, Mollie."

"Sounds like a bunch of girls like Joanie. Who makes a hate club past the age of twelve?"

"True, but still...."

"Oh well. Doesn't matter. If he calls, I'm going out with him. Life's short my friend." Mollie threw her purse on the hotel chair and dug through her bag for her pajamas. She looked to the suddenly quiet Jack and saw the tears in her eyes.

"They told you, huh?"

Jack bit her lip.

"Jack, I'll be fine. They're just overly cautious because I had cancer as a kid. If you had found the lump; then they'd probably do nothing. Since it was me; they cut it out and test it. That's all. I'm fine."

Jack smiled. "I know. I know." Jack grabbed her night clothes. "I just can't believe how much shit has happened to you in the last month. It just sucks."

"Things are looking up."

"Are you talking about Paul Bunyan, aka, Craig the Neanderthal?"

"You're funny, but he does rather put me in mind of Paul Bunyan. Dark hair, broad shoulders, mmm, a girl could spend all day dreaming of that."

"Now that just scares me, Molls. I've never seen you like this. You're almost giddy, and you don't even know anything about this guy. I just can't help wondering...rebounds often cloud the vision, and it's not even been a month."

"You don't have to remind me. Trust me. I know how long it's been. I know how pitiful I must look, but honestly, all that seems like a lifetime ago. Heck, Jack, it doesn't even feel like that was real. Seems more like a bad dream. Now I'm awake and I want to live. I have the chance to do something spontaneous, and it feels so good."

"Mollie, this guy *might* just be after sex."

"I'm a big girl, Jack."

"But he could be a real pig."

"Then *I* will figure that out."

"I just hate to see you get your heart broken—again."

"One date won't lead to heart break."

20

"You're not a one-nighter kind of gal, Molls."

Mollie shrugged. "He makes me feel alive. That's enough for right now. I will deal with later when later comes."

Jack nodded slowly without much commitment to the agreement. "Please, just be careful."

"I will. Remember, Jackie, I am the Unsinkable Mollie Hinkle."

"Let's just hope Craig isn't your iceberg."

"He's not. He's the strong, out-doorsy type, with a big warm heart. Nothing like an iceberg. Besides, no one who loves his dog like he does could be a totally bad guy."

"What dog? I didn't see a dog. He told you he had a dog?"

"No," Mollie answered as she disappeared into the bathroom. "I just figured he's the dog type."

Jack shook her head and sighed. "If they have a third leg, they're the dog type."

Mollie emerged from the bathroom changed and ready for bed. "Ha, ha. You're such a word smith. Maybe you should write with Joanie."

"Shit. Joanie. I suppose I should see if she's all right." Jack pulled her phone out of her pocket. "Of course, the battery is dead."

"Use mine." Mollie tossed her phone on the bed. Jack turned it on. "You have twenty three messages."

"Ignore them all," Mollie said flatly.

She sat by Jack and touched up the paint on her toe nails as Jack talked. Evidently Joanie would be back late.

Jack hung up. "Seems Joanie and her new man are driving somewhere to see something."

"That's all she told you?"

"No, she named names, but I didn't really give a damn."

"Aren't you worried about her?"

"No. I do worry a little about my car, but not about Joanie. She's a cat. Cats always land on their feet."

"Funny, Jack."

"Trite but true." Jack was about to reach for the remote when Mollie's phone rang. Jack flipped it open and answered, "Mollie's phone, yeah…just a sec."

She handed the phone to Mollie with a shake of her head. "Timber."

Chapter 3

They woke a little past one in the afternoon. Mollie was up first. She ransacked her suitcase, tossing clothes from her bag to the hotel chair.

"What should I wear, Jack?"

Jack rolled over and tossed an arm over her eyes. "A chastity belt."

"Come on. Wake up and help me. We agreed. I'm an adult. Remember?"

"I don't recall coming to any agreement of the sort."

"Well, then consider it a decree. Now help me."

Jack lifted her arm just a bit and cast her friend a skeptical look. "I'll help because I like to see you happy. I just wish I could shake the feeling that this isn't going to end well."

Mollie ignored Jack's ominous mood. "Just think, all of this might be destiny. I mean last night, he was drawn to me when I needed someone the most; like some sort of cosmic destiny. They say God puts…."

"Now you see why I worry?" Jack threw her hands in the air. "Dump the bullshit, Molls, or I'll have you committed. Cosmic destiny…sounds like a name for a nuke. So, where is Mr. Bunyan taking you?"

"Dinner at his house," Mollie answered.

"You're joking, right?" Jack froze and shook her head.

"No. The closest place for dinner is an hour away, and he gets up at five a.m. for work."

"Oh, God. You do realize that a man asking you to dinner at his house, on a first date, is a euphemism for 'come on over baby, my pecker's hard'?"

"Seriously, Jack, you're truly annoying me with this." Mollie planted her hands on her hips. "I am *not* a child. I am *not* fragile. Please, I came with you guys to get *away* from all the pity and protection. Keep it up and I'll...."

Jack dropped her head like a whipped pup. "You're right. Let's have a look in your suitcase."

Jack helped her put together an outfit: a tee shirt and bib overalls. "Are you sure? What about the halter dress? It always caused Justin to do a double take."

"No, definitely go more casual. You don't want to look like an uppity city girl do you?"

"No." Mollie stared at the outfit Jack had chosen with a frown. She'd only brought it in case they went hiking. It wasn't exactly date wear.

"It's perfect. Remember, you've already agreed to a very casual get-together. If you show up dressed to the nines, it will totally give away that you are working hard to impress him. That gives him the upper hand. Go with, 'well, it was what I threw on this morning cause you didn't go to any effort to put together a real date, ya prick, so this is what you get'."

"All right," Mollie agreed half heartedly. She changed and checked herself out in the mirror. To her, the bibs seemed about as attractive as a burlap sack and hid most of the curves to her petite body. She chewed the side of her cheek as she looked herself over in the mirror. Maybe Jack was right. She did feel safer with casual and understated, especially when she remembered the way she responded to his kiss. He was a complete stranger to her and still her body warmed and melted to him without the least bit of restraint. It was only logic imposing self control that made her stop his hands from roaming all over her flesh.

Mollie plugged in her curling iron, using it first to smooth the suitcase wrinkles from the denim. Then she went to work on her hair. She was half done when the antique rotary dial hotel phone rang.

"I'll get it." Jack grabbed the phone and frowned at Mollie.

"Hello," Jack said into the receiver, her tone definitely bitchy.

"What the hell did you say your name was?"

Mollie gasped.

"Oh, right, Ron, how the hell did you get this number?"

Mollie came out of the bathroom to kick her and whispered, "Be *nice*."

Jack stuck out her tongue. "So, you can read. That's a plus. What else qualifies you to cold call a girl you hardly know and ask her out on a date? That is where you're heading, right? So, who are you sniffing out? Me, Mollie, or Joanie? Me? My, you *are* brave. A man who can read the phone book *and* is ballsy enough to challenge the dragon lady."

Mollie smacked Jack on the back of the head. "Stop being a shrew."

"What the— Damn, Mollie that hurt. Sorry, Ron, I'm being abused here. Look, I'd love to go out with you, but I have to keep Mollie company tonight."

Mollie shook her head and frowned.

"Oh, Mollie and Craig have a date, huh? No, she didn't mention that." Jack was quiet a moment, and then she sprang to her feet, lifting the phone base from the night stand and gestured with it as she talked, her voice rising, "The hell I am. I'm not intimidated by a little chicken shit man like you. Yeah, I know how to dance." Pause. "Bring it, Buddy. Hate to make you look pathetic, but I will." Pause. "Fine. One minute late and I'll kick your ass."

"He asked you out?"

"Yeah. You act surprised I can get a date."

"Seriously, Jack? You're a total bitch."

"I'm tired of games. Let all men be forewarned. No simpering damsel here."

"So, do you like him?"

"I don't even know him. Unlike some people, I reserve judgment until at least I've known a guy for more than twenty freakin' minutes."

"Speaking of fast first dates, what do you think about Joanie? She must be having one hell of a time. She didn't come back last night." Mollie returned to wrapping clumps of hair in the curling iron.

"I'll try her cell."

Pause. "No answer."

Mollie's worried face peered at Jack from the bathroom sink. "Should we phone the police?"

"For Pete's sake, no." Jack snorted and laughed. "Joanie is gone all night with a stranger. What else is new? Remember…Joanie…meow."

Mollie rolled her eyes and released another curl from the wand.

Jack searched through her own bag. She pulled on a size too small baseball shirt that stretched "Angel" across her ample bosom and a pair of ripped jeans.

Jack joined Mollie in the bathroom brushing her blond hair until it shined, then clipped it at the nape of her neck. She quickly applied her make-up and returned to the bed to wait on Ron.

"So, this guy—Ron—wouldn't it be great if he was the one?" Mollie asked.

Jack shot her a disgusted look. "I met him once. Are you feeling fourteen again? Why don't you settle for a Harlequin and leave the real men to the adults."

"Kiss it. I just think love at first sight would be…."

"A sorry case of co-dependence."

"Don't you want to fall in love?"

"Yeah, with Santa. He and love are both about as real."

"That's so sad," Mollie answered. "I believe in love."

"Really? Still? After the month you've had, you still believe in knights in shining armor and all that jazz?"

"Of course. Justin was one bad apple."

"They're all bad apples. Don't be taken by the sauce they smother themselves in. They are each and every one cut from the same cloth with one thought continuously on their minds—get laid. Think they're anything but…and you're headed for heartache."

"My dad's a good guy." Mollie challenged.

Jack was silent a moment. Her hard face softened. "Touché," she answered, but cut Mollie's victory short by adding, "I dare you to name one more."

Mollie's blank face brought a "hah-hah" and declaration of victory from Jack. Jack turned her attention from harassing Mollie to a box of food on the floor. She rummaged through it. "What's your choice…peanut butter and Ho-Ho's, or beanie weenies and Ho-Ho's? I'm so ready for a hot meal. Maybe I can get that guy to stop somewhere with plates to eat dinner."

"I doubt you'll even have to ask." Mollie jumped off the bed and looked out the window when she heard the gravel outside crunch. "He's here already." Mollie looked at her watch. "He's a full half hour early."

Jack peaked through the curtain. "Is he just going to sit there?" she whispered to Mollie.

Mollie shrugged. "Maybe he knows he's early. He seems pretty anxious."

"Pathetic if you ask me."

"Be nice, Jack," Mollie sighed. "He seems like a really nice guy."

"You don't even know him." Jack stepped away from the window and plopped herself on the edge of the bed. "Why don't we all do a double date? That's the saner thing to do."

Mollie thought a minute; then shook her head. "I want to do this like an adult. I dated Justin for four years and barely knew him because every date was a party or a double. And Craig doesn't seem like the type to date that way. He'd probably think I was a complete child if I showed up with my posse."

"That's a problem because…?"

A knock on the door ended the conversation. Mollie looked through the peak hole, though she knew who it was—a well-dressed, handsome Ron fidgeting at the door with a bouquet of cut flowers. Mollie turned to Jack and said, "That typically predictable piece of slime from the male species has garnered the courage to face his destruction."

Jack shrugged and slipped her bright red toes into her gold sandals. "A little dramatic, Mollie, but at least you're beginning to get it." She grabbed her purse and slung it across her shoulders. "Look, it's time you realize that men have but one ambition. An ambition which makes them putty in our hands. They want to win the game...they think by scoring. But the true winner is the one who learns to use the other's weakness to their advantage first. You," she pointed to Mollie, "are simply a naive who's bound to one day get annihilated in the cross-fire of our war."

"Who's at war, Jack?" Mollie laughed.

"Men versus. women, or vice versa—it simply depends on who's on top on the given night."

Mollie groaned and shoved her through the door.

"Hi, Ron," Mollie said. "Take good care of her...don't worry about getting her home soon."

She was still waving good-bye when Craig pulled up. Mollie was shocked that he, too, was early. She took a deep breath and tried to look nonchalant. He swung the car door open and stepped out. "Is that Ron and your friend?"

Mollie nodded.

"I shoulda known."

"Why's that?" Mollie asked.

Craig shrugged. "Ron likes feisty women."

"How but you, what's your type?"

Craig shrugged. "Guess I'll let you know if I ever figure it out."

He laughed and she couldn't help but smile. It seemed like an honest answer. And she had to ask herself, did she have a type of man? Not really. Justin was a far cry from Craig, so the two didn't exactly fit a type. She scanned the well-constructed frame of Craig Coulter and grinned. He was still dressed in his state trooper's uniform.

Not a fair fight, Mollie thought. Mr. Coulter in a uniform could make a nun swoon. The tan fabric clung to his hips and muscled thighs. The color accentuated the brown of his skin, the corded muscles at his throat and on his arms. His shirt was crisp and form fitting from his broad shoulders to his narrow waist. A white tee-shirt peeked out from the top contrasting the dark hair and skin at his throat. Mollie sighed, "So, you're a cop."

Craig nodded his dark head. "One of Montana's finest."

Mollie secretly agreed, then blushed, fearful he might be able to read her mind.

"Ready?" he asked, his hand lightly touching Mollie's back as he escorted her to the car. He opened her door, waiting until she was in before he closed it. Mollie's eyes followed him as he crossed in front of the windshield. She shamelessly checked him out from head to toe. His hair was so black, it reflected shades of blue in the sun, though he did have the tiniest brush of gray at the temple. His jaw was firm and darkened with afternoon stubble. His nose was straight and just large enough for his square face, with a scar at the bridge.

He climbed into the car, which suddenly felt too small for his large frame. He looked across at Mollie, his brown eyes liquid pools flecked with gold. "You look adorable."

"Thanks…I think."

"You think?" He looked confused.

Mollie let out a giggle. "I'm sorry. Puppies are adorable…babies are adorable, but I'm bad to parse a compliment."

"Oh no. I guess I will have to up my game. I've never dated a woman with a solid vocabulary."

"Really? So, who do you date?"

Craig shook his head. "No one exceptional. That was my point."

Mollie smiled and nodded. Looking him over, she wasn't sure she needed to know who, or how many, she had to compete with. How many of the 400 hate clubbers were actual girlfriends? What she was certain of was that she doubted Craig spent too many weekends alone. If he chose to find company, she figured he could. Mollie gulped and suddenly felt inadequate. She had so looked forward to this moment, but now that it had arrived she felt dumbstruck. Surely, whatever she managed to utter would be childish and uninspiring now that she considered how cluttered the playing field probably was.

Craig slipped his Honda into gear and drove out of the hotel lot, the gravel crunching under the tires. "I came straight from work. I didn't want to be late." He winked at Mollie.

She blushed and tried so hard to think of something witty to say. Nothing came to mind.

"I got held up at Jim Gunning's ranch. He just built himself a hay wagon and wanted to get it authorized for tags."

"So, you like being a cop?"

"I guess. Hell, it's a job. Nothing ever happens around here. I don't know why they waste money paying for police."

"So, do you wish it were more exciting?"

Craig's eyes narrowed a moment; then he shrugged. "No. No, I don't wish for excitement. I suppose I like it here. There aren't too many places left where the night's biggest crime is a teen who forgot what field he parked his dad's car in after having a few too many beers."

"Very quaint."

Craig chuckled. "But then maybe this isn't where I belong. I have never, ever had any part of my life called quaint."

"Really? So, what is it typically called?"

"I'd rather let you judge." He flashed her a grin that warmed the blood.

Mollie bit her lower lip and couldn't help but think he didn't belong in a boring little town. Mollie asked, "I can't help but wonder if this is your natural environment. You seem more like the jungle type. Or maybe like a lion at a busy oasis who lies patiently in the grass. He looks calm until prey crosses his path, and then he pounces."

"You're quite creative."

"Am I right?"

"I've had my share of accusers."

"Oh, I didn't mean it as an accusation. A lion has the right to be a lion."

"Until it eats its handler."

"Hmm…." Mollie thought quietly, scanning Craig's face for the truth. "I suppose the trick to dealing with the lion is to either keep it caged or very well fed."

Craig let out a laugh, a full bodied laugh that made his countenance glow. With the corners of his eyes crinkled in humor, he looked like a very tame lion indeed. Mollie was pleased she had made him laugh. It really shouldn't matter that he liked her, but it did.

It was a short drive. Craig's house was only a few blocks away from the hotel. Arriving at his stucco ranch, Mollie stepped out of the car and walked beside him toward the house. She checked it out in the daylight. It was a solid house. The lawn was neatly cut, but void of any decoration. No flower beds, no gnomes, not even a name on the mail box. She supposed he had either just moved in or cared nothing for aesthetics. She looked at the yard…no sign of any party. No chairs, no trash, nothing. Just the pit was there, with the fire doused, she could barely tell it was used last night. Craig must have gotten up early or stayed up late cleaning up.

She began to doubt her dog theory, until she heard a bark. The porch's metal underpinning bowed as a pair of paws clawed the dirt, pulling the massive form of a honey beige mutt from under the house. He shook, and dust flew like a cloud around him. He turned to his master and his body twitched with pleasure as he alternated between bark and whine. It was the biggest dog Mollie had ever seen. He pranced like a stallion a little to the right, a little to the left, and then he bolted toward them. Mollie continued her walk up the sidewalk as she patted herself on the proverbial back for being right about the dog. She was so pleased with her astuteness that she didn't notice he bypassed his owner, ducking his attempt to grasp his collar. Instead, the dog focused on Mollie and leaped. He lunged, all paws off the ground and collided with her chest, knocking her off balance and into the empty flower bed. Mollie felt the breath purge from her lungs as she hit. She gasped and tried to breathe as the horse of a dog licked and sniffed her neck and cheeks.

Craig grabbed the dog by the collar and pulled him off. "Bad dog, down!" He held the dog at his side, trying to calm him, but the dog kept straining to get to Mollie.

"I'm sorry Mollie. I don't know what's got into him. He usually jumps on me. It's kind of his thing. I never dreamed of this. He usually hates people, hides under the porch when there's anyone around."

"It's all right." Mollie answered. Craig ordered the dog to heel. The dog sat. His whole hind end wagged with his tail, and he whined, but he remained seated. Craig grabbed her hands and pulled her to her feet. His eyes scanned her backside, and Mollie thought for a moment that she might faint if he brushed the dirt off for her. He cleared his throat and shook his head. "Looks like Brutus got your, um…well…he got you dirty."

Mollie quickly brushed the dirt from her backside. "I'm fine." The dog whined. Then as if unable to control it, he let out a single bark. Mollie leaned over and scratched the dog's ears and rubbed his thick neck. Lowering her nose close to his she laughed. "You definitely know how to say hi, don't you?"

The dog barked and wagged his entire back end in approval.

"Now behave, Brutus," Craig admonished, tossing a two foot long raw hide bone from the porch into the yard. Brutus chased after it, grabbing it by one end and dragging it under the porch through the breach in the underpinning.

"Sorry," Craig said, "not making much of a first impression."

"It's all right. That's what dogs do."

"Not my dog…well, not usually." He unlocked the front door and stepped back, allowing Mollie to enter first. Mollie thought of Jack's dating theory and felt a moment of hesitation. She swallowed hard, suddenly realizing she was no longer on neutral territory.

Chapter 4

She stepped over the threshold into Craig's domain. It was perfectly clean and empty. There were no pictures or bric-a-brac…nothing personal cluttered the space. Mollie wasn't sure what that said about him. The only thing she was sure of was Brutus' slobbers were beginning to dry, making her neck feel tight. Rubbing her chin with the back of her hand, she felt the grainy smudge of dirt. Looking at Craig, reminding herself to act like an adult, she cleared her throat and asked, "Do you mind if I use your bathroom," adding nervously, "to wash up?"

"Of course," Craig answered, "right this way. I really am sorry. Brutus doesn't normally like people. I always figured he was abused. I found him abandoned at a campground in the mountains. He was so skinny. I never dreamed he would survive, but he did. Now he is my loner buddy who lives under the porch. Well, until now. "

"That's sweet of you."

"Not really, I make him work for his keep. He keeps the place free of prairie dogs. Damn things dig up everything. If he gets lazy: then off to the pound with him."

"I bet," Mollie laughed.

"Believe me. I made him sign a contract." He led her to the only bath in the little house. The house consisted of a living room, a miniature kitchen, a short hall way which lead to a bathroom on the left and two rooms to the right: Craig's bedroom and an office. He took Mollie into the bathroom and took a clean washcloth and towel from the linen closet. Mollie soaked the cloth and added soap washing off her face, neck and arms. Finished, she wrung out the washcloth and turned to Craig for the towel. His eyes were intense, as though he were looking past her flesh and into her soul. He handed her the towel wordlessly and watched as she dried off. When she finished, he gently picked the stems and twigs from her hair. He wrapped a curl around his finger allowing his thumb to glide over it. Mollie's breath caught in her throat. She couldn't inhale or exhale with him so close, and from the look in his eyes, Mollie knew he was aware of his affect on her.

"I better get the groceries," he said pulling his hand from her hair. She said nothing, but her eyes followed him as he left the room.

Mollie's cheeks flamed. She splashed them with cold water, and then buried her face in the towel. What was wrong with her? *Snap out of it, Molls,* she heard Jack's voice in her own head. But there was no snapping out of it. Had he asked her to strip so he could mount her against the sink, she might have said yes. Or more likely, she would have just started disrobing because she had trouble verbalizing a sensible thought when he was so close.

She moved slowly to the kitchen where she found him emptying a grocery bag. He pulled one plastic-wrapped pack of lunch meat out of the bag after another. Mollie grinned, her body and her mind returning to normal. So, dinner was to be bologna, ham, salami, pickle loaf, or whatever other highly preserved treat he had in the bag. What would Jack say about that? Either he was a novice at seduction—or, she thought a bit saddened—he hadn't planned to go to much effort to seduce her.

Craig saw Mollie eying his "dinner." It was his turn to blush. "I lied, Mollie. I can't cook. Hell, I can't boil water. I don't know why I offered to even try and provide you with food. I almost got cans of soup, but then one of the guys at work suggested I make cold subs—swore to me even a moron could do it." He shrugged as he perused the growing stack of meats on his counter. "I guess I'm the moron who can't." He wadded the plastic bag into a tight ball, suggesting, "How about I shower and change and take you somewhere for a real dinner?"

Mollie looked down at her bibs; two big paw prints on her chest, and her bottom was still moist.

"I guess you'd need to change too." Craig thought of his choices when Mollie stepped forward and shoved him toward the bathroom. "You go shower and change. I'll rescue your dinner."

He looked at her skeptically, but she shooed him away with a wave of her hand. "Go. Get. Trust me. I can make what we in the northeast call a 'grinder'."

Craig nodded as he turned and walked backward down the hall. "I'll make it up to you. I know this is a lame first date."

With Craig gone, Mollie turned her attention to the kitchen. She left out the salami and ham and put the rest in the fridge. There she lucked into all the fixings for pizza—a stick of pepperoni, a bag of shredded mozzarella, and a jar of pickled peppers. In the bag were lettuce, tomato, and mayo. Mollie started to work peeling and washing the lettuce and slicing the tomato, and then on to assembling the sandwiches. She needed Italian dressing, but there was none to be found, so she mixed the mayo with peppers, garlic salt, and onion powder. Spreading it on the sandwiches, she folded the bun together and wrapped them in foil, shoving all six in the oven. Craig had gotten chips and a bottle of wine. Mollie shoved the wine in the freezer to chill. She was shutting the freezer door when he appeared in the doorway.

His hair was still damp from the shower, and he smelled of soap and aftershave. His cheeks were shaved smooth, though his dark facial hair left a permanent shadow to his jaw. She felt inclined to touch his chin, to rub her thumb across another scar, which had been covered in whiskers. But she stayed where she was, frozen, leaning against the kitchen counter for support.

"Find everything?"

"Yeah," Mollie answered. Her pulse quickened as he came further into the room. His presence in the tiny space overwhelmed her.

"Good." He leaned against the counter next to her. "I apologize again."

"I don't mind. I'm used to cooking," Mollie answered, adding, "I'm the oldest of three. I have two little sisters, and when my mom was sick, I kind of took over the house."

"She all right?"

"Yeah, she's a fighter. It took her two years of chemo and a mastectomy, but she won."

Craig's voice was serious, reverent, "Breast cancer?"

"Yes, but like I said, it's a finished battle and my family– my dad, my sisters and me– we're all the closer for it."

"Really?"

"Certainly, my little sisters, well they're fourteen now, but they're ten years younger than me, and they're twins. We weren't real close with such a big difference in age. I was in high school when they were in elementary school. We were kind of like two separate families until mom got sick. I moved back home and helped them out."

"That's quite a sacrifice."

"No, it felt good. I got to know my little sisters and take some of the weight off my dad. Proved to myself I could accomplish whatever I set my mind to. I helped my family get over their hurdles and still graduated on time. It has been four years, and she is still clear. One more year and she will be considered cured."

"You're a hell of a person, Mollie."

"Oh, anyone would have done it."

"You really believe that?"

"You don't?"

Craig shook his head, "Not at all." He looked down at her as she stood beside him, a full head shorter. She tipped her gaze up to meet his. He brushed the hair from her bangs back into its place behind her ear. "The first time I saw you, I wondered if your hair was as soft as it seemed."

"And?" She breathed, relieved she didn't stutter her one word answer.

"It's softer, so silky." His fingers trailed down her cheek, "I suddenly feel like I'm heading into a velvet trap." His voice was husky; his thumb stroked the smooth skin of her cheek as he asked, "Who are you, Mollie?"

"I'm Mollie Hinkle," Mollie answered, her voice barely above a whisper.

He pulled Mollie into him, his hands gentle on the back of her neck. She relaxed against him as he stood there against the counter, his lips drawn magnetically to hers. He was in no hurry, and neither was she. Mollie was never one to read the last chapter first. She relished the suspense, the subtle nuances of a story and Craig, she decided, had more than one plot line. He kissed her chin and trailed his lips down the sensitive hollow of her throat. Her heart pounded there. Her body was definitely stirred by his touch, and Mollie instinctively knew he was as eager as she was. She sighed.

His lips were suddenly hungry. Powerful hands dug into her soft flesh like they couldn't get close enough or touch deeply enough. His lips returned to hers. The tenderness faded, replaced by an eagerness that left Mollie breathless.

Neither heard the car door slam. Neither heard Brutus bark. Neither heard the front door open and then close, but both heard Jack's siren voice at the kitchen door, "Mollie!" Then more innocently, less vocally, Jack added, "You slippery Sam. I thought we were double dating on this one."

"No." Mollie stumbled back from Craig, her mind still fuzzy, her body still humming.

"I'm certain you're just nuts."

"Oh, well, my bad." Jack sat at the table and stretched her legs out on the chair in front of her. "But since we're here, the more the merrier." Jack smiled. Mollie eyed Craig, who didn't look half as disappointed as she felt. Ron stood in the doorway, shaking his head with a look of "hell if I know" to Craig.

Mollie, frustrated, turned her attention to the stove, checking on the sandwiches. Jack peered from her post at the table and exclaimed, "Great! Mollie Specials. Mollie makes the best grinders.

She learned it from her *daddy*. Mollie really is his pride and joy. He's so proud of *his* little girl."

"I'm not a little girl," Mollie said through ground teeth.

"I know that, but to him you are, and I promised to look out for you." Jack turned her gaze to Mollie. "It was *my* idea to take you away after such a crushing break up."

"I'm not crushed," Mollie spat, opening the cabinet drawer with plenty of force, grabbing a pot holder and slamming the drawer closed. She pulled the oven sheet off the rack and let it slam onto the top of the stove. Her eyes blazed as she turned to Jack, who seemed completely at ease to be on the receiving end of Mollie's anger. Not a blond hair was ruffled. Mollie, on the other hand, would need a bucket of ice to cool her hot head and flaming cheeks.

Craig turned to Ron, who stood wide eyed and silent in the doorway. "Hey, Ron, why don't you take Jack into the living room and find a game on television? I think the Steelers play today. You're from Steeler country, right, Jack?" Jack nodded, an easy smile on her face.

"Good then– you two find the game. Mollie and I will bring in the food. We have plenty."

Jack stood. "See, Molls? We'll have fun– together. Good *clean,* wholesome fun your dad would be proud of."

Ron grabbed Jack's arm and pulled her through the doorway to the living room before Mollie could take aim with any object available on the counter.

Craig grinned and pulled her in for a hug.

Mollie looked up at his smiling face and asked, "What's so funny?"

"Spunky little thing, aren't you?"

Mollie sighed, her anger with Jack subsiding, a little. "She thinks I'm senseless around you, so she thinks she needs to guard me."

"Do you think you need protection?"

Mollie felt her knees go weak as she looked into the eyes of the man who drove her pulse to near heart attack levels and made her body so very warm in some very intimate places. Hell, yes she needed protection. She needed an entire convent of nuns to surround her and extinguish the constant smoldering this man had ignited.

Mollie licked her lips, which suddenly felt dry, and managed to say, "No."

"Good." Craig let go of her and grabbed a piece of chalk. He wrote on the board next to the fridge, "went fishing." He grabbed two sandwiches and the bag of chips. He took Mollie's hand and pulled her toward the back door. She laughed, pausing only long enough to grab the bottle of wine from the freezer. She followed close behind Craig as he led her to his garage, where he had a late model truck parked, keys in the ignition. He started the engine, and Mollie laughed, her head thrown back, her heart as light and carefree as a teenager.

Without thinking, she reached over and squeezed Craig's hand. No matter how this turned out, she had this man to thank for making her feel, for the first time in her life, like she was made of flesh and blood.

Chapter 5

With a smile that glowed near nuclear, Mollie stuck her face out the open window and breathed the freedom of Big Sky Country. Montana's nickname was most appropriate. The clear blue stretched endlessly in all directions punctuated only by the many layers of clouds. Full and fluffy ones were held up by thin, wispy strands, only to be topped off by the high, heaven brushing tufts of white. Gathering overhead, they created a ceiling as timeless and endless as an ever rolling sea.

Humbly thriving below the grand sky were the waves of brown and streams of green that covered the plains. This was farm land. In any and all directions were the fields that fed the world. Huge tractors and combines, large hulking machines as large as semi-trucks, worked the thousand acre crops.

It was a polar opposite of the city Mollie came from. Pittsburgh was all glass, steel, and concrete sandwiched between mountains and rivers. It was a city built on industry, its smokestacks belching out the gray clouds that filtered the same sun that shone so brightly on this wide open land.

"It's so different from home." Mollie looked out the window at the passing landscape.

"It took me a while to get used to it," Craig admitted, "mostly the lack of trees."

Mollie looked out again and gasped, "You're right! I can't believe I didn't notice that. I'd been too preoccupied with self-pity, evidently."

"Well, we flew out here, so the change was abrupt. Locals say there's too much wind and the harsh winters kill the saplings."

"So, you aren't from around here! I thought your accent was wrong. When did you move here?"

"About a year and a half ago."

"From the south?"

Craig nodded. "Virginia."

"I knew it! So, why here?"

"Followed a girl."

"Oh," Mollie answered, annoyed by her instant jealousy. Maybe Craig was right. Females were emotionally "in" from the beginning.

But not her. Not anymore. Mollie was a new creature. She wouldn't even ask about the girl, though she was dying to know. Instead she asked, "So, do you ever miss home?"

He shrugged. "I miss the ocean. I used to spend a lot of time there. Pretty much land locked now."

"And your family? Any of them live close by?"

"No. But that suits me fine."

"Oh." Mollie sighed. "That's too bad. Though after last night, I don't miss mine either. Well, I miss my mom, and my dad, and of course, my sisters, but the rest?" She let out an exhausted breath. "With everything going on, it's great to be away for a while."

"So, when does *a while* end?"

"You mean when do we go home?"

Suddenly distracted by the sudden change out her window, Mollie paused before answering. The land started to roll more, and suddenly pine trees growing in sporadic clumps along the road, saturated the horizon. Large boulders rose from the flat earth as if sprinkled by an unknown hand on the greening grasses. She turned her attention back to Craig and had to consciously think to answer his question. She was inclined to simply gape out the window and revel in the splendor. "You know, I'm not real sure when we plan to go home. Joanie plans to be a free-lance writer, and she can because her parents will keep replenishing her bank account. And Jack is between jobs. She's an excellent chef, one of the best, really, but she got fired a week before we left."

"Poisoning men?"

Mollie laughed. "Aren't you a wise guy? No, it wasn't her cooking that got her fired; it was her mouth."

"Shocking, are you sure she didn't kill any men while she was there?"

"Certainly not." Mollie's fake indignation was ruined by the smile she couldn't contain.

"So, Jack and Joanie are free spirits; how about you?"

"Me? I will officially be out of a job if I don't renew my teaching contract by the end of August."

"So you work at a school?"

"Yes, I teach Freshman English, and I really enjoy it. I just don't…oh, it's just been a crazy year. My parents want me to take a year off to sort everything out. I don't know if there's anything to sort. To be honest? I'd rather just not worry about it." She winked at Craig. "And per your recommendation, I refuse to think about anything that causes me worry. Your philosophy on life feels most beneficial to my spirit."

Craig winked at her. "Glad to be of help."

"Oh, you have. And wow." She turned back to her window. "It is so absolutely beautiful here." The plains disappeared completely. High pinnacles of bared rock blocked the horizon. The vegetation at the mountain base was lush and tender, supported by the veneer of fertile humus.

"Where are we headed?"

"The mountains."

"To go fishing?"

"Well, no, I just wrote that to throw off our scent from your blood hound."

Mollie laughed again, rolling her head against the back of the seat. "She means well."

"Not mad anymore?"

"No, that's just Jack. She'll annoy me again by midnight. I'll have to shout her down; then we'll be friends, and then she'll do it again in the morning. That's just how we get along."

Craig nodded.

Leaning out the window, Mollie gasped. The trees thinned and revealed the daring drop within inches of the narrow dirt road.

"Whoa." Mollie sat back and turned her head to Craig. He looked at her and smiled.

Mollie rewarded him with a very brief smile, but then admonished, "Eyes on the road." She added with another gander out her window, "No second chances from a tumble over that edge."

"Nope, no forgiveness there."

"So, do many cars slide over these mountains?"

Craig shrugged. "Not since I've been here."

Mollie's cheeks were pink from the cool air coming through the open window, and her lips seemed prepared to curve into a smile at any given moment. Her eyes were bright and alert windows to her curious nature.

"I can't watch the deadly drop off any longer, so hmm…what's your passion? You said earlier that being a cop was just a job. What is it you love?"

Craig offered no answer.

"You must have something you love to do," she coaxed.

Craig scratched his head and then shrugged again. "How 'bout you? What's your passion?"

"I told you. I'm a teacher.

"So, if you love it so much, why do you question whether or not to return?"

Mollie wasn't certain she was ready to answer the question. How lame would he think she was if he knew the truth? Fortunately, they arrived before she had time to answer.

"Wow," Mollie uttered as she scrambled out her door. Rendered speechless until excitement burst from her in a squeal, she turned to Craig. "It's so beautiful." She spun round and round, compelled to absorb every sight from every direction. Here she stood, on top of the world. In any and every direction, there was perfection; a certainty of skill that rivaled the works of man's greatest artists. It had to be a work of creation, not chance. A whisper that Heaven was a step away.

Mollie heard Craig's footsteps come up behind her, and she turned, ready to express her elation when warm hands on her waist turned her around until she faced a grove of pines. His hands lingered at the curve of her hips as his cheek brushed against her ear, and he whispered, "See? Right there?"

She looked over her shoulder at him and swallowed hard. His body radiated heat. Without thinking, she rested her head against his, and he pulled her tighter, his thumbs stroking the tiny area of flesh exposed between her tank top and her bibs. His hands and body seemed to be melting into her, but his eyes looked straight ahead. She followed his gaze. There sat a little brown rabbit. Its big, unblinking eyes so innocent and vulnerable, he looked like a stuffed toy.

"I see him"

The rabbit's nose twitched, but he kept nibbling the grassy stems.

"What're the chances I could catch him?" Mollie whispered.

Craig chuckled. "Without a trap or a gun? Zero."

Mollie elbowed him. The movement brought his head up. He sniffed the air, and in a moment, he was gone.

"He heard you."

Craig laughed, his head tipped back. He spun Mollie toward him. "Since when do rabbits understand English?"

"He was a very smart rabbit."

"I see." Craig kissed the tip of her nose. "Next time, I'll write you a note. Come on, you need to see this." He pulled her by the hand up over a roll in the meadow. A stream sparkled in the sunlight like molten silver. Mollie squatted by the water and dipped a hand in its coolness. Speaking to herself in a low, reverent tone, she said, "All I have seen teaches me to trust the Creator for all I have not seen."

Craig kneeled beside her. "Experiencing profound thoughts?"

Mollie kept dipping her hands in the water and explained, "Nathaniel Hawthorne. You know, I often wonder if there really is a Heaven; then I see places like this…where the beauty is so masterful, so beyond the perfection of man…it gives me hope."

Craig's eyebrows drew together, and he looked worried. Mollie caressed his cheek like one would a frightened child, and she smiled.

"You need hope, Mollie?"

Her eyes were moist as if hiding unshed tears, but she tweaked his nose like he was a naughty child. "Don't we all?"

Reaching out, she plucked a tiny yellow flower from the earth. Then she picked its blue neighbor, then a purple little sprout. Standing, she moved across the lush earth gathering plants and stuffing them in her pockets. Turning to Craig, she mindfully ignored his look of confusion and concern, and asked, "Do you know what these are called? They look like what my mom would call blue bells and buttercups, but they're just slightly different. Do you know their names?"

"No."

"Oh well, it'll give me something to do later," she said as she plucked a white lacy sample from the ground and added it to her collection.

Craig nodded. He reached out and took her elbow and pulled her close. His hand crept to the silky skin of her neck, his thumb caressing the smoothness. Her eyes closed and then fluttered open again to find him looking at her, examining her. She wondered if he was pleased with his perusal, and as if in answer to her silent question, he wrapped an arm around her waist and kissed her. Her body was soft and pliable; his hard and unyielding. He squeezed her so tightly, the air escaped her lungs for a moment. She took a shallow breath and laid her cheek against his chest. He kissed the top of her head and asked, "What are you doing to me Mollie?"

"Me?" Mollie choked, her throat dry. "I didn't do anything. I'm just being me."

He held her tighter, inhaling the scent of her skin. "I know. That's the problem."

He pulled away and looked down at her tucking the wayward hair back from her eye to its place behind her ear.

"I'm a problem?" she asked with a slight frown.

He kissed the tip of her nose. "You're perfect. *That* may be the problem." With that, he turned and took Mollie by the hand and walked her across the field. His jaw was set, and he looked grim. His hand touched hers, but Mollie knew he was far away.

She trailed behind him a few steps before an explanation presented itself. Why would he kiss her and then become so quiet and brooding? She thought instantly of the girl he came here for. Alarm shot through her. Could he still be in love with her, or worse yet, still attached? Even married? Mollie felt her stomach turn and threaten nausea. She stopped in her tracks and jerked on his hand. He stopped and turned to her.

"You can't say that and walk away. Why do I bother you? Are you married? And by married I also count being separated either physically or emotionally. Married is married."

Craig's laugh was short. "I'm definitely *not* married."

"Well, then, what is it?"

Craig shrugged.

"Oh, come on, I deserve to know why. Why do I bug you?" She squeezed his hand and goaded, "Got a guilty conscience because you're hiding something?"

"No, not at all," he assured her.

Mollie refused to budge, waiting for an answer.

Craig threw a hand in the air. "All right, yeah. I feel some guilt. The thing is you seem so damn sweet. I feel like I'm trying to seduce a saint and that feels so damn wrong."

Mollie laughed so hard her eyes watered. She paused long enough to wipe her eyes and then couldn't help but laugh again. She wrapped her arms around one of his, leaned her cheek against his thick bicep, and surprised herself when her voice came out a throaty purr, "Well, then maybe I'll have to seduce you."

She patted his belly, and then released his arm as she strolled across the field and resumed collecting flowers. She stopped when the ground she walked on gave way to a steep slope. She stood on the edge of the mountain basin that wrapped for miles around its crest. At the very bottom was a lake. Clear blue water twinkled the sun's reflection up at her.

"Wow, that's just breathtaking." Her feet moved closer to the edge. It wasn't a steep drop, but a steady roll to the bottom thousands of feet below. The spirit of adventure tickled at her soul. Mollie wanted to climb to the bottom, just to say she did it. She turned to Craig. "Take me down there. I want to say I climbed a mountain."

"I don't know." Craig shook his head.

"You ever do it?"

"Yeah, plenty of times. There's good fishing in the lake."

"Is it hard?"

"No, they bite pretty quick."

"Not the fishing, the climb."

"I've never had trouble"

"So let's go."

"But you're a—"

"A girl? Are you seriously going to say it's because I'm a girl?"

"No," he said. Mollie's eyes challenged him, and he modified his answer. "All right, yes. You seem very girly."

"You're lucky I'm feeling gracious, or I'd kick your fanny. Now, come on, I warn you, I'll do it on my own if you don't go with me." She took his hand and tugged him closer.

He led her down the least taxing trail, keeping a slower than usual pace, but she kept up well, chattering the whole way to the bottom.

She came to a patch of snow and stopped. "Snow?"

"There's always snow up here in the high spots."

"This is so neat." She rolled a snowball in her hands. "I wish I'd brought a camera. My students would appreciate this. And my dad. Oh, and my little sisters. Snowball fights in August. They'll think I've gone off my rocker when I tell them." She grinned, tossing the ball of snow in the air and catching it again. "Watch out, officer, I'm armed and dangerous."

"That you are."

"Don't worry, I'd never attack and unarmed man."

"And I'm definitely unarmed."

Eying the handsome man with the magical hands and eyes that seemed to read her soul every time he looked at her, Mollie's eyebrow shot up, and she couldn't stop the smirk on her face. Dropping the snowball, she brushed past him as she resumed her trek down the mountain and said, "The hell you are."

Craig's laugh echoed in the scooped out hollow of the basin. Without a word, he grabbed her hand and held it as they walked silently to the lake. He led her to a large boulder on the edge of the crystal blue water. Scooping her up as if she weighed nothing, he set her on the rock. Mollie scooted to a comfortable spot and took in the sight. Craig leaned against the rock, his hips touching her legs, his arms crossed in front of his chest. He explained to her the history of the place. Old Baldy, as it was called by local residents, was carved from a glacier millions of years ago. It was naturally barren, so it was stocked each year by the state game commission who dropped fish in by helicopter.

Mollie listened intently, though her mind couldn't truly focus on facts now that he was so close. Mollie wondered what kind of woman could steal the heart of a man so austere in his every mannerism, yet so attentive as to notice a rabbit on the edge of the woods? Justin never would have noticed. Never would have thought this place special enough to even bring her here. Mollie looked across at him, listening as he talked but not hearing a single word. She enjoyed the sound of his voice. It was steady and strong with the slight southern drawl. She liked the way he gestured as he talked. Liked the way he stroked the small of her back when he kissed her.

Oh my, those kisses. He had probably just ruined her for all men. As a matter of fact, that mystery man who was her childhood creation of perfection was beginning to take on a face in her fantasies, and he had dark hair and warm brown eyes that narrowed to near slivers when he was troubled by deep thoughts, and Mollie was aware enough to know she was part of what troubled him. And it wasn't because he thought she was a saint. It was something else.

Mollie simply didn't know what. Maybe Jack would know if it was a good or bad sign.

Mollie interrupted, cutting Craig's story about a bear attack off in the middle. She'd never been coy, had never been anything but honest and direct because she, more than most, knew that life was fragile and short, and wise or not, all determinations to maintain her cool forgotten, she succumbed to curiosity and asked, "Did you love this girl you followed out here?"

"What?" Craig looked baffled.

"The woman you followed her. Did you love her? Did something happen to her?"

"There's no woman. Never has been. Hell, I wouldn't cross the street for a woman, much less a continent."

Mollie's eyes widened, a little shocked by his answer. "In the truck," she reminded, "on the way up, you said you came out here for a girl."

Craig had an a-ha look of understanding. "Emmy Lou Who."

"Pardon?"

"Ron's niece. He came out here to live with her after her mother, Ron's sister, died. She's in high school and doesn't want to leave her school and friends. You know how kids are, and Ron, being single and pretty much career impaired, volunteered to come out here and live with her. I just came along for the ride."

"Oh, that's sweet," Mollie said, her eyes moistened and relief spread relaxation throughout her body. She gave Craig a playful punch to his arm. "Now you tell me, how can I ever seduce a saint?"

"I'm no saint, that's for damn sure." He looked at her seriously. "A smart girl would ask herself, how can a thirty-year-old man have absolutely nothing in his life to stop him from moving two thousand miles away at the drop of a hat?"

Mollie shrugged. She was twenty-four, and what did she have? If she decided to stay here, all she'd have to do is quit her job, sublet her apartment, and convince her family and Jack that she wasn't crazy. So, she supposed she couldn't pack and fly the roost as quickly as she thought.

"So, why could you?"

"Because I don't love anyone. Or anything. One person, one place is as good as another."

"Really?" Mollie took a deep breath. Craig's eyes were clouded and his forehead looked pinched and worried.

"Really," Craig answered. His stare challenged her to believe him.

"Unable or unwilling?"

Craig smirked and looked to the horizon. Mollie could see he had an answer, but she doubted he'd share it. She wasn't out to psychoanalyze him or rake him over hot coals with her questions, so she let him off the hook. Instead, she rubbed her thumb against his furrowed brow. "I think you judge yourself a bit too harshly, Craig Coulter."

Craig shrugged. "Proves you don't really know me, Mollie Hinkle."

"No, I don't. So tell me about you."

"There's nothing to tell really. I'm the second son of three brothers. I've gone to college enough years to be a brain surgeon, but I barely scraped through with the liberal arts degree I've got."

"Middle child bad boy, hmm?"

"I suppose you might say that," he admitted. "I've done my share of damage."

Mollie took his hand and held it. "I don't think you're so bad. You've been nothing but a gentleman."

Craig shook his head. "My intentions for you are way less than honorable, Mollie."

"I don't believe you."

"I've got a glove box full of condoms that say otherwise."

Mollie blushed and grimaced in embarrassment, but she continued her argument once she recovered. "If your intent was sneaky and nefarious, you wouldn't have just said that."

"Unless I said that to gain your sympathies by making you think I'm showing you the 'vulnerable needing your love to heal me' side, while the whole time I'm just out to get laid."

Mollie thought a while. She scanned Craig's face. It remained nearly emotionless and unreadable, but Mollie thought she saw a real sadness, a real disconnect that she didn't believe was phony. She leaned her lips next to Craig's ear, her finger's stroking the opposite ear as she spoke the honest, direct words that came natural to her: "I think you know how to persuade me without weaving a web of deceit." Pulling back, she looked up at him. "Am I right?"

Craig looked from her smoldering eyes to the icy waters of the snow-fed lake before him and announced. "Look at me like that much longer, I'll have to jump in for a swim."

"Seriously?"

"Hell yes," Craig laughed, "That water's less than forty degrees. I hope that's enough to cool me off."

Mollie grinned. He was such a handsome man when his face lit up with humor. She wished he felt this happy all the time, wished she knew what pain caused the wrinkles in the corners of his eyes. She leaned in kissing him lightly on the lips, tracing his smile with her thumb. "You should always be this happy. You're a beautiful man when you laugh."

"You," Craig said, touching the tip of her nose like she was a child, "shouldn't trust bastards like me."

"Sir, I've known bastards, and you, sir, are no bastard."

"You put me in the odd position of having to convince you otherwise."

"Why?" Mollie asked. "For your safety or mine?"

Craig's face clouded, and his nostrils flared. His heart pounded against her palm. Did she make him nervous? Her, mild Mollie Hinkle, made his pulse race? No, that couldn't be. No man had ever found her irresistible. She kept her hand on his chest reveling in the feel of its beat.

He took her hand in his own, the sadness in his eyes returned. "Seriously, what are you doing with me, Mollie? You're old enough to know better." He didn't give her any time to answer before he grabbed her hips and scooted her down from her perch, pinning her between a rock and a hard place.

Chapter 6

Craig took a step back. Mollie sighed. His hands slid down her arms stopping when they reached her hands. He held on gently, lifting them to his lips and giving each one a tender kiss. She tugged on his hand to bring him back, but he shook his head and stepped farther away.

Mollie blushed, her gaze dropping to her feet. She didn't know why he had stopped kissing her, and she was surprised, and a bit ashamed to admit she was annoyed by his timing.

None of this was at all her style. Perhaps it was because she felt pressured by time. It no longer passed by in a steady tick; it was on fast forward, a zip in her ear. Her life was on the move, and she didn't have time to over analyze every thought and emotion. She just wanted to live.

The warmth his body created was quickly replaced with chills. She shivered and bit her lip to stop her teeth from chattering.

"We need to head out of here," Craig said quietly pulling her to his side and rubbing her arms to warm them up. "You're cold, and it's getting dark. It'd be dangerous to try to get out of here at night."

Chewing on her lip, she nodded and wordlessly followed as they made their way back up the mountain.

They walked for several minutes before he stopped and turned to her. Embarrassed, she looked away, pouting. Why? Because he treated her *with respect*? What was wrong with her?

His warm hand brushed under her chin, lifting her eyes to meet his whether she wanted to or not. She closed her eyes a moment and tried to compose herself before opening them and facing this intimate stranger.

"Mollie." His voice was rich and smooth. She looked at him and tried to smile, but it was a sad, watery eyed failure. Craig frowned. "Ah, Mollie…" He pulled her closer, the tip of his nose nearly touching hers. "I honestly don't know what to do with you. I never met a woman I wanted to still respect me in the morning."

Mollie grinned in spite of herself. Then she turned scarlet, her cheeks flaming. As she realized he knew she was disappointed, he pulled away. She bit the side of her cheek. "It's all right. I suppose I just…I was surprised. Contrary to my behavior down there." Mollie pointed to the lake and then blushed again, shaking her head, unable to voice her thoughts. What should she say? *Look, I'm not a tramp, even though the only way I could throw myself at you any more obviously is by doing a striptease or a lap dance?*

Craig seemed to read her mind. He grinned and kissed the top of her head. "I think you're a fascinating woman, and it causes me great pain to leave these…" He paused, leaned close and kissed her lips, gently flicking his tongue between them, quickly tasting her sweetness before pulling back and saying, "…very perfect lips." He kissed her again, leaving her near breathless. "But bears and coyotes come out of those woods after dark."

Mollie's eyes snapped open, and she searched Craig's face for the truth. He was dead serious. A new surge of electricity tingled through her, but this time it was fear. She began her ascent again, leaving Craig behind her as she scrambled up the loose rocks.

Reaching the top, Craig asked a winded Mollie, "Shit lady, you trying to win gold?"

"I saw *When Bears Attack* and I've no intention of tangling with one."

Craig laughed and pulled her to him. Lifting her off her feet, he tossed her over his shoulder and carried her to the truck. Opening the door, he set her inside and closed it quickly. He tweaked her nose through the open window. "There, my dear. Safe and sound."

Joining her, they shared the sandwiches as the sun set in a red glow over the mountain. Craig used a pen knife to dig the cork from the neck of the wine bottle. Once opened, he handed it to Mollie, who took the first drink. She handed it back to Craig, who shook his head. "I'll stick with water. I need to drive back."

"Oh well, we can save it."

"No, enjoy. Besides, it's open."

Mollie read the label. "And it's Raspberry flavored. My favorite."

"Really?"

"No. I didn't even know wine came in flavors other than red and white."

Craig grinned. "There was a whole wall of bottles. I took a guess and went with the girliest, fruitiest bottle I could find."

"Hey now, I drank a beer yesterday. It was *awful,* but I drank it."

"Maybe this will be more to your liking."

Mollie hugged the bottle to her chest. "You know, this really isn't like me. This wine and the beer last night…that's like more than I drank in college."

"Dear God, did you go to a convent?"

"No, but I was busy…with my mom and all."

Craig grimaced. "Yeah, you said that."

Mollie took a long swallow. "Wow. That is good. I wouldn't have guessed it had alcohol in it."

Craig reached for her hand and held it tight, his thumb rubbing tiny circles on her skin.

"So, do you think your friend is completely nuts by now?"

Mollie laughed, her head tilted back against the seat. "Oh, Lordy, I forgot about Jack." Mollie covered her mouth with her hand and giggled. "She's probably got your friend driving all over the country."

Craig grinned. "I'll have to thank Ron. He could easily find me if he wanted to. I don't have that many good hiding places."

"So, you hide a lot?"

"Not hide, I guess. But I'm finding I prefer solitude to people."

"Seriously? You *prefer* to be alone?"

"Of course. Wouldn't you? People are annoying."

"Seriously? You seriously think people are annoying?"

"*Seriously,*" he echoed with a grin.

"Oh, no. That's sad. And hardly true." She studied the bottle top as she thought about all the people in her life. Most loved and supported her. True some had hurt her. She said without any real conviction, "Most people are all right."

Craig shook his head. "There are two types of people: those who are out to change you and those who are out to get something from you."

"So which one am I?"

Craig clenched his jaw and shrugged. He took the wine and took a swallow.

"And what about Ron?" Mollie asked. "Ron doesn't seem like a changer or a user."

"Ron is definitely a changer. He's always trying to improve my life. And you're a changer too. I'll bet you a real dinner that by the end of the night you'll try to change how I view the world. You'll want me to see the beauty and goodness of sunsets, fluffy kittens, and ask me to say, *God bless us every one.*"

Mollie gave him a punch to the ribs. "There. Bet you didn't see that one coming, Ebenezer."

"Damn. Your bony little knuckles hurt. I didn't realize you had an abusive streak. I'm even more intrigued."

"You're a sick man, Craig Coulter. You remind me of Jack. Maybe that's why I like you."

"Thanks. From what I've seen, Jack's psychotic."

"Nah," Mollie answered. She took the bottle back from him and sat cross-legged in the seat turned toward him. "Jack is my self-appointed protector."

"Why's that?"

"Well," Mollie answered slowly, not sure whether or not to air her life history. She took a long drink, wiped her mouth, and then smiled at Craig. Taking a deep breath, she admitted, "This hasn't exactly been a banner summer for me, and I guess Jack just thinks if she watches over my shoulder carefully enough then I'll not suffer any more harm."

"What happened?"

Mollie looked at him seriously. "You really want to know?" Craig nodded. "I'll sound truly pathetic, and you'll probably not respect *me* in the morning."

"Never. Tell me. Why was this summer so bad?"

"Well, right now, at this very minute, I should be on my honeymoon."

"Really." Craig's voice was harsh, and he gripped Mollie's hand a little tighter.

"Really." Mollie laughed. "I was the first *bride* in history to be left at the altar."

"At the altar?"

"Yeah, during our wedding vows, he got cold feet. He just said he couldn't do it and took off."

"What kind of asshole does that? Are you all right?" Craig's voice was heavy with sympathy and concern.

Mollie cradled his hand to her chest. "Please, don't feel sorry for me. Cause if you do, I will either have to kick your butt or never tell you the whole horrid tale. It all sounds horrible, but trust me, it has worked out for the best."

"Why's that?"

"Because, it made me realize that I never want to settle for less. I want it all. I want a man who is completely silly for me. I want real, honest death do you part, for better or for worse. I won't settle for anything less, ever…again. It may never happen in my lifetime, but it beats a lie."

"So, your marriage would have been a lie?"

"Well, not a lie exactly, but it wouldn't have been real love."

"How can anyone tell the difference?"

Mollie thought a minute, and then she shrugged. "I'll just know." She was quiet a minute longer, and then asked, "Do you have any idea how hard it is to get season tickets to the Steelers? People who have them pass them on to their next generation. My dad had them. Good ones a friend had given him when his business transferred him to Saudi Arabia. My dad loved those tickets. They were his pride and joy. But when my mom's cancer bills stacked up, he sold them. And he did it happily. He said he was just grateful he had them to sell. Then when they had to sell our house and move to a much smaller place right before Christmas, Dad never complained. He worked so hard trying to get the place unpacked and decorated. He did it all, from the tree to the yard. Can't say it was very pretty, but it was decorated." She laughed. "My mother was so overwhelmed, the exhaustion, and the guilt caused her to just break down. She got angry and started ripping ornaments from the tree and throwing them on the floor. Dad yelled at her. The only time I ever remember him yelling at any human being. He told her to grow up and learn to appreciate what was really important in life. Mom just fell on the couch and cried, begging my dad to let her die before she ruined the whole family. Dad simply told her she owed it to him, and to us, to get well after all we had done. He hadn't sacrificed so much just to be left alone with three kids to raise." Mollie brushed a tear from her cheek and allowed herself to be pulled closer to Craig's warm body. She toyed with the buttons on his shirt as she finished her story. "My dad told me later that money and houses didn't matter at all if he didn't have my mom to share them with." Mollie looked up at Craig. "My dad was right and as far as I'm concerned. I'm lucky as hell Justin got cold feet. As I stood there, in my gown, with everyone staring at me... all I could think was, 'thank God.' I was crazy to think he was the one. Just crazy.

"But, Jack," Mollie continued, "Jack thinks I was devastated, but actually, I felt liberated. I felt like I had been given a new chance at a better life. I know that sounds crazy. I may *be* crazy, I don't know."

She looked up at Craig, who looked troubled.

"What is it?" she asked. "I told you I'd look pathetic."

Craig shook his head. "No, it's not that. I'm just wondering why you didn't leave him at the altar if you knew he wasn't the right guy."

"Because I didn't know until that moment."

"You didn't know whether or not you loved him?"

Mollie shrugged. "I thought I did. I dated him for three years. We had troubles, but I always tried to work them out. It wasn't until

the night before the wedding my mom came to me for *the talk*."
Mollie laughed and made air quotes. She sighed and added
seriously, "Anyhow, I could see the confidence my mother had in
my father's love…the trust she had in him to always have her back.
To her, my skinny, gangly, nerdy father is a real knight in shining
armor. I realized that he was perfect in her eyes…that even on his
worst day, she wouldn't change him. After *the talk*, I thought about
Justin. I thought about how often he got annoyed with me…how
often my personality…you know my very nature…just grated on his
nerves." Mollie shrugged and took a drink. "It just made me think,
is this as real as what my parents have? Would he, on my worst day,
given the worst situation. . .Would he still want me?"

"So, I called him and I painted a worst case scenario for him
and asked him if he knew that was the future, would he still say 'I
do'?"

"And?"

"He accused me of trying to talk him into calling off the
wedding so I didn't look like the bad guy."

"Sounds like you hit a nerve," Craig offered.

"I was evidently right."

"So, what evil picture did you paint that changed his mind?"

"Cancer."

"Cancer?"

Mollie nodded. "I had cancer when I was eight. If it came back,
would he want to be with me?"

"You had cancer? Damn, Mollie…."

"Please, don't say you're sorry. I already have Jack to pity and
protect me. She's been hard at work doing it since we were little.
Trust me, the Queen of England doesn't have more a willing and
eager handmaid than I have in Jack. She went so far as to shave her
head so I wasn't the only bald freak in the mall."

"I suppose that explains Jack's insanity."

"A bit." Mollie laughed. "Though at times, she is nearly
certifiable. But the operative word is 'had.' I *had* cancer. That
doesn't make me a victim."

"True. So, he decided at the wedding?"

"Yep. During the vows."

"I'd like to have seen Jack's reaction to that. Do you have it on tape?"

"You're such a heel!" Mollie laughed. "Okay, maybe you should feel a little sorry for me. And yes, we do have it on tape. She called him an effing bastard, threw her bouquet on the ground and hurtled a pew to get her hands on him. She was like a purple tornado of taffeta with fists flying. She bloodied his nose and busted his lip. The minister pulled her off of him, but not before Jack got in one last kick and screamed, 'I hope your dick falls off' or something like that." Mollie squeezed his hand and laughed so hard her eyes watered. "What would I do without Jackie?"

"I'm beginning to like her. She's my kind of gal. I'd enjoy punching him myself. What a son of a bitch."

"Oh, well. I can't really blame him. Truly," Mollie said without any anger in her voice, "who would want to knowingly take on that kind of burden?"

"Someone who loves you." Craig pushed her hair back and tipped her chin until she looked at him. "You're extremely lovable, Mollie."

He wrapped her up in his arms and pulled her into him. He kissed her lips, her ears, and the tender skin down her neck and across her collar bone. His hands roamed the exposed skin of her arms up to her shoulders then down her back. Then he pulled back, yet again. His hand stroked her cheek as he asked softly, "Is this what you want, Mollie? I would like nothing better, but I don't want to do anything that will make you regret you ever met me. You've been hurt, and I don't want to take advantage of that. Be another pain."

Mollie shook her head. "And to think you tried to convince me you were a louse."

"The ironic thing is, I'm probably no different than your boyfriend."

"You left a woman at the altar?"

"No, but I have a history of being a dick."

"Well, I only judge people by how they treat me. I don't care about other people's opinions." *Even four hundred hater groupies on the internet.*

"Even my mother thinks I'm a dick."

"No!" Mollie gasped.

"Oh, yes. She's probably my most vocal critic. Even sent me away to military school when I was sixteen trying to redeem me."

"By shipping you off?"

"In her mind, it was the right thing to do. Hell, she was a single mom with three boys to raise and a high profile career as a circuit court judge. She just wanted to keep me out of jail. Out of the press. And keep me from doing too much harm to the local female population." He took a deep breath before adding, "Look, Mollie, I'm not proud of what I was or am, but to my young, testosterone-soaked brain, women were no more important than a meal."

"That's scary."

"Yeah, I told myself it's what women deserved. When I was sixteen, I had one make my life a living hell, and I was the one punished for it." Craig admitted and then went silent.

"What happened?"

Craig made no move to share the story.

"Please?" Mollie asked. "I've told you my humiliating truth."

"Yeah, but you were the victim." He ran a lazy hand through her hair and then admitted, "I'm the bad guy in this story."

"All stories have two sides. And I can't imagine you having a black and unredeemable heart."

Craig laughed. "You're too much."

"Come on. You owe me. Tell me the story." Mollie poked him in the ribs until he agreed to talk.

"It was a long time ago…on a dark and stormy night…."

"Stop!" Mollie giggled. "Tell the story for real."

Craig took a deep breath and looked at her as if searching for a way out of making any disclosure. He leaned forward and kissed her. She allowed him to kiss her, but as his lips trailed down her neck, she cleared her throat and said, "I won't give up. You can kiss me all night, but I still want to hear what happened."

He shook his head as he pulled back. "It was worth a try." Mollie motioned for him to talk. Craig sighed. "All right. I met this girl during summer vacation, and she made my life crazy."

"So, you loved her?"

"Love? Hell no."

"Well then, how would she make your life crazy?"

"She complicated things."

"Because you cared for her?"

"Not at all. I mean she knew how to drive a guy absolutely insane."

Mollie looked confused. "Without loving her?"

"Ah, forget it, Mollie. I can't explain it. For you, everything is tied to love. You probably can't understand why someone would be obsessed with someone they don't love."

"Ahh...sex. Was she your first?"

Craig covered his face with his hands and groaned. "Holy shit, but I'd rather tell my mother this story. Hell I'd rather tell my Grams."

"So, she was your first?"

"Yes. Yes, she was my first. And she was a few years older than me, and far more experienced. She had me wound so freaking tight, if she said jump, I'd say 'how high and when could I come down?' But the deeper I got into the whole relationship, you know, the more I got to know her, the crazier everything got. One time, we went to a movie, and in the parking lot, she banged her car door into this old lady's car, and the woman told her she should be more careful. Well, Angel, that was her name, waited until the woman was in the theater, and then she took a tool box and busted out the window of the old lady's car. I was shocked. I mean I had had my fair share of mayhem, but to do that? And hell, the old woman was polite to us. Another time, she chased a cop all over town until he stopped and told her harassing an officer is a crime. She told him cops followed people all the time; she just wanted to let him know how it felt. Needless to say, we both ended up getting breathalyzers and the third degree. It was insane. She was insane. I didn't know what to think. I mean, I liked certain things about her. Hell, she knew things no teenage girl should."

"No details needed, please."

Craig laughed. "Things that are shocking to a kid, Molls. Don't go getting all gutter on me."

Mollie snuggled into his shoulder, helping herself to the wine while he resumed his story.

"Then she started talking about marriage and kids and wanting to meet my mom. It was too much. I didn't want all that. I told her I couldn't see her, and then I did my best to hide from her, but I swear, she was a stalker. I should've told my mom, but I couldn't. Maybe if my dad were alive, things would have been different. All I had was my mother, who was never home. And my Grams. And I figured telling the old gal would give her a coronary. I could've talked to my brother, Tres, but he had a girl and was never around either. So I told her to get lost. Told her I thought she was crazy, and I didn't want to see her or talk to her ever again. Then I avoided her. Went back home to Virginia, hoping she'd never find me. Then my mother came to me and accused me of rape. She said Angel was filing charges against me. I couldn't believe it. It was a total lie. But my mother sure did buy it. She came into my room screaming at me that if I had done this, she'd have me prosecuted to the full extent of the law—there'd be no Kennedy kid gloves for me. I swore I didn't do it. Hell, I hadn't been anywhere near her for months. But Mom, well she didn't ever believe much that came out of my mouth. Instead, she hired an investigator who, fortunately for me, told her the girl was lying. Mom told me I got lucky, but until I learned to respect women, I'd just keep getting myself in trouble. So, off to military school for me."

Mollie kissed his cheek as one might kiss a boo boo. "I'm sorry, Craig. That's just awful."

"That's not so bad. That's where I met Ron. He's my family."

"So, you still don't get along with your mom and brothers?"

He shook his head and rubbed his eyes. "The kicker of the story is, the girl I had my problems with? She was my brother's wife's sister. And I'm solely responsible for them breaking up and being separated for fifteen years."

"How could it be your fault that they broke up?"

Craig sighed. "They were forced apart. They *fell in love*," Craig said the words like they were a part of a fable, "as teenagers, but didn't get married until three years ago."

"Why'd they wait so long?"

"Because of the chaos I created with Angel, my mother and Sam Privett, my brother's wife's father, severed the ties between them. Jenna, Tres's wife, thought he dumped her; he thought she dumped him. Same sordid tale you see every day on Oprah."

"I still don't see why that's your fault. If they loved each other, they shouldn't have let people tear them apart."

"I helped my mom keep them apart. I pretended to be Tres when Jenna sent some guy to tell Tres she was pregnant. I told him to tell Jenna to prove it was mine, me of course pretending to be Tres, before she started making claims. She got the message and evidently just fell apart and...." Craig closed his eyes and frowned. "She was pregnant and scared, so she married another guy. My brother didn't know he was a dad until three years ago. Thanks to Uncle Craig."

"Oh, Craig. That is sad. But you were young, and you said yourself that your mom asked you to do it."

"A lot of people got hurt. My nephew, my brother, his wife...hell, even Angel ended up dying of a drug overdose. And it was all me."

"Craig, you can't...."

"I don't want to talk about this anymore, Mollie. I can think of better ways to spend the time till the wine wears off."

"Craig you can't blame yourself for...."

"Shh, Mollie. I'm serious. I'm not looking for absolution. I just want you to understand I've never been a nice guy."

Mollie offered Craig the bottle, but he refused. "I need to drive you off this mountain safely."

"That you do." Mollie lifted the bottle in a toast. "Here's to you, Craig Coulter. My newfound protector."

Craig pulled her close, the taste of wine still on her lips and tongue. He kissed her until she was breathless and boneless, her body melding to his. He held her, his hand cupped behind her head, pressing her cheek to his shoulder. "I'm not a good man, Mollie. You'll end up hating me."

"No, I won't. I'm not a crazed teenage girl. I'm not asking for hefty promises or declarations of love. I enjoy being with you. And at this point in my life, that's all I'm looking for."

Craig wrapped her body tightly in his arms and lowered her body onto the seat.

Chapter 7

Jack flipped the door open before Mollie had a chance to touch the knob. She stood there, door in hand, foot tapping until Mollie entered the room. She closed it with both hands, quickly securing it with lock and dead bolt as if she expected an intruder to come crashing into the room. She then turned to Mollie, but said nothing, instead she shot her a look of parental disapproval: cheeks sucked in, eye brow arched high, nostrils flared, arms crossed over her chest, and foot still tapping hollowly on the carpeted floor.

"Sorry," Mollie answered, avoiding Jack's gaze as she headed to the bathroom. Jack wasn't thrown off the nagging trail as she followed Mollie to the bathroom door. Leaning against the doorframe, she simply said, "Well?"

Mollie turned on the water, dipping her fingers in the stream, waiting for it to warm up.

"Well nothing."

Once the water warmed, Mollie turned it down and used it to lather her hands and wash her face, preparing for bed.

Jack let out and exaggerated sigh and stood poker straight. "It's almost dawn, for crying out loud."

"We shared a bottle of wine. You didn't want him to drive drunk."

"You could have called."

"I forgot my phone." Mollie dried her face as she reminded Jack, "I thought we agreed I was an adult. I thought we agreed you would let me enjoy this date without interference."

"I don't recall...."

"Don't, Jack." Molly shook a finger at her friend. "You were totally irrational. I was embarrassed. You're lucky I'm still speaking to you."

"I...."

"You were crazy." Mollie threw the towel in the corner. "Dear God, you have to lighten up."

Jack looked at the floor. "I was just...."

"You were 'just' nothing, Jack. You were out of line."

"Maybe."

"Maybe?"

"All right. I was bad. I acted like a total freak, and I truly am sorry." Jack looked at the floor. "Forgive me?"

"I should kick your fanny, but I won't. I will forgive you, but you have to stop, okay?"

Jack nodded. "So, will you tell me what happened?"

Mollie sighed, a contented sound of pleasure as the memories replayed in her head. "I have never had so much...gosh, fun doesn't even cover it...I have never *enjoyed* myself so much. I don't really know how to explain what I'm feeling." She wrung out the washcloth and laid it over the side of the basin. Her cheeks blushed as she thought of how to describe her date with Craig. She leaned against the sink and asked ever so hesitantly, "Do you believe we all have a soul mate?" As soon as the words were out of her mouth, Mollie's cheeks turned scarlet, and she groaned, "Oh, why am I asking you that; you, of all people? Of course, you don't." Mollie grabbed her toothbrush and squeezed paste across it as she kept talking, "Let me guess, you don't believe in soul mates, but you do believe in inmates because love is like a sentence. Am I close, Jackie?" Mollie brushed her teeth, spitting and rinsing.

"I guess it doesn't matter what I believe. Do you think you found your soul mate? Did you, you know...?"

Mollie blushed. "No, he was a gentleman, and as for thinking he's my soul mate? Well, I realize it's ridiculous to think you can love someone without really knowing them, but I will admit I'm very intrigued. I had fun. I didn't think a single time about my problems. When was the last time I could say that?"

"I am glad for that," Jack admitted.

Jack followed Mollie out of the bathroom as they got into their beds and tucked themselves in for the night. Stretching, Mollie rolled over and shoved her hands up under her pillow. Jack flipped off the light.

"Oh, speaking of soul mates, evidently Joanie's a believer."

Mollie turned her face toward Jack in the darkness. "Is she back?"

"No. Joanie ran away from home, Molls." Jack's voice oozed false concern.

"Ran away?" Mollie propped herself up on her forearms.

"Yeah. She called from Nevada. Says she and that guy, Mitch…says she's in love. Ugh, I could just vomit. I had to hear all about it…like I give a shit. *I just adore him, Jack. He's sooo real.* She'll probably marry him in some sleazy chapel."

"I can't really say I'd be surprised. Joanie never was wrapped together too tightly. I think any time a guy shows her more than a second's attention she thinks she's hit with Cupid's arrow. Such a twit."

"Meow! What's up with you? It's not like you to be catty, that's my job."

Mollie dropped her head onto her pillow. "I suppose I can tell you now…." Mollie plucked at lint on her blanket. "Joanie and I had a bit of a tiff before we left."

"And you never told me?"

"I never told you because I didn't want you and her getting into it during the ride." Mollie sighed. "You can be so protective of me, Jack. I'm a big girl. I'm smart, and I'm stronger than you think."

"Guilty as charged. And I apologized. I said I'll back off." Mollie could hear her sit up, probably crossed-legged in the other bed. "So, tell me what happened. All the dirty details."

"Justin happened," Mollie added flatly, "Not that I really give a damn, but it hurt my feelings because she didn't know I didn't give a damn."

"Wow," Jack said and said it again, "Wow." Finally gaining her balance she asked, "So, how did that happen? How did you find out?"

"The night before we left on this trip, I went to see Justin to assure him there were no hard feelings, and to give him back his grandmother's ring. Anyhow, I knocked on his door, and there was no answer. I didn't want to leave the ring in the mailbox or anything, so I used my key and, well he was home, but he couldn't answer the door 'cause he was *busy* in the kitchen with Joanie."

"Oh hell no. Seriously?"

"As a heart attack."

"Oh, God, Mollie that's awful." Jack's voice held the wicked sting of venom. "When I get my hands on that bitch…."

"That's why I didn't tell you," Mollie answered. "I don't want you to do anything."

"Nothing? The back-stabbing little bitch just gets away with it?"

"Karma will get her."

"Then call me Karma."

"Jack, I'm warning you…."

"Fine. It may kill me, but fine. I won't kill her."

"Good girl," Mollie said with a sigh. "If it makes you feel better; Joanie begged, 'Please, don't tell Jack. Please, Mollie, please don't tell Jack.' She kept crying and pleading for me not to tell you. Heck, she chased me all the way to my car without her shirt even buttoned, scared to death." Mollie laughed, the situation funny in hindsight. "I assured her she'd be safe. So, I mean it, no retaliation. Promise me, Jack?"

Jack took a deep breath, "I already promised to let her live."

"Jaaaacccckkk…are you leaving open the possibility of brutal harm?"

"Maybe."

"Maybe not. You'll do nothing."

"Nothing?"

"Nothing."

The room was quiet a minute then Jack laughed. "You got to at least let me do this…next time she calls I'm going to tell her." Jack lowered her voice to a sinister whisper, "I know what you did last weekend."

Mollie laughed till her sides hurt. It felt good to feel so unburdened. Jack was right. This trip, this time away, was just the medicine she needed.

Mollie laughed again. "You may do that. She deserves that much. She left me with an image I'll never be able to wipe from my memory. It was like walking in on a very badly staged porno. Oh, my, Justin is such an ass. Why didn't you warn me?"

"Uhh!" Jack screamed. "I didn't warn you? I believe I said I was wearing black to the wedding to demonstrate my mourning."

Mollie laughed. Jack had bemoaned Mollie's relationship with Justin since day one. Sobering, thinking of Jack's reaction to Craig, Mollie decided maybe her friend's gut was better than her own. "What about Craig? Do you really think he's that bad?"

"Do you still love Justin?"

Mollie shook her head. "Don't think I ever did."

Jack nodded. "I can tell you Ron seems like a good guy, and he thinks the world of Craig. So, at this point in time, I have no major reason not to trust him."

Relief washed over her, and she smiled, until Jack added, "The problem is, I don't trust you."

"Me?"

"Yeah you. You were ready to walk down the aisle with loser man two weeks ago, and now you're madly in love."

"I never said I was madly in love."

Jack imitated Mollie, *"Oh, Jack, do you believe in soul mates? Sound familiar, Mollie Dollie with the head for follies?"*

"I wish I could erase Justin, and I wish I had more time to get to know Craig. With Justin, I have to admit, I think I dated him because I was over twenty and felt that I should be making the connection with someone. I wanted to be married, and I still do. I want a happily ever after. I want that more than anything in the world." Mollie was quiet a minute. "You know why Justin walked away, Jack?"

"Evidently not for Joanie…cause she's in love with Mitch and Justin's still calling you. Which, by the way, since you've abandoned your cell; he's calling me, which is pretty ballsy, so definitely desperate. For the record, you take him back; I will assassinate the little pecker drool before the wedding."

Mollie laughed. "Pecker drool?"

"I found an insult thesaurus online. I'm trying some new things out."

The giggles that erupted between them made Mollie feel like she was a kid again. Once the fit was over, Mollie sighed. A contented happy sigh. "You know, you don't have to worry. I doubt there's any way Justin and I can work out our issues. He doesn't love me. I talked to him the night before the wedding, and I told him to imagine life with me at its worst—imagine I have cancer, and it consumes all his time and money. Would he still want me? Would he sacrifice a family for me? If all the chemo I had as a kid made me infertile, then what? I knew in my heart it would scare the hell out of him, but I had to know…was he really in this for just the better, or was he willing to do the worse too? My only wish is that he'd have called it off right then and there. I really thought he would. You don't know how shocked I was when he showed up at the church."

"What would you have done if he hadn't run away?"

"I would never have known true happiness."

"But Molls, what if you're doing the same thing with Craig? What if you're just looking for a relationship?"

Mollie thought quietly. "I see what you're saying, but this DOES feel different. I know it sounds crazy, but I feel like I know him. There's no awkwardness. I don't feel compelled to hide who I am from him, and maybe it's just physical, but when he touches me; I swear it's like I'm electrically charged. I have *never* felt like that before." Mollie rolled over onto her side, facing her friend. "But you make a good point. Maybe I *am* just looking for someone to love me. Maybe I'm just afraid my life will end before it ever begins. I don't know. All I do know is that when I'm with him I feel alive, and if it doesn't end well, and I end up on the short end of the stick? Well, this feeling, this wonderful feeling of life, is well worth it."

Jack nodded, a sympathetic smile on her face and tears in her eyes. "Mollie?"

"Yeah, Jack?"

"I…." Hot tears rolled from Jack's eyes and made a wet spot on her pillow. She took a deep breath, wiped her eyes on her pillow, and cleared her throat and ordered. "Tell me all about your evening."

Mollie recanted every detail of her evening till the sun glowed around the edges of curtained window.

"Goodness, it's morning! We better get some sleep."

"Yeah, we better. Night." The room was quiet for a long time before Jack whispered, "And Molls, I do believe in soul mates. There is a special someone just for you."

"Really, Jack?"

"Really."

"Maybe one for you too?"

"Hah! Don't overly stress the cosmos. It might implode."

****

Craig returned home to find Ron rummaging through his fridge.

"Don't you ever go home?" Craig teased as he dropped his keys on the table and poured himself a cup of coffee.

"Emmil's still at band camp. It's boring there without her. So, tell me, what's the scoop? Anything happen?"

"Nothing happened," Craig said simply as he carried his coffee from the kitchen to the living room.

Ron followed right behind him. "Good, 'cause, I know we're brothers in booty scores, but I think Mollie should be left out of the game."

"Why's that? Thought me getting laid was the answer to my every problem?" Craig sat on the couch and propped his feet up on the coffee table. "Since when's that changed?"

"Mollie's different. She's not your kind of girl."

"I disagree. She's clearly my kind."

"Craig it's just…you can't."

"Can't what? I said nothing happened. It was just a date. Hell, she'll leave any day."

"Then stay away from her."

"Stop talking bullshit. She's an adult. I'm not doing a damn thing wrong. I was a *gentleman.*"

"That's freaking scary. I mean no offense, buddy, but I know you. And I would never let you near any woman I loved. You're a sneaky bastard."

"Why is it that any comment that starts with, 'no offense,' is always offensive?"

Ron plopped himself in the recliner. "Don't give me that wounded shit. I know you. I know where you've been, what you've done, who you've done what with." Ron laughed, while Craig frowned.

"You didn't say anything to Jack, did you? She's a big enough pain in the ass."

"No, but she told me something I think you should know."

"Like what?"

"Girl's got problems."

"I could have told you Jack was a crazy bitch."

"Not Jack, Mollie. She's had a rough road."

"She told me all about it."

"Even the cancer?"

"Yep, even the cancer."

"Well, then, you know why you can't screw with her. Even if she does have a fine ass."

Craig shot him a look that clearly conveyed to Ron that he'd gone too far.

"Ooh, something did happen," Ron snickered. "Or did more happen by nothing happening?"

"You're the clever one with all the answers. I'm sure you'll figure it out."

"Oh, damn, you got the bug. She's crawled right under your skin, and it's made you all bitchy." Ron shook his head and gave

Craig a lame frown. "Here you thought the Roninator was bonkers for falling for a girl so quick." He pointed to Craig. "See, buddy, it happens."

"I like her," Craig answered simply. "That's as far as I'm willing to go."

"But for you, that's like miles, screw the baby steps, you're just going to fall head over heels 'in like' with this girl. You know, Craig, it's harder to find a girl to like than it is to find one to love."

"You're full of shit," Craig laughed. "You really have some of the most bizarre theories on love and relationships."

"No, no. Hear me out." Ron leaned forward in his chair counting his points on his fingers. "First of all, every time I walk into a bar, I fall in love with the ladies. I love their smell and their shape. Oh, how I love their shape, especially nicely rounded…."

"Get to your point."

"Yeah, yeah, to the point. I have been in love so many times, head dizzy, obsessed with being with a girl, but rarely have I found a woman that I want to talk to, a woman I want to try to make laugh, a woman I like enough to want to make her get into me."

Craig neither agreed nor disagreed, but he listened.

Ron continued, "So, it's a rare and beautiful thing when you find that person you wouldn't mind just sitting on a porch and knocking back a beer with."

"And that's 'like'?"

"Yes. And it's better than love."

"You're a strange man, Ron Stiles." Craig sipped his coffee. "And I think you lost your penis since we got here."

"Don't try to change the subject. I'm right. You know I'm right."

"Well then, o' wise one, what the hell is love?"

"Real love? The kind poets yap about? Well, that kind of love comes like a bolt of lightning…but you won't even know it hit you until you realize there's a person you'd walk through the fires of Hell to reach. Someone you'd willingly die for. Some people never love. Spend fifty years in like and never reach love."

"You sound like Mollie."

"She must be the introspective, intuitive type like me," Ron said with a wink.

"Or completely starry eyed and irrational."

"And that's why you shouldn't hurt her."

"I will be at my most noble."

"Somehow, buddy, that just doesn't make me feel any better."

"When did Mollie become your responsibility?" Craig gripped his coffee mug and grimaced.

"I'm your friend, and I just want to warn you, if you hurt a girl with all the shit she's going through, karma will come back and bite you so hard on the ass you'll walk pigeon-toed for the rest of your life."

"Pigeon-toed?"

"It's late. The metaphors start to lose their magic pre-dawn. I'm just sayin', don't play with this girl. Promise me?"

"You insult me, Ron. When have I ever lied to a woman? It's not my fault women don't listen. I've been honest with Mollie. She knows exactly who she is dealing with. Feel better?"

"Sure." Ron pinched his chin between his thumb and forefinger. "I guess that's the most I could hope for...unless you just stop...."

"Not seeing her isn't an option." Craig said nothing more as he stood, abandoning his coffee and his friend, and went to bed slamming the door behind him.

Chapter 8

Mollie rose the next morning, her mind alert and awake even though she only had a couple of hours of sleep. Tossing the covers aside, she crept to the bathroom, closing the door without a click. Jack's snores were muffled by the pillow over her face. Only her lips were visible.

Mollie turned on the water and stepped into the shower. She hummed as she bathed, enjoying the warm water massage. She thought of the day ahead and wondered when she would see Craig. When he dropped her off at the hotel; he said, "See you tomorrow". Mollie assumed that meant today, even though it was technically already *tomorrow* when they said good-bye. Or maybe he was simply being polite? No, she would see him. She knew it. She supposed he had to work, so most likely it would be after four.

Shutting off the shower, she dried off and used the towel to wipe the steamy mirror clean. A vibrant-eyed woman looked back at her. Mollie almost didn't recognize herself. She looked so…happy. The shadows that had lingered in her eyes, and the furrow between her brows that she had thought was a permanent part of her facial landscape, was gone.

She felt good…and powerful.

She pulled on her panties and was about to slip her arms into her bra when she paused. The tiny cuts near her armpit were healing where the little lump was removed. It had been over two weeks since she had the biopsy done. Surely they knew something by now?

Mollie ran a hand through her damp hair and sighed. She didn't fear cancer. She beat it once and was certain she could do it again. She just didn't feel like it. When she was eight, she had been diagnosed with neuroblastoma, during a check-up. The tumor was located near her spine; further tests found one more. The tumors were removed and Mollie spent the next year undergoing chemo and radiation treatment. It sapped her strength as it caused her to become anemic. Her parents withdrew her from school, so she could rest and avoid infections.

Mollie thought withdrawing from school was great, at first, until the second week of isolation made her stir crazy. In the beginning friends came by, but the visitor stream trickled to near nothing rather quickly. A few stopped in every couple of weeks, but only one came daily.

Jack.

Jack had been there rain or shine for their favorite pastime, Monopoly. Mollie grinned at the memory of Jack whipping the pants off of her, completely ruthless in her play, never feeling sorry enough for the kid with cancer to ever let her win.

Finally, almost exactly one year from the start of treatment, Mollie's red cell count was high enough to return to school. But the excitement was ruined when Mollie realized she'd have to go back with a still bald head. Jack quickly pointed out how *stupid* Mollie was to care, then sauntered off to the bathroom where she proceeded to shave her head with beard trimmers.

Mollie stood and watched, awed by her friend's kindness and beauty. Bald Jack was stunning. Mollie could still picture Jack in her bathroom rubbing her bald head and educating her in haughty style. "Whatever you wear; wear it with attitude, and people will be impressed." Jack looked closely at her image in the mirror. "We just need…." A thought came to her, and she grabbed Mollie by the hand and dragged her down the hall to her mother's bedroom, where Mrs. Hinkle's eyes went from round surprise to teary-eyed in seconds. Hand on hip, Jack informed her, "Mrs. Hinkle, we need to go to the mall. We need hats, scarves, and I think we should get our ears pierced." She thought a moment. "No, I'm certain. We *have* to get them pierced."

Dressing quickly, she decided to sneak out and find Jack some breakfast. Jack was a natural born eater, and Mollie knew it would please her to get something besides a pop tart.

She searched the tiny town, going up one street and down another, but found nothing more than a little grocery store. Mollie inquired about a hot meal and was shocked when the cashier flipped off her light and dragged her out of the store. "It's my break," she said with a wink as she grabbed Mollie's arm and dragged her a street over to cook her up some eggs and bacon with a side of gossip.

Mollie returned to the hotel with breakfast and an exuberant story to tell. She set the plates on the dresser and shook Jack until she groaned and sat up.

"You'll never...never in a million years believe me."

"Let's see...." Jack stretched and yawned. "So far this week, we've driven over a hundred miles out of our way to attend a party neither one of us wanted to go to...Joanie stole my car and ran away with some guy leaving us stuck here...the bitch. You met your soul mate and morphed into a moony-eyed pain in the ass who wakes me up before dawn so that I may feast on another pop tart...another good reason to kick Joanie's ass." Jack fell back against the pillows. "Let me sleep, Molls. It's my only comfort."

Mollie waved the plate under her nose. "I brought you real food...which I shouldn't let you have...such ingratitude."

"Food?" Jack threw back her covers and sat up. "Where did you get food?"

"I was talking to the lady at the grocery store, and she was really nice, and she offered to make us breakfast...so she took a break from work and made us some eggs."

"You've got to be kidding me?"

"So quaint."

Jack frowned. "Sounds like a scene from *Deliverance*. Did you hear any banjos?"

"No. No banjos, and she had perfectly fine teeth. You know, you're like a racist toward small towns."

"Small towns aren't a race."

"I know, but you know what I mean. You've got like small town phobia."

"Well, for saints like you, Mollie, it ain't a big deal. I bet if you asked Ron, he'd tell a different tale."

"Because he's black? Get over it, Jack. Sue, the lady who made the eggs, said she liked him. She did call him 'colored,' but I don't think she thought of that as rude. She said, and I quote, 'That colored boy is good people, a right fine young man. Got to respect what he did for his niece.'"

"What niece?"

"Ron's niece. Craig said her name's Emily. I guess her mom, Ron's sister, died a couple years ago, and Ron moved out here to take care of her. He didn't want her to have to change schools and everything, so he just moved here. Isn't that sweet?"

"Wonder why he didn't tell me about her?"

Mollie shrugged. "In Ron's defense, there are things about me I haven't told Craig, not because I'm not interested, but because I want him to like me, not feel sorry for me or anything. And quite honestly, if I were raising a child, I wouldn't go making her part of my dates unless the person was a definite keeper."

Jack shot her a look. Mollie placed her hand over her heart and patted it. "Oh my," she cooed, "I do believe for the first time in my little girl's life, she wants to be a keeper."

Jack tossed a pillow at Mollie and grabbed her plate of food. "Bacon grease eggs, I haven't had these since Grandma died," Jack admitted. "Makes me feel a little misty eyed. Queasy, but misty eyed."

Mollie laughed. She knew how Jack felt about the woman who had raised her. Jack was fourteen when her grandmother passed away, leaving Jack with a drunken father who tried but never could quite manage to grow up. "I think you'd find that one in every third person in this town would remind you of your grandma. She'd have cooked breakfast for a couple of strangers."

Jack grinned. "That she would, Mollie, that she would."

Mollie hurried and swallowed her bite of food. "Did you know Ron owns the bar in town? But he doesn't run it, because evidently he gets checks from a bank back east that more than pays for his living expenses."

Jack nodded. "He did tell me he owned the bar. Said he was going to open it, but then saw how much work it was going to be and kept putting it off. He didn't mention any checks…good lord, are these people all private eyes?"

Mollie shrugged. "Well, seems the bar houses the only restaurant too, and since he's not running it, there's no place to eat in town, which evidently is a real disappointment to everybody. Sue, the cashier who cooked all this? She said they've tried to talk him into opening it back up and he says he will…if he could find a manager." Mollie's eyebrows raised, and her voice held so much hope that Jack stopped chewing.

"What are you getting at?"

"Well…I just couldn't help but wonder…what if…wouldn't it be wild if you could help Ron out?"

"Yeah, I'm going to ask some guy I hardly know if I can open a restaurant in his bar—a bar that's two thousand miles from home!"

"I like it here," Mollie said quietly. "Sue said the county needs a teacher."

Jack gave her a hard look. "You've totally lost your mind. This isn't a mail order bride love story Molls. Keep your head out of the clouds and your feet on the ground. Who changes their life that drastically that quickly?"

Mollie dropped her fork. "I almost forgot! Joanie and Mitch got married in Vegas! Of course Sue says his mother is just livid…she being the head of the Baptist women, and now her son has ran off and got married in sin city and all."

"I don't know what's more shocking…Joanie getting hitched or you just making yourself at home with the locals."

Mollie flipped her the bird and resumed eating.

****

Later that afternoon, Ron arrived unexpectedly to beg Jack to go with him to dinner. Jack tried to bow out, but Mollie practically shoved her out the door to the car. She waved good-bye from the parking lot and then turned and found herself unwilling to wait alone in her hotel room. The sun was too bright, the air too sweet to stay inside, so she walked down a gravel road that was behind the hotel. It wound its way through the miles and miles of farm land. It was hypnotic, these fields with their perfectly spaced rows continuing endlessly across thousands of acres. Crickets chirped, and somewhere, a tractor hummed. Pronghorn leaped through the tall grass, prairie dogs stood on their hind legs, sniffed the air, and glanced around, watching for danger. Mollie walked until she could no longer see the hotel on the horizon. As a matter of fact, she couldn't see anything. She had passed two houses, and an abandoned-looking barn. None of which were still in sight.

She decided to head back. She turned to retrace her path when she saw, off in the distance, a gathering cloud of dust. A vehicle approached. She stepped to the side of the road so it could pass unhindered, but instead it stopped.

Mollie's initial fear of being alone in the middle of nowhere was replaced with relief when she recognized Craig. Then her heart thumped with the awareness of his presence.

"Need a lift?" he asked. Those simple words made her blood pressure climb and her cheeks blaze.

Mollie nodded, but made no move toward the car. Craig reached across the seats and swung the door open. Mollie climbed in, wishing with every thought that she was a bit calmer, a little smoother when she came in contact with Craig Coulter. He made her feel like such an adolescent.

"You walked here from the hotel?"

Mollie nodded. "Ron and Jack left around three, and I was bored, so I went for a walk."

"I tried to call you before I left the station, but you weren't there."

"Oh," Mollie gasped, realizing she had, as usual, forgotten her cell phone. "I left my phone on the dresser. I swear, I'd forget my head if it wasn't attached."

"I had to ask Jerry where you went."

"Jerry?"

"The guy who runs the hotel. He said you went out the east road about an hour ago. You realize you made it over three miles? I was starting to get worried when I didn't spot you after the first mile. This place has a near zero crime rate, but things can happen anywhere." He reached across, grabbed her hand, and brought it to his lips and kissed it lightly.

Mollie turned and looked out the window. Craig sounded like a caring boyfriend...one Mollie could count on when things got tough, but she knew better. He barely knew her. *Oh, Lord, I just want this too much. What's wrong with me? I just want to wrap up in those thick arms and say love me, I know you've only known me for three days, but isn't that enough to build a lifetime? A lifetime isn't so long, because for some it may just be a matter of months....*

Forcing composure, Mollie turned to Craig and grinned. She could see the confusion in his eyes, but having no answer; she ignored it, trying instead to change the subject. Mollie babbled about anything she could think of—her parents, her sisters, her job, her childhood—whatever came to her mind she talked about it.

Craig listened.

Mollie stopped abruptly. "I'm sorry; I haven't let you say a word."

Craig grinned. His eyes sparkled. "I like to hear you talk. I could listen forever."

Mollie's heart sped up, forcing extra blood to her cheeks. "I guess that's good. I'm...I always seem to chatter."

"Well, I have all night to listen. You available?" Craig asked as he approached the hotel.

"I suppose. Though I did have big plans...."

"Big plans?" Craig asked a bit seriously.

Mollie laughed. "I'm joking. I can't even think of something to say I might do."

"Good then. You're all mine."

Chapter 9

Pulling into the driveway, they found Ron's car parked in his yard.

"Looks like Ron is reliving glory days. He thinks the Celtics screwed up by not calling him." Craig shook his head as he pulled his car next to Ron's. They got out and leaned against the car and watched with amusement as Ron attempted to alley-oop and hook shot his way to Jack's heart—or so Mollie assumed. Jack seemed unimpressed.

Ron caught them watching and shouted, "Think fast." Then he hurled the basketball at Craig. "How 'bout a little game?" Ron asked.

"Not tonight." Craig tossed the ball back.

Mollie rounded the front of the car and stood beside Craig. Ron threw her the ball. "How 'bout you, Mollie? You game?"

Mollie looked up at Craig, then to Jack, who was already pink cheeked from exertion. "Come on, Mollie, don't be scared, I'll take it easy on you," Jack taunted.

"They're just afraid of losing." Ron nudged Jack and both made clucking noises.

"Fine," Mollie agreed, "What's the bet?"

"Loser makes dinner," Ron offered.

"And cleans up," Mollie upped the ante.

"And buys the food because the fridge is empty," Craig finalized the deal.

All agreed, and the game began. Mollie and Craig versus Ron and Jack. There really was no competition between Jack and Mollie. Jack played circles around her, making Mollie's head spin. Mollie wasn't surprised by her friend's lack of mercy. Fortunately, Craig carried her—both figuratively and literally. He grabbed Mollie by the waist and lifted her up to the basket where she was able to do a slam dunk.

It felt good to be breathless and happy.

Ron named each shot, swapping his personality for the Roninator, basketball player extraordinaire. The score was tied at eighteen, the winner to be called at twenty. Ron stood before Mollie and rolled it up one arm and down the other. He only stopped to spin it on a finger as he said, "I think I'd like lobster. You know how to cook a lobster, Mollie?"

Without a word, Mollie snatched the ball mid-performance and took off dribbling clumsily. Squealing with delight, she pulled up at the end of the drive and hurled the ball in the air. Arms flailed, legs sprung out like a jumping jack, she sent the ball sailing through the air toward the basket. Breathless, she watched as the ball hit the rim with a thud and circled once, then twice before dropping through the net. With a whoop and fingers in the air, she announced to them all, "I am the unsinkable, unbeatable, indomitable Mollie Hinkle."

Craig grabbed her around the waist and lifted her from her feet pressing her body against his as her arms waved high in the air.

"Abominable?" Craig teased.

Mollie laughed harder, her head thrown back, exposing her throat as she chuckled. Composing herself, she brought her attention and her gaze to his, laying her hands on top of his shoulders. Her smile was broad and genuine; her thumb stroked his stubble roughened cheek as she repeated, her voice lilted with humor, "Indomitable."

"That you are. Now give me a kiss."

Mollie gave him a simple kiss on the forehead. Craig lowered her until they were eye to eye. "That won't do," he informed her before he kissed her. Mollie's body melted into his. She knew he wanted so much more, but she wasn't sure if what he was searching for could be satisfied with any physical touch. She felt his hunger, could feel his need. She knew because she felt it herself.

"Break it up," Ron said. "The neighbors will talk."

Craig let Mollie slip back to the ground, though he kept his hand on her lower back, his thumb finding the groove of her spine through her shirt.

Ron offered Mollie a high five and sincere congratulations. Jack nagged at Ron as if they'd been married for years, "If *you* hadn't been showing off...."

Ron grinned and pulled Jack in for a hug. "Oh, come on now, Jackie, just wanted to show you my stuff."

"Blow an easy win like that again, I'll show you my stuff."

Ron squeezed her tighter and said in a loud whisper, "Besides, sweetie, I just saved you from a lousy dinner."

"So, what are we having, Ron?" asked Mollie.

"A meal that will curl your toes, little lady."

"I can't wait," said Mollie.

"And you won't have to. As soon as I get back, your dinner will be first on my to-do list."

Mollie looked to Jack, expecting her to look surprised, but she seemed to already know. "Where are you going?" Mollie asked.

"It's parent's week at Em's camp, and I need to go there for a couple of days. I tried to get Jack to keep me company, but she's too busy."

Jack glared at Ron. Mollie's face scrunched in displeasure. "What's wrong with you? Go, let me have some peace, for crying out loud."

Jack looked from Mollie to Craig then shook her head. "I don't want to go. Ron will think I'm easy."

Ron laughed, nearly dropping to his knees. "Do you see why I love this girl? She's a hoot."

Mollie gasped. Jack looked like someone punched her in the gut. Craig's eyes were big as saucers for an instant, and then he rubbed his chin and watched his friend as if to see how he would recover from this one.

"Why's everyone staring at me?" Ron asked, arms outstretched. "So, I said it. I said the L-word. Unlike you people, I'm not afraid to say what I'm feeling. I know you dig me, Jack. You're just too big a chicken-shit to even consider that we mesh."

"I am not a chicken-shit."

"The hell you aren't. If you weren't; you'd go with me, and don't be using the excuse of respect...I already offered you your own room."

"I don't want you to pay my way."

"Well, then, you pay for the rooms. Just come with me. I don't want to drive up there alone. It's in the mountains; it's beautiful up there. I'd like for you to see it."

"No," Jack answered flatly.

"Fine then, Craig that leaves you. Looks like you and I are going on a road trip."

"No," Mollie blurted. Craig couldn't leave now. She looked at Jack. "Stop being a big wuss. Go with him. He'll be a gentleman, right, Ron?"

"Of course I will."

"I just don't think I should..." Jack said.

"I'd pity you, Jack, if you were staying on my account," Mollie threatened sweetly.

Jack seemed to consider the consequences, then answered with a sigh, "Fine, I'll go, but I'm warning you." She pointed a well-manicured finger at Craig. "Well, you know. Just trust that I will make your life a hell."

"Jack," Mollie scolded.

Jack quieted. Ron offered to take her home so she could pack; they would leave tonight. Jack looked as tortured as a mother leaving her child in day care for the first time. She hugged Mollie, asking her over and over if she was sure this was the right thing to do. Mollie assured her repeatedly, finally just ordering her to leave.

Jack and Ron left. As the car drove away, Jack looked out the back window as if she expected Mollie to change her mind and run after her.

Craig took Mollie by the hand and pulled her toward the house. Brutus came to say hello, but this time Mollie was prepared and dodged the ever-friendly beast at the door. Once inside, Craig kissed her lightly. His face hovered above hers for a moment as if there was something he wished to say, but he said nothing more profound than, "I need to shower and change. I was going to do that before I picked you up, but after I called and couldn't get hold of you, I went straight from work. I was afraid I'd find your perfect, little body broken in a ditch along the road." Mollie felt the color creep up her neck. It was impossible to stay calm with his body so close, and his words so gentle, yet provocative, in their simplicity.

"I'll just...." Mollie's voice was hoarse. She cleared her throat and licked her lips before finishing, "I'll just watch television."

His thumbs traced the outline of her brow. She could feel her eyelashes brush against his roughened palm. Framing her face in his hands, he lifted her chin and kissed her again. His lips caressed, explored, his tongue teased, tasted, absorbed. Pulling back, he looked down at her. Her eyes remained closed, her cheeks pink, her lips red and full. She opened her eyes to find him studying her. "Penny for your thoughts?" she asked.

He grinned, appearing all the more devilish. "You don't want to know."

He kissed her lightly once, then again. Then he backed away, finally turning and heading for the shower.

Mollie sat on the couch, not bothering to turn on the television. She wished she knew what went on inside of Craig's head. What was he thinking when he stared through her? Her eyes closed as a tingle ran through her body. It didn't take a genius or a crystal ball to know what he wanted, and she needed to decide how far she wanted this to go. Would it be a mistake to make love to him? She didn't know. But no matter what happened, she would never be the same. Love should complete you, make you better, stronger. Craig taught her that.

In an instant, she turned several shades of red and fidgeted in her seat as if there was someone in the room who could read her thoughts. She just admitted she loved this man, this near stranger, who felt as comfortable to her as Jack.

Were she and Ron completely insane?

She had to answer, yes. This was the worst time in her life to fall in love. She might have cancer. What man wants to date a girl on chemo? And even if he did want her, how could she stay? Her doctors were at home. Oh, it was too unfair. She wanted not only to live, but she didn't want to take the time to fight, even for her life. She just wanted to feel. She just wanted to be normal. Her pouts were interrupted by the ringing of the phone, sitting on the table in front of her. Without thinking she grabbed it and said, "Hello."

It was a woman's voice on the other end—a strong, confident voice. "Put Craig on the line, please." The please was not polite, but perfunctory.

Mollie panicked, and then felt the rising nausea of jealousy.

"Is there a problem?" the voice demanded.

"No," Mollie squeaked.

"Then get my son."

"Your son?" Mollie felt relief flood through her veins; then another wave of panic marched in. It was *his mother*. Mollie squirmed on the couch, looking nervously toward the bathroom door.

"Yes, my son. And I don't care how busy he says he is, put him on the phone."

"Yes, Ma'am," Mollie answered. Placing the phone on the table, she went to the bathroom door. "Craig?"

He didn't answer.

Mollie returned to the phone. "Sorry, Ma'am, he can't hear me."

"The phone's cordless, right?"

"Mmm, hmm."

"Then *take* it to him."

Mollie gasped. "I can't."

"Why not?"

"He's in the shower."

The woman laughed. "That's never bothered any of the other women he's dated. What's your name?"

"It's Mollie, Ma'am," Mollie said, adding, "Mollie Hinkle."

"Are you over eighteen?"

"Of course," Mollie blurted. "I'm twenty-four."

"You sound shocked."

"Well...I...."

"This your first date?"

"No."

"Really? You've made it through a date without showering with him. I am impressed. You seem like a nice girl. I'll give you some advice: run now."

Mollie gasped. "That's not very nice."

"Just trying to help. Don't sound so offended."

"But you're his mother."

"So?"

"So, you shouldn't be so mean."

Barbara Coulter laughed, "You evidently don't know my son."

"I know he's kind and decent."

Barbara Coulter's laugh ended abruptly, her voice harsh, "I'd give a year's salary for that to be true." She sighed, giving off an air of condescension. "Well, tell him his brother, Tres, had another boy. This morning, before breakfast. Weighed eight pounds, three ounces. Name's Charles Winston Coulter the fourth. I'm visiting them this weekend. Tell Craig if he'd like to come, there'll be a ticket waiting for him at Great Falls. Should I get one for you?"

"No, Craig and I are just friends."

"Really? A friend?" She inhaled deeply. "Why this is a change of events. Well, there will definitely be a ticket for you. You, I have to meet."

There was no good-bye, just dial tone. Mollie stared at the receiver as if she didn't know what to do with it. Craig emerged from the bathroom, his cheeks smooth and his hair damp. Mollie placed the phone on the table. "That was your mother. She said you're an uncle again."

Craig shrugged and went to the refrigerator for a beer.

Chapter 10

Mollie followed him. "Don't you want to know what it is?"

"The ultrasound said it was a boy."

"They can be wrong."

"Was it?"

"Well…no," Mollie answered.

Craig frowned and took a long drink.

"Don't you care? Aren't you excited for your brother?"

"I'm happy my brother finally has all he deserves."

"Then call him and congratulate him."

Craig ignored her question as he moved past her to the living room. Mollie followed, not giving up. "Your brother has a new baby. It's a big deal."

Craig flipped on the television. Mollie sat beside him and leaned across his lap until she could see his face. He tried to avoid her eyes, but couldn't. Sighing, he flipped off the TV and turned his attention to her. "Look, I don't know what you want from me."

"Just call him."

"What am I supposed to say? Glad you got to be around when this one was born?"

"Oh, Craig, that's absurd. Just call and acknowledge that he's had a child."

"I'll send flowers."

"Craig." Mollie grabbed his leg and gave it a shake. "Call him. Get all this behind you. You can't move your life forward until you let go of the past."

"I don't need, or want, my life to move anywhere. I warned you not to try to change me."

"But they're your family."

"Why are you making such a big deal out of this?"

"You can't be serious. It's a baby...a new, fresh life."

A child, oh, if only she could have one she'd climb Mt. Everest and shout her news to the world. But she knew with all the chemo and radiation; it may never be possible. All she might ever have to look forward to was being an aunt. And if that was all she could have; she fully intended to spoil her sisters' children to the max. She couldn't understand how Craig could shrug the honor of being an uncle away so easily. "A baby is monumental." She handed him the phone. "Call him."

Craig put the phone back on the table.

"Are you afraid to talk to him? Is it because he acts like your mom?"

Craig laughed. "She was her charming self on the phone?"

Mollie blushed. "She was, um, direct."

"My mother's a rude bitch. She says whatever's on her mind. She went from lawyer to judge to senator by being hard-nosed and domineering." He stroked her cheek, his eyes soft. "But that doesn't make it all right to hurt people. What did she say to you, Mollie? You don't deserve...."

"Don't worry about me. She was polite...in her own sort of way."

"Did she tell you I'm not to be trusted? I'm the Big Bad Wolf and you're Little Red Riding Hood?"

"Something like that." Mollie grinned. "Should I be wary?"

Craig pulled her in and wrapped his arms around her. He nuzzled his lips against her ear as if telling her a secret. "I'll make you a promise."

Mollie nodded as it was the only response she could muster with him so close; his breath was warm and enticing against her ear.

His kiss was light, barely brushing his lips against hers. "I promise I won't take advantage of you: no lies, no coercion, no tricks, and definitely no games. I won't take anything from you that you aren't willing to give."

Mollie pulled back and searched his eyes. She saw pain. She saw a man hiding so much hurt.

"I might be insane, but I trust you. And I want you to trust me."

Craig's eyes narrowed as if confused.

"Take my advice and call your brother, or better yet, go see them. Your mom is arranging you a plane ticket. She said you can pick it up at the airport."

"Not happening."

"I don't truly believe you don't care about your brother's baby."

Craig leaned back against the couch and ran a hand through his hair. "Why can't you let this go?"

"Because I just don't get it; he's your brother."

"Not all families are the Hinkle's. I've made my decision. Drop it."

Mollie nodded. She squeezed his hand and smiled at him, her eyes stinging with unshed tears. "I'm sorry. I really should mind my own business."

"Ah, shit. Stop looking like a kicked pup. I don't mean to be a prick, but I'm done with it. They don't need me around reminding them that I screwed things up."

"But you didn't do anything!"

"I lied to my brother. I never told him Jenna was trying to contact him. Hell, she told me she was pregnant, and I withheld that fact from my brother."

"But you were only sixteen…it was up to your mother to make the wise decisions."

"I never told her about the conversation. I figured Jenna was a lunatic like her sister."

"See? You were trying to help your brother. You have to forgive yourself. Then you'll be free to have a relationship with…."

"For God's sake, Mollie…enough. You're making a big deal out of nothing."

"You just have to get past the fear."

"Fear?"

"Yeah, you're kinda like Jack. You act like a prick to stop anyone from hurting you."

Craig's jaw clenched and he stood. His voice was clipped, "Stop being naïve. And dammit, don't make me your salvation project. If you think I'm a sweet guy waiting for love to fix him, you're a fool."

Mollie said nothing. She studied her hands, unable to look at him.

Craig continued, red faced, "Don't waste your time and your hopes trying to make me something I'm not. How the hell can I be any more direct? How can I make you see I'm not what you think I am? Son of a bitch…it's like you don't listen."

It took every ounce of courage to look him in the eye, but she did, "You're right. You are a prick."

Mollie stood to leave, mumbling a few unintelligible words as she gathered her purse and headed toward the door. She opened it, but he moved in behind her and shut it. Mollie stood frozen, staring at the door, waiting for him to speak. He put his hands on her shoulders and turned her to face him, "Don't leave me." He pulled her close to him and buried his face in her hair. "I don't want to hurt you, but I don't want you to think I'm more than I am." Mollie hugged him tight and laid her cheek against his chest.

He sighed and stroked her hair. "You really want to know what I was thinking earlier?" Mollie nodded. He pulled her a little tighter. "I was thinking I need to screw you until you can't walk straight then whatever the hell it is you're doing to my head will stop. I don't want you in my head, Mollie. I don't want to think about you every minute of every day. I don't want to give a damn about you or what you think. I want to relieve myself of you."

Mollie was dumbstruck for several moments. Then she took a deep breath and gave her head a shake. Looking up at him, she said, "Wow. I'm speechless. I'll never accuse you of being silver tongued. I suppose this would be the appropriate time to storm out in an insulted huff."

Craig shook his head. "I'm being honest, and you did ask what I was thinking."

"Yes, I did. Watch what you ask for, eh? Well, I'll neither get mad, nor ask you to explain. I will assure you, I don't want anything from you that *you're* not willing to give. I'm not trying," Mollie said and paused to swallow hard, feeling guilty for all her daydreams, "to rope you into a relationship or some sort of commitment. I mean I have to go home soon. I have my own life to get back to." Craig said nothing, but his stare made Mollie more nervous. Her already pink cheeks grew warmer. "Friends?" She smiled up at him.

Craig shook his head and walked away. "Damn it, Mollie...."

She sighed. "Relax. I don't expect you to fall in love with me and carry me off into the sunset on your white horse. I say we call today a night, and maybe tomorrow, if you feel like it, we could go fishing or something." Mollie grabbed the doorknob again. "Until then, lighten up. You're too serious."

"You don't have to run off." Craig pulled her away from the door, his hand gentle on her arm. "We can do that now."

"No. I best go."

Craig kissed her, his hands cradling her head, twisting into her hair. He nipped at her ear and said, "I'm sorry."

Mollie grinned in spite of herself. "Well, you *are* the only person I know in this town."

"Thank God." He kissed her again before breaking away to gather the fishing gear from the kitchen closet. Then he went to the fridge for the container of worms.

"Yummy," Mollie said, "dirt and worms. Right next to the hotdogs."

"Where do you store your bait?"

"My dad and I always use fake worms. They don't spoil."

"That's not real fishing."

"Try to tell my dad that. He says he's never had much luck on the river with live bait. Gets the most bites with the fake ones, but they have to be white. I guess city fish expect their dinner to glow in the dark."

Craig led her out the back door, across the yard, over a gently rolling bank that opened to a stream. The rocky bedded water cut through the endless meadow. The trees lining the river rustled in the ever blowing wind, and the sun shone off the water in a liquid shimmer. "What a beautiful little stream."

Craig laughed. "It's a river."

"No way," Mollie argued. "The Ohio, the Allegheny, the Monongalia, now, those are rivers. You could never get a boat down one of these. It's what, a foot deep?"

"In some spots, but it's very deceptive. In some places it's over your head. The water's so clear you can see the bottom whether the water is one foot or ten. See right there? In the shade of that cotton wood?"

Mollie nodded.

"It's at least five feet. So, watch where you step."

Craig rolled up his pant legs and stepped into the water. Mollie followed suit. He held out his hand, helping her into the water. As her first foot took the plunge, she squealed and nearly lost her footing on the surprisingly slippery rocks. The cold gripped her ankle, making it ache. Craig grabbed her around the waist and laughed. "Oh, yeah, the rivers are mostly fed from melting mountain snow. Water's real cold."

"Really? Now you tell me." She adjusted to the cold with further squeals, though she attempted to muffle them as she dipped the second foot into icy water. She slipped and slid until she slowly gained her balance on the slime covered round rocks. Once she was totally in and numb to her ankles, Craig escorted her down-stream. Mollie held her own, only having to grab his shoulder for support a few times.

"So, we are traipsing through the freezing water instead of just walking along the bank because?" Mollie asked.

Craig shrugged, "Just how it's done. The guy I bought the land from called that field rat'ler field, so I guess I've just always been a little hesitant to check out if the name was appropriate. I just stick to the water."

"So, since I live on Squirrel Hill you'd assume there are lots of squirrels?"

"Probably wouldn't give a damn. Squirrels aren't poisonous."

Mollie laughed. "We do have a lot of squirrels. My dad battles them over his bird feeders. I kind of like the squirrels better than the birds. There was this one that would climb the metal pole…a metal pole! Can you believe that? Anyhow, the squirrel would run off the birds and just sit there and eat. Have you ever watched them eat? They're so cute. They have little hands, just like little tiny humans. He'd hold onto the sunflower like a cookie and nibble on it. That's far cuter than anything a bird can do."

"I like squirrels. My dad used to take me squirrel hunting every fall."

"Oh," Mollie said. "Well, did you ever look at their hands?"

"I know skinned out, they look like you're eating rat."

"That's gross."

Craig laughed. "Don't worry. I quit hunting squirrels long ago."

Mollie was quiet a moment. She remembered him telling her his dad had died of a heart attack when he was young. She pulled in close to him and wrapped her arm around his. Craig looked down at her and smiled. It was a small smile, barely a twitch, but his eyes were soft and the stress on his face was eased. The glint of sunshine off the water made his eyes sparkle. Even the scars on his face seemed softened. Curious, Mollie asked, "How did you get the scars?"

"The one on my nose came from a game of wiffle ball."

"Wiffle ball? Lordy, what kind of wiffle ball do you play?"

"It was my dad's game. We'd play in the foyer of our house. The batter would bat from the stairwell then you had to slide down the banister and get to the front door to score. I was sliding down the banister, and my little brother, Trip—he was so much smaller than Tres and I, so he had this little guy complex—well, Trip didn't want me to score so he punched me in the face. That didn't really hurt, but I lost my balance on the railing and fell and busted my nose on a table. I had five stitches across the bridge. Trip hid from me for a week. He was scared to death I'd kill him." Craig laughed at the memory.

"Did you kill him?"

"No, I suppose I deserved it. I harassed that poor guy every day. I was the one who gave him the awful nickname, 'cause he was a clumsy little kid. God, I teased him constantly. I think that's why he's so feisty now. Without my torture, he'd probably been a mellow sort of guy."

Mollie nodded. "How 'bout the scar on your chin?"

Craig frowned. "That story isn't so much fun."

"Well, how'd you get it?"

"A woman hit me with a ball bat, knocked out two of my teeth and sliced my chin open."

"Wow. What did you do to deserve that?"

"I didn't deserve it."

"No?"

"No, her girlfriend was a consenting adult. If she was pissed at anyone, it should've been with the tramp that cheated on her."

"Oh," Mollie gasped, "She was gay?"

"Evidently."

Mollie laughed. She imagined telling Jack and laughed a little harder.

Craig growled at her. "I'm glad you find it amusing."

"Can I tell Jack?"

Craig shrugged and shook his head. "So you can both laugh at me?"

"With you! We'd be laughing *with* you!"

"But I'm not laughing."

"But you should be. It's a funny story." Mollie's eyes gleamed, twinkling with laughter tears.

"This is a good spot." Craig stopped at the bend in the river where the low-growing cottonwoods bent to offer shade. Craig worked on the tackle, finishing Mollie's pole then turning to his. "You don't fly fish?" Mollie asked. "Isn't that the thing in Montana?"

"I'm an eastern boy, remember? Here…." Craig offered her bait.

Instinctually, Mollie held out her hand. He dipped into the bait can around his waist and placed a fat, squirming worm in the palm of her hand. Mollie squealed and jerked her hand and body back, twisting in fright and surprise. Her footing lost on the slippery rocks, her feet slid out from under her. Craig grabbed for her, but down she went, backward into the six-foot fishing hole. She dropped her pole, which was swept away by the current, but Mollie didn't see it go. She was submerged in freezing water. Craig yelled and lunged for her. In a single swift motion, he grabbed her under her shoulders and pulled her out.

His voice was sharp, "What the hell? It was just a worm."

Mollie held onto his arm for balance as she sputtered, coughed, and tried to catch her breath. She was cold, and her teeth chattered. "You should have warned me! You don't just hand a girl a worm!"

"You said you fished."

"I said I fished with fake lures!"

"It was just a damned worm. You act like the damned thing would bite. You could've drowned."

"Don't be so dramatic." She pulled her soaked hair away from her face. "It was barely over my head…besides, I know how to swim."

"You could have broken your damned leg."

"My *damn* legs are fine."

Craig grabbed her by the arm and started walking her back the way they came. "Let's get you back before you freeze to death."

Mollie tried to pull her arm free. "I said I'm fine."

It was as if he didn't hear her. His grip on her arm remained, and he nearly dragged her from the water. Not once did he look back at her. He trudged on silently, pulling her behind him. Mollie huffed, but followed. The wind whipped right through her soaked clothes, making her shiver. As they neared the house, Mollie jerked her arm away and snapped, "You're as bad as Jack."

Chapter 11

Craig neither spoke nor slowed his pace as he led Mollie back to the house. Mollie crossed her arms over her chest and decided if he wanted to be a grump, so be it. She wasn't going to be chastised. She didn't fall on purpose. As they reached the front porch, Mollie took a different course, heading toward the road with every intention of going back to her hotel.

"Mollie," Craig called from the yard.

Mollie slowed, but never turned.

"Come in and get dry."

"I've been enough trouble, and…and I'll pick you up a new fishing pole. It'll be on your porch tomorrow."

Craig grinned. "How are you going to do that? Don't you need your purse?"

Mollie bit her lip. Her purse was sitting on his counter. Would he get it if she demanded? She doubted it. Craig didn't take orders.

"Come on, come get your purse."

From where she stood, she was on the low ground, he was on the high. She tapped her foot as she looked up at him. He smiled down at her and bowed his head as if offering a truce. "Come on, Mollie. I was just worried about you. The current's swift and you could have really gotten hurt. I'll be nice. I promise."

Mollie stormed past, careful not to let her shoulder brush against him. She'd get her purse and leave. Her progress was delayed by Brutus, who blocked the door, whining to be petted. Mollie tried to sidestep the dog, but he was like a furry, panting, lovable monolith. Mollie sighed hard as she leaned down to stroke his ears and rub his chin.

"That's it, buddy, slow her down, so she's not mad at us." The dog agreed with a single bark and a wag of his tail.

"Us? Hmmph." Mollie shot him a wicked look. "I'm not mad at Brutus. He may be a dog, but he has manners. You," she stood and faced him, "act like I jumped in the water on purpose."

"I was…alarmed…I…." He took her hands in his. "I was scared. You can't be mad at me for that." He moved a step closer. He was so close Mollie could feel his heat. He rubbed her arm and said, dipping his head, "I'm sorry. I'm an ass. Let me get you some dry clothes, then I'll make it up to you. Please?" She didn't budge. "For Brutus?" As if on cue, the dog whined and sat against Mollie's leg.

"Sorry about the pole." Mollie's contrition softened a little.

"I don't care about the pole. I didn't like thinking about you getting hurt."

Mollie shook her head. "Am I so pathetic that everyone feels like they have to baby me? I went ass over tin cup into a fishing hole. That's funny, not tragic."

Craig grinned at the memory. "Maybe I was afraid of Jack. I've already been beaten up by a woman; don't want to add another to the list."

Mollie rolled her eyes. "Jack's not my girlfriend."

"But she'd still seek revenge, right?"

"I can control Jack."

"Not if you snapped your pretty, little neck."

"Pretty? Little? I suppose if you're going to use flattery…."

"You want flattery?" Craig pulled her into him, kissing the tender skin of her neck. "You are, by far, the most beautiful woman I've ever seen."

Mollie laughed. "Don't push it."

"Oh, but you are." His lips trailed up her neck to her ear, nibbling the lobe. "And your body is perfect. It fits just right into mine." He pulled her closer, molding her to him. "See? I wonder if you weren't made for me."

Mollie closed her eyes and enjoyed the warmth, savored the feel of his kisses as his lips met hers. His hands moved down the small of her back, and she shivered.

Craig stepped back. "You're freezing."

No, I'm smoking, Mollie thought with a blush.

"Let me get you something to wear." Craig led her to his bedroom where he dug out a hoodie and sweat pants. Laying them on the bed, he offered to dry Mollie's clothes while they ate. He kissed her on the forehead and left. Mollie looked around the room. It, too, was nearly empty. Craig definitely didn't bother with decorating. He didn't even have any family pictures around. There was a clock on his nightstand, nothing else. He didn't even have a bedspread, just sheets and a thin blanket. But it was made. Tightly. Maybe that was a habit learned in military school. Mollie felt her heart sink at the thought of a young Craig being sent away from home. Was he scared? She would've been terrified. She didn't even stay at the hospital without her mother or father. Poor Craig, to lose his dad and then be sent away from home, no wonder the guy didn't trust anyone.

Mollie heard clanking in the kitchen reminding her Craig was waiting for her. She stripped, pausing a moment at her bra and panties. They were soaked. She chewed her lip as she debated what to do. The clammy itchiness made the decision for her. She pealed them off also, carefully wrapping them inside her clothes. She pulled the sweats on, cinched the waist tightly and dragged the hoodie over her head. She checked herself out in the dresser mirror, running her fingers through her hair and wiping the mascara smears from under her eyes. Satisfied, she opened the door and called to Craig, "Do you have a dryer?"

"Yeah, right there in the hallway. Do you know how to work it?"

"Of course." Mollie opened a linen closet. It was filled with the same neatly folded sheets and blankets as on the bed. Behind the next door, a stacked washer and dryer. Mollie put her clothes in the dryer then started the machine.

"You should get a clothes line," Mollie said as she came through the hallway. "With all the wind, you'd probably have dry clothes more quickly on the line."

"No thanks. I'm trying to warm the planet. It's too damned cold here in winters."

Mollie's laugh ended in a gasp when she turned the corner and saw Craig had set the table for a candlelight dinner. All right, so the candles were citronella, the dining ware was paper plates, and the fare was the worms' neighbor, the hotdogs. Mollie looked at Craig, who seemed suddenly bashful, possibly even embarrassed. "How thoughtful; thank you."

"It's nothing."

"No, this is wonderful. Mollie flipped off the kitchen light to heighten the glow of the candles on the table.

"You're seriously impressed?"

"Of course." Mollie seated herself while Craig stood by the table as if he was still trying to figure her out. "I suppose," Mollie chattered, ignoring Craig's confusion, "if you had just dated a guy, well a girl, like Justin, you would understand. He would never have thought to light a candle or cook me a hotdog. Buy me things? Yes. Take me out to expensive restaurants? Of course. Talk to me? Make me something? Listen to a word I have to say? Hell no. I'm so glad you live in God's country and can't try to buy me off."

Craig took his seat. "You're something else, Mollie."

Mollie helped herself to baked beans and a hot dog. "Is that a compliment?"

"Yes. I can't believe I am about to say this, but I think I've fallen in respect for you."

Mollie licked mustard from her finger as she checked out the seriousness of Craig's confession. She burst into laughter. "Well, I respect you too, Mr. Coulter."

The candles were near spent by the time they finished dinner. Dishes were done by tossing them in the trash. Mollie mixed up a pot of hot cocoa, while Craig built a fire in the fire place as the temperature dropped outside from the day's high of 80, to the night's low of 45. Craig explained this was normal for Montana as

Mollie carried in two mugs of cocoa and sat on the couch with her legs crossed. Craig tended the fire until it blazed. He rested on his heels and brushed his hands together. He looked back at Mollie with a satisfied look. She patted the couch and he joined her. Mollie handed him his cup of cocoa. He sipped it and sighed, "Mmm. I could get used to this."

Mollie nodded and let her head drop against his arm.

"You should just stay here, tonight. I don't like the idea of you being in the hotel all by yourself."

"You said yourself this wasn't exactly a high crime area," Mollie reminded.

"I know. I'd just…I don't want you to go. I'll sleep on the couch. You'll be safe, I promise."

"I trust you."

"Good, then it's settled."

"But what will people think?"

"Who cares? I don't care."

"I…."

"Come on, Mollie, they all probably think we're doing the nasty anyhow. Your reputation was ruined as soon as your friend ran away with Mitch."

"True," Mollie admitted, not wanting to leave anyhow. She didn't feel like being alone. "All right, but I'll sleep on the couch. You have to work tomorrow."

"I might be a cad, but even I won't make a *girl* sleep on the couch while I take the bed. Do you want to insult me?"

"No."

"Besides, it's a comfortable couch."

"Well, then I guess."

Craig leaned in and kissed her, then kissed her again, and again until the clock sped its way to well past eleven.

"What time do you get up?" Mollie asked as he nibbled on the bit of collar bone he could expose in the oversized garb.

Craig groaned.

"Seriously, you need sleep."

"I don't want to leave these." He kissed her lips.

"You won't be safe without sleep. You could wreck."

"Fine, if you're tired of my kisses...."

Mollie kissed him. "I would never tire of your kisses, but it is bedtime." Mollie stood and stretched, not remembering until she saw Craig's eyes pop that she had no bra on and the fabric clung to her naked breasts. She quickly dropped her arms and hunched her shoulders. Craig grinned and escorted her to the bedroom where he tucked her in and gave her a chaste kiss good night. She listened as he grabbed blankets and clicked off lights.

She lay there for over an hour, watching the clock tick off the minutes. She heard the crack and snaps of the fire and had the sudden urge to sleep there, in front of the warm and cozy glow. She grabbed her pillow and ripped the blanket from the bed and padded to the living room. She moved as quietly as a mouse, careful not to disturb him.

As she curled into fetal, sleeping position on the floor, Craig's voice startled her. He commanded from the darkness, "Come here, Mollie."

He scooted over, lifting the blanket, making room for her on the couch. She moved as directed and nestled into his warm, hard chest. His hands stroked her hair, his lips kissed her forehead. He didn't offer any sensual temptation, he simply snuggled her against him. She listened to him breathe, felt him fade into sleep. Mollie smiled and put her hand against his chest, his heartbeat soothing under her hand. Mollie's body relaxed, and she drifted off to sleep without her usual worries and fears for her future.

Chapter 12

Mollie woke the next morning as Craig tried to sneak away, but their limbs were too tangled for success. Sliding to the floor, he crouched beside her. Mollie tucked her hand under her cheek. "You should have taken the bed. I seem to have taken over the couch."

"My pleasure."

Mollie smiled.

Craig pulled on the tee-shirt then sat, watching her.

A blush crept up her neck from his scrutiny, but before she could ask what was up, he stood. Hands on hips, he paced as if making a tough decision.

Mollie sat up and crossed her legs under her.

"If I called off work, would you spend the day with me?"

Mollie tried not to grin from ear to ear, but it was a futile effort. Resting her elbows on her knees, she locked her fingers under her chin. "I suppose. With Jack gone, what else have I got to do? You're the only person I know in this whole town."

Craig shot her a look. Mollie leaned back and put her feet up on the coffee table. "Don't look at me like that, Craig Coulter. You are." Mollie pretended to be uninterested, taking pleasure in teasing him. She squealed and tried to bolt when she realized he was about to pounce, but she was far too slow. Within seconds, he had her scooped up, on her back, and pinned to the couch with his weight.

"You're a little sour in the morning, Mollie Hinkle. I think you need sweetened up." Craig nibbled on her neck, his whiskers tickling the sensitive skin. Mollie twisted and thrashed, giggling until her eyes watered.

"Please, please, stop," Mollie begged.

"Why will you stay with me?"

"Because you're so much fun?" Mollie tried to get away.

"That all?"

"Because I can't imagine a day being fun without you in it?"

Craig halted his assault. His eyes were searching, but for what? Mollie wondered. He kissed her. "I suppose that'll do."

"It better, because I can't take much more."

"Can't hardly resist me, huh?" he asked with a wink.

Mollie sat up and put her feet on the floor. "Torturing me for sweet nothings. How is it exactly you got the reputation for being so smooth with the ladies?"

Craig turned toward her, and Mollie yelped and ran off, locking herself in the bathroom.

Craig leaned against the door. "Coward. I expected better of you."

Mollie laughed, pressing her forehead against the wood. "It's too early for me to defend myself. Make me some tea…and some toast, then I'll be better armed."

"Help you in the shower?"

"Go away, beast!"

Craig laughed and moved on to the kitchen.

Mollie emerged from the bathroom several minutes later. He made the toast. A bit too brown, slathered in a few inches of butter, but to Mollie's rumbling stomach, it looked delicious. Next to it sat her steaming cup of tea. The coffee maker on the counter gurgled and spit. The aroma and early morning sunlight filled the room. Mollie sat at the table. "Coffee smells so good. Tastes like mud, but smells delicious." She wrinkled her nose and sipped her tea. "I should run to the hotel to change and shower. Then I'll be less *sour*."

"I'll run you over after you eat."

Craig poured himself a bowl of Fruity Pebbles, silently offering a bowl to Mollie, who declined. She sat cross-legged in her chair and took a bite of her toast. She chewed and swallowed, then said, "I never guessed a Casanova like you to be a Fruity Pebble kind of guy."

"They're the best. Fruit Loops cut the roof of your mouth, and when they sit in milk, they just sink and get soggy, whereas Fruity Pebbles…milk soaks in just a bit, and they're still perfect." He took a bite with an exaggerated, " Mmm." Before his next bite, he asked, "And why can't I be a Fruity Pebble kind of guy? And for that matter, what makes you think I'm a Casanova?"

Mollie shrugged. "Well, you've done your best to convince me you're a cold-hearted creep, and so did your mother. Also, every time you look at me, you look at me like I'm naked. " She hid behind her mug, pretending to take a long drink.

"You really believe that?"

"You do have a definite rakishness."

Craig shoveled cereal for several quiet minutes, then added, "It's that obvious I see you without clothes?"

Mollie sat her cup on the table and nodded. "Totally obvious. You're a bad, bad man."

"So I've been told." He looked across the table at Mollie, and if eyes ever smoldered, Mollie thought, his did. He promised with a wink, "And you'll not be able to resist me too much longer."

Lifting the toast to her mouth, she paused; eyes open wide.

Craig laughed. "Just joking. I promised you'd be safe, and I'll keep my word. No nefarious seductions." He grabbed her by the hand and pulled her from her seat. "Let's go have some fun today."

He took her to the hotel, and Mollie showered, blow dried, and dressed. She finished up and opened the bathroom door to find Craig gone. She went to the window and pulled back the curtain. There he stood by the door, a bag in his hands. Opening it, she asked, "Why are you outside?"

"I…." Craig shrugged and held the bag out to her. "I ran over to the hardware store and got you this…then I forgot I'd locked the door, so I've been standing out here waiting for you to get done dressing."

Mollie took the bag and pulled out a book. It was a guide to Montana wild flowers.

"I noticed you were pocketing all those flowers in the mountains, and I figured you'd probably like to know the names of them."

Mollie grabbed him by the shirt and pulled him in for a kiss. "You're so thoughtful. This," Mollie hugged the book to her chest and said, "is the most wonderful gift."

Craig blushed. "It's just a book."

"Oh no, it's not. It's perfect, and to think the only thing I've given you is a lost fishing pole."

"Screw the pole. Let's get lunch."

They drove to the nearest town with a population big enough to support a McDonald's. They ate and then he accompanied her to local gift shops while she picked up presents for her sisters. Then on to the post office so she could mail them home. "I appreciate you running me around. I've been sending gifts home every couple of days since we left because I know how my sisters love to get a little something. But with Joanie running away with our rental car, we've been stuck with what we can get in Windham, and no offense to Windham, but the shopping is rather restricted. I suppose if Joanie doesn't come back soon, we'll have to fly home." Mollie grumped after handing her packages over to the post master and walking out into the bright afternoon sun.

"Are you in a hurry?"

"No, I just," Mollie thought of her biopsy and sighed, a frown appearing on her face as she said, "I just can't ignore my...um, obligations forever."

"Why not?"

"Because I'm an adult," Mollie grabbed his hand and said, "but let's not worry about that now. I'm having fun. Thank you again for my book, and for a wonderful day."

"I had fun too. Thank you, Mollie."

"For what?"

Craig kept a hand at her waist as they walked back to his car. "For reminding me I can still have fun."

Stopping herself mid-breath from saying, "aw, how sweet," she realized quickly that was the last thing he would want to hear, so instead, she kissed him. Stepping back, she wiped her lip gloss off his lips and said, "Life's short. It should be fun."

"Honestly, I hadn't felt hopeful or happy since I was a kid and my dad was alive."

"I'm sorry, Craig."

"Don't let that bother you. It was a long time ago. I imagine he's up in Heaven, drinking beer and smoking cigars…that doesn't cause cancer in Heaven."

"Really?"

"Really."

Leaning toward him, she kissed him again. "You're full of surprises. Fruity Pebbles and now Heaven."

They reached the car. As Craig slipped it into gear, Mollie asked, "Shock me with one more."

Craig thought a minute, then he confessed, "I installed one of those underwire fences to keep Brutus from running off. I know he's just a mutt, but I like having him around. I hated the thought of him wandering off. I even tried to get him to sleep in the house, but he won't give up his kingdom under the porch."

"He's a good dog. I wouldn't want him to leave either. Now, imagine, the love you have for your dog—imagine how crazy your nephews could make you."

Mollie bit her lip. Her mind jabbed at her for overstepping her bounds. She promised to drop the subject. Why didn't she learn? Glowing red, she gave him a sheepish smile.

"Fine. I'll call my brother. I don't know what I'll say, but I will call."

"Promise?"

"I said I would, that's enough."

Mollie pressed his hand to her lips. "Thank you, Craig."

"I suppose you're a good influence."

They spent the rest of the forty-minute drive discussing music, movies, books, and hobbies. Mollie felt she could talk to him for days on end without ever getting bored. Arriving home, Mollie recognized Ron's car. They were back. Swallowing the lump of disappointment didn't make her heart feel any better. Jack's return brought reality with it.

"Did you miss us?" Jack asked as they got out of the car.

"Not really," Craig answered, good humor making his comment less offensive, more taunting.

"You're still the friendly one aren't you?" Jack shot back without malice.

"Just honest."

Ron snickered; Jack tossed out a quick, "I bet."

The kitchen table was loaded with grocery bags. Ron and Jack began unloading them in a well-coordinated effort.

Ron heated a skillet, melted butter, and added seasoning while Jack dumped in a bag of shrimp. "Em's doing great," Ron announced as he stirred. Jack husked ears of corn and nodded. Ron continued, "She's going to do the whole month of band camp. She doesn't even miss me. I think she just wanted me to come up and give her more money and her iPod. I had lunch with her, and she was like um, thanks, see you later, Uncle Ron. At least I had Jackie to keep me company or I'd have been heart broken. Oh, that reminds me...." Ron put a large pot of water on to boil. "I've got big news, buddy. Jack has agreed to go into business with me."

Jack coughed and turned bright red.

"What?" Mollie asked turning to Jack.

"Ron suggested we open the restaurant. Remember, Mollie, you said the town needed one?"

Mollie was stunned, her mind reeled. Her best friend took a quantum leap.

"I know it's impulsive," Jack explained.

"You're staying here?" Craig asked, his voice not hiding his utter shock.

"Well, yeah. You got a problem with that, there Paul Bunyan?"

"I can't think of anything better for the town, besides maybe a drought."

"Oh, kiss my ass, Coulter. You just keep your nose clean, and you won't have any trouble with me. You got a spare room I can borrow till I find me a place?"

"You can sleep with Brutus, under the porch, I guess."

"You're a real gentleman." Jack wadded a grocery bag and threw it at him.

Craig pulled a couple of beers out of the fridge and handed one to Jack. "Here's to one more Easterner invading the unsuspecting little town of Windham."

Jack laughed, lifting her beer to Craig's.

Mollie choked back, threatening tears. She tried to be rational. She was being completely selfish, but she couldn't help wonder why Jack had a dream come true? And why was banter between her and Craig suddenly so easy? Mollie felt like an outsider, and she didn't know what to say.

"Oh, damn," Jack said much too loudly. "Mollie, I forgot to get you creamer for your after dinner coffee. Well, let's run and get it and let Ron work his magic. He claims to make the best shrimp scampi in the West."

Mollie was about to object, but said nothing as Jack took her hand and nearly dragged her out of the house.

Opening Ron's car door, Jack climbed in. Mollie was shocked, this was so unlike Jack, using a date's car. She was usually so rigid about maintaining her boundaries that she'd not even accept anything but going dutch on dates.

"Ron leaves his keys in the car—how very freakin' quaint, huh?"

"What's come over you, Jack?"

"I'm crazy, Mollie. I'm behaving like a mad woman, and quite honestly, I don't care."

Mollie said nothing. Jack gushed on, "I told Ron everything."

"Everything?" Mollie asked still confused.

Jack nodded her head.

Mollie asked, "What was there to tell?"

"My dreams, you know those dreams that I have told you *all* my life and have threatened you with bodily harm if you told?"

"Your restaurant and Christmas dream?"

"Yeah!" Jack turned a face full of animation toward Mollie. "And I don't really know why. I just did, and Ron he just listened and then said, 'Well, Jack, why are those just dreams?' That's what he said, and you know for the absolute first time in my life, I actually believed it really could happen. I could have everything I've ever wanted; I just have to allow it."

"With Ron?"

"Well, I won't go that far. I've only known him a few days, but someday, maybe. Ron also suggested I make over his bar, and I thought about what you said, and I went for it." Jack looked stricken. "You did say that, Mollie. I never would've been so hasty if I didn't think I already had your blessing."

Mollie nodded, trying to find some excitement and happiness for her friend. "So, you'll be staying here?"

Jack shrugged. "Yeah, but look, it's not like I have anything at home. A rented apartment and what? Junk that would fit in a few boxes?"

Mollie realized her problem was envy. It wasn't a good feeling and it shamed to her very core. Jack had done everything for her, and if anyone in this world deserved to be cut a break, it was her.

"That's great, Jack," Mollie lied.

"Mollie," Jack said, squeezing her hand, "you know if anything happens, you know with anything, then I'd be right there by your side."

"That's not it, Jack. I'll be fine. I really am truly glad this is happening for you." Mollie felt her eyes sting. She looked out the window, searching for any distraction to stop the threatening tears. "I'm just jealous." She smiled weakly at her friend. "I'm jealous because Ron wants you here." Mollie felt the first tear fall, and she brushed it quickly away. "I'm jealous because I realize I want something I know I'll probably never have." She looked her in the eye. "I want him. It's crazy, and I keep thinking hopefully it's just like you said, a rebound, or even just a desperate attempt to experience something before it'sits too late. Whatever the reason, I can't convince my heart that I don't love him."

"Maybe you should tell him?"

"That proves you have gone insane." Mollie laughed. "You know men, and a guy like Craig? How do you honestly think he'd react?"

Jack frowned. "I don't know, Molls. It's possible he might run for the hills, but then it's possible he might not. I mean, look at me, I just signed on the dotted line for a fifty thousand dollar loan. All because I feel like some human, other than you, finally gets me. It's all crazy, and maybe I'll regret it, maybe I'll get a broken heart, but hey, they heal, right? Now, I'm betting right now, you're probably thinking, I wasn't considering my best buddy."

"You don't have to make your life revolve around me."

"I didn't say revolve. I said I *was* thinking about you. You see…now you don't have to see this as time limited. With me here, you have the perfect excuse to stay or to visit as often as you like. I mean, now you can catch him at your leisure."

Mollie nodded and smiled. Jack was right, but then she was also wrong. Whether or not she had a lifetime to work on Craig Coulter was still up in the air, or more specifically sitting in a lab on a Petrie dish.

Jack parked the car in the store lot. Mollie reached for the handle and then stopped to ask, "Do you think I'm crazy Jack? It hasn't even been a week."

Jack thought a moment before answering, "No, I think it's a matter of time consciousness. We know our time here wasn't permanent, so it made every feeling more intense. Some would argue these feelings may be less than real, but I think it just causes us to be better focused. Like when a person faces death, and suddenly priorities shift, and things become crystal clear."

Mollie nodded and silently absorbed Jack's words. Jack grimaced. Mollie squeezed Jack's arm as they walked into the store. "Thanks, Jack. I can always count on you to be my voice of reason."

"Yeah, anytime," Jack answered then said nothing more.

Chapter 13

At the end of the evening, after dinner and the dishes were done, Ron and Jack left. It was nearly eleven. The kitchen was silent, all but the hum of the fridge and the tick of the wall clock. Mollie had a million things on her mind, but nothing to say. Nothing that was safe to admit. She cleared her throat. "It's late. I better get back."

Nodding, Craig watched silently as she slipped on her shoes. Last lace tied, she stood.

"Well, maybe I'll see you tomorrow?" she asked.

Craig nodded again. That was the only movement his body made. Molly supposed he was as stunned and freaked out by the change of events as she was. He didn't budge until she opened the door to leave.

"Wait." He pulled a jacket off the hook by the door. "It's cold outside."

Slipping it on, Mollie said, "Thanks." It was thoughtful of him, but the gesture brought a lump to her throat. What did she think, that he'd say, "I love you, stay with me?"

Craig zipped her into the oversized thing, his fingers lingering under her chin. Gentle hands pulled her close, and he kissed her. "I'll walk with you. Keep you safe from local bandits."

Mollie laughed. "That's hardly necessary."

"Probably not, but still…seems the right thing to do."

She stepped out the door, and he followed, taking her hand and holding it as they walked. The air was crisp, the wind cold and

119

bitter, and the sliver of a moon did little to penetrate the velvety darkness. There was silence. No sirens, no motors, no sounds of life other than an occasional barking dog.

As they approached the hotel, the lights from the parking lot made the place glow like a theater stage set for the next scene. Outside the circumference of the light, Craig stopped, pulling Mollie up beside him.

"Guess this is good night."

"So it is." Mollie's answer was slow, hesitant. "Thanks for a great day...and dinner."

"You got us dinner." He reminded her.

"I did, didn't I?"

"Yes, you did, abominable Mollie Hinkle."

Her laugh echoed in the stillness making her bring a hand to her lips. She leaned forward and whispered, "Indominitable."

"Yeah, yeah, that's what you keep saying."

"I say what I mean, Craig Coulter." Mollie teased poking at his ribs.

"Good, then you'll answer me honestly when I ask...what's wrong?"

"Nothing."

Shaking his head, Craig asked again, "You've been quiet since Ron and Jack got back. What is it?" He touched the side of her cheek.

"I swear, nothing is wrong." Mollie insisted.

"So it's me?"

"No, no." Mollie squeezed his hand. "It's just...I guess I'm shocked that Jack will be staying here. It's a sudden change, ya know?" Craig nodded and looked appeased by her answer. Mollie quickly, intentionally changed the subject by saying, "So, are you going to use the ticket your mother bought and go see your brother?"

"Trying to get rid of me?"

"No." Mollie pulled him toward her and answered quietly. "I'd never try to get rid of you." He wrapped his hands around her waist and brought her close. She rested her cheek against his chest.

Sighing, he kissed the top of her head and rested his cheek against her temple. Fingers stroked the flesh at the curve of her back. "So, do you think Ron has a ghost of a chance with Jack?"

Mollie shrugged.

"Ah, come on, she had to tell you something, dragging you out of the house like that."

"For creamer."

"You don't like coffee."

"No, I don't," she admitted with a grin.

"So is my buddy going to get his heart broken?"

Mollie looked up at Craig, his face nothing but shadows. "I don't know. Jack screws up almost every relationship with some irrational, stupid move. Ron seems to challenge her—in a good way, but Jack's track record is bad. And it's only been a few days. Is it even possible for two people to fall in love in such a short period of time and it be real?"

"Last week, I would have said no."

"And this week?"

Craig brushed a curl from her eye and buried his hands in the silky strands. Head tipped back, she looked up at him, wondering what he was thinking as his eyes studied her. Finally, he answered, "My brother met a girl, and in one summer, he fell enough in love with her to wait fifteen years until he could have her. I always thought he was crazy. Until now."

"What changed your mind?"

"I was minding my own business and along came this beautiful woman. I stole a kiss, and her lips were sweet as honey, but only half as sweet as the heart and soul I found right…" He placed his hand above Mollie's breast,"…here."

Mollie's heart soared.

"Good night, Mollie." He kissed her good-bye, his lips barely brushing against hers.

"Good night," she parroted, not fully realizing that meant he was leaving until he was gone. She wanted to cry out for him to stop. To stay with her, but instead she watched him walk away. He turned before rounding the corner to his house and waved good-bye. Mollie waved back, her hopes soared so high, so fast. She felt dizzy.

Could he feel what she felt? Tossing caution to the whipping wind, she let her feelings guide her across the road and down the same street she had just walked.

Mollie had no idea what she would say, but that didn't stop her or even cause her to pause as she knocked on his front door. Only a second or two lapsed before the door opened and only the screen door separated them.

"Mollie," Craig breathed, his eyes locked in on hers.

"I hope you don't mind."

"Mind?" Craig pushed the door open and pulled her inside. He glanced at the clock on the wall. "It's been seven minutes. What the hell took you so long?"

"Are we crazy?"

"If we are, then sanity is overrated."

Mollie stepped into his arms. Her hands stroked warm, hard forearms, to biceps too large for her hands to span. He brushed the hair back from her face, his lips touching her forehead in a kiss. They lingered there as he spoke, his voice husky and electric to her ears. "Want to watch a movie? Make popcorn?"

She closed her eyes and shook her head. Craig's lips traveled down, planting kisses to her temple, cheeks, and finally to her lips. Mollie wrapped her arms around his neck and held on. His lips on hers, was all she wanted, for the moment. To feel him close, to feel his breath against her skin, the warmth from his body penetrating her own. This was what she wanted. His hands moved down her spine to the small of her back, his fingertips sliding under the fabric of her shirt caressing the sensitive skin around her waist.

Craig pulled back and looked down at her; a knowing, satisfied grin twitching the corners of his lips. "What do I do with you?"

"Hmm?" Mollie answered her brain still fuzzy, her body several degrees above warm.

"You're making me crazy."

Mollie said nothing. She bit her lip and touched her hand to his heart. Its pounding comforted her.

He kissed her again, his lips light against hers; his hesitation obvious. "I don't want to mess this up."

"I don't either. You may run when I say this, but I have to be honest with you. I know it's only been a few days, I know I shouldn't feel this way. I know it makes no sense, but..."

"But it feels right?" Craig finished her thought.

"It feels perfect," Mollie answered.

Craig grinned and lifted her off her feet. "More perfect than anything I've ever felt."

Mollie nodded and kissed him, her fingers combing through his hair. She held his cheeks with her hands, so he couldn't break away from her kisses as he carried her through the house to his room. Laying her down on his bed, he kissed her slowly, tenderly teasing her lips. She tried to pull him in for more, but he drew away. His lips trailed down her throat where they lingered at the hollow, igniting the sensitive skin, causing her breathing to speed and her pulse to pound in her throat.

"Craig?" Mollie interrupted his caresses. She leaned over and snapped on the bedside lamp. She touched his cheek, rubbing her thumb across the stubble that had grown since dinner. Resting her head on a pillow, she said, "Tell me this isn't a mistake. Even if you have to lie, tell me this won't change how you feel about me?"

He kissed her. "This feeling I have when I touch you, hell, even when I see you. I don't want it to end, but I won't lie, part of me is afraid that if we do this, somehow that feeling will be gone. It scares the hell out of me."

Mollie snuggled into his chest. "I want to be close to you. More than anything I've wanted in a long time." She played with the collar of his shirt. "I'm no expert. I just know I've never felt like this. I've thought I was in love, but it was nothing like this. This feeling of being alive, of being so completely content just to be next to you, I don't want to ruin that." Mollie's eyes glistened with tears.

"Ah, sweetness, how could this be more perfect?" He pulled her in and kissed her. His mouth moved to her ear and he traced the contours of her lobe with his lips and tongue. Mollie's body arched against him. His breath was hot against her skin as he whispered, "Tell me you love me, Mollie. Tell me you'll be mine, forever."

Mollie's bones turned to liquid, her heart pounded as she told him what he wanted to hear, over and over again, beginning the onslaught of his desire. He couldn't touch her enough. His hands pulled and tugged at clothes, removing them hastily, sloppily. Seams groaned as clothes were shed without buttons or snaps loosened.

They lay naked next to each other. Craig touched her gently. "I've never seen anyone so beautiful. You're all I've imagined and more." He kissed her slowly, his tongue teasing. His hands circled a nipple, causing it to grow firm against the palm of his hand. Mollie sat up and shoved Craig's shoulder until his back was against the bed. She moved on top of him and kissed him. His teasing was relentless. She decided to tease him in return. She kissed him, stopped, then kissed him some more. She had planned to be merciless, to return each volley to match his game. She realized too late that she was easily outplayed. She moved above him and straddled his hips. She saw the change in him immediately. Gone was the soft set of his jaw, the moist patient look in his eyes—they turned hard like the rest of him, his jaw clamped, his pulse pounded visibly in his throat.

Mollie felt his hand on her hips, firm as iron clamps. He lifted her body and placed it down on his own. Mollie gasped at the feel of him as he wedged himself deep inside her. She shifted her hips to accommodate the size of him. After a few minutes, her body adjusted and she began moving her hips. She was embarrassed to be so naive and unskilled, her hips moving unsteadily.

Craig tried to remain calm, tried to remain in control, but he couldn't keep his eyes off her. She was a sight he couldn't resist, even if it was to be his undoing. She was so perfect. Her body built to fit his, her breasts not too small or too large but perfect for her body. Her waist so little he could nearly wrap his hands around her. Her movements weren't calculated or rehearsed, they were natural and flawless. He lifted his hips and shoved himself further inside her and she gasped. Her hands gripped his chest. Her nails dug into his flesh. He couldn't take much more. He had to find some way of slowing this situation down.

Mollie gained confidence as she watched the change she brought over him. He, so perfect and flawless, begged her to slow down. His hands twisted into the headboard. His muscles bulged as he gripped the wooden rails. The tension in his neck caused the corded muscles to flex and pulse. He was at her mercy. He begged her to stop. And part of her wanted to stop—to prolong this strange feeling of euphoria building inside her, but part of her wanted to take him to the point of no return.

Distracted for a moment by the thought, Mollie let him regain control. In a single move, he was up, his arms around her waist as he lifted her and rolled her over. Mollie could no longer think of anything but his body in hers. It was wave after wave of pleasure until she felt his hand slide under her hips, lifting her body from the bed to meet him. He drove deep, causing her passions to build in a torrent of heat until her body crashed. She barely heard his own strangled gasps over her own as he found his own place of peace.

He held her tightly and kissed her everywhere he could touch, her lips, her nose, her eyes—anywhere and everywhere. He held her close until their breathing slowed to normal. She started to get up, but he pulled her back and tucked her into him. He kept one arm around her waist as he used the other to cover them with the blanket. He snapped off the light, whispering in her ear, "Stay with me."

Chapter 14

The ringing dragged Mollie from the midst of a pleasant sleep. A sleep so steeped in relaxation that her mind seemed cloudy as she groped the floor next to her for her purse, blindly rummaging through it for her cell phone. She pulled it free and flipped it open, her greeting a croak with her sleep thickened voice.

The voice on the other end brought her immediately awake. She untangled her limbs from Craig's and moved smoothly from under the covers, careful not to wake him. Her eyes adjusted to the low light from the hallway, and she looked around for something to cover herself. She found Craig's shirt and slipped it over her head.

"Just give me a minute to go to another room," she whispered as she glanced over her shoulder to make sure she hadn't disturbed Craig. He didn't even flinch.

"Just Jack, but I don't want to wake her." Mollie crept from the room, trying to be silent on the groaning floorboards. She pulled the door closed without latching it, then crouched against the wall in the hallway. "Yes, I was in bed. It's only 6:00 a.m. here…When did you try to call?…I'm sorry, uh, Jack and I were sightseeing…Uh, sure. Haven't really seen anything special. Mountains and stuff. I'll tell you all about it when I get home…Soon…I miss you too."

She leaned her head against the wall. "I know I should call more…No, I haven't been *ignoring* you or the *situation*…Well, don't. Everything will be just fine. I promise…."

"No!" Mollie said a little too loudly. Then she said much more quietly, "I'll see about coming home in the morning. Until then, open nothing. Do nothing…I know it's not fair of me. I know your life is in limbo too, but please, I can't do this right now." Mollie's voice cracked; and she took a deep breath. "Please…understand?"

A tear slid down her cheek, "I'll always be your girl. Everything will be fine. I promise."

Mollie hung up the phone. She couldn't stop the tears that sprang to her eyes. She went to the bathroom and leaned over the basin as the water ran into it. She wouldn't think of this. *Just two more days, God, just two more days, and then I'll deal with everything.*

She washed her face and returned to bed. Craig was still fast asleep. She crawled in slowly. Her body was cold, and she couldn't stop it from shaking, even when she snuggled in against him. He pulled her close, kissed her temple and asked, "You all right?"

She nodded against his chest. His body went heavy.

Mollie closed her eyes, but couldn't sleep. She should tell Craig everything. The truth about the biopsy, and the lump, that turned her summer upside down. She knew she should, but she knew she wouldn't. If she pretended hard enough, she was certain she could make it go away, at least for a little while longer.

She pulled his arm tight across her and clung to it. As she lay in the dark listening to him breathe, she couldn't stop the tears that rolled down her cheeks and soaked her pillow. She wished she could just be happy and forget about what if.

****

The rude ring of an alarm clock ushered in the morning. Craig was up and out of the room within seconds. Mollie ran a hand over the warm areas his body left in the bed. A slow, satisfied smile crept across her face as she listened to him shower. When the water stopped, she expected him to return and give her a good morning kiss, a hello, something. But he didn't. He dressed in the bathroom and moved straight through the hall without as much as a glance in her direction.

She frowned and rolled over. Cabinet doors opened and closed in the kitchen, but no call to her. Maybe he thought she was asleep?

She climbed out of bed and dressed. Shuffling to the kitchen, she grabbed her purse from the hall floor where she left it.

She found Craig there, dressed for work, pouring himself a cup of coffee. He had dark circles under his eyes and a frown on his face. He barely made eye contact with her as he took a swallow. "Your phone ring last night?"

"Yeah, um…Jack. Worried I didn't come back."

"I see. You want a ride to the hotel before I leave for work?"

Mollie shrugged. She expected a good morning, a smile, possibly a kiss to verify last night meant something. He offered nothing but an emotionless face, eyes narrowed as he watched her.

"I can walk. Don't want to make you late."

"You won't make me late. I'm enough of a gentleman to offer the girl a ride home in the morning."

Mollie's jaw dropped. She was about to ask him what the hell his problem was when her phone buzzed, and buzzed until she pulled it out of her purse and hit ignore. It immediately lit up again with a call. Justin. Did he have radar that told him it was a horrible time? She turned the phone off.

She walked to the door and turned the knob. Craig cleared his throat and Mollie stopped, hopeful.

"Tell *Jack* I said good morning."

Mollie looked back at him, her brows furrowed. "All right." Half out the door, she stopped and asked, "Is there something wrong?"

"Why would there be anything wrong? Last night was the best I've had in months. I guess Ron's right; I needed to break the dry spell."

Mollie's mouth dropped open, her mind went blank. She blinked back tears and hurried to escape before she was overwhelmed by them.

The door slammed behind her, caught by a burst of wind. Brutus pranced and tried to slow her retreat, but she stepped past him. She made her way to the hotel, though her vision was clouded with tears. Once inside, she dodged Jack and locked herself in the bathroom.

"Mollie?" Jack knocked on the door. "Please…talk to me." Jack was approaching the panic zone when Mollie finally opened the door, dressed in her robe, with a towel wrapped around her head.

"What happened?" Jack stayed right on her heals.

"Nothing," Mollie said, but the tears flowed again.

"What did that prick do? What did he say?"

Mollie shook her head and climbed under the covers. "He didn't do anything. He's exactly what he claimed to be. He told me he was incapable of love, was opposed to any serious relationships, and was just looking for fun. I knew that, so shame on me for thinking there was more to him than there was."

"You guys…?"

"Yes. And it's over."

"I'll kill him."

"You'll do no such thing. If you have any feeling for me, you'll not say a word. I don't want him to think I'm nursing a broken heart over him, understand?"

Jack sat on the bed and rubbed Mollie's arm. "I understand, Molls. Sometimes self-respect is all we have. It'll be hard though. I'd love to bloody the bastard's nose."

"I know, Jackie, but don't." Jack plopped down beside her. Mollie smiled up at her. "I just want to rest. I'm so tired."

"Do you feel sick?" Jack put a hand on her forehead to check for fever. "You need a doctor?"

Mollie laughed a little. "Calm down. I'm physically fine. I just need to get some sleep. I need you to concentrate on getting your future started. One day I expect to see you happy and settled, maybe even a couple of kids I can spoil."

"Oh, Mollie." Jack sucked in a sharp breath and started to cry. "I'm not staying. I'm going home with you. I don't want to be here having fun while you're suffering."

Mollie sat up and hugged her friend. "Oh, for goodness sakes. I'm not going to be suffering. Screw Craig. He doesn't deserve me anyhow. Do you really think I plan to go home and lick my wounds? I wouldn't give him the satisfaction. Besides, you've taken care of me for too long. It's time for you to have a life of your own."

"Being your friend has never been a chore, Mollie. I've always counted you as the one blessing in my life."

Mollie hugged her tighter, tears dropped on her shoulder. "You're the best."

Jack pulled away and wiped at her tears with alacrity. "You're making me blubber. You know how that annoys me." Jack blew her nose on one of the shirts that were strewn across the floor. She offered a corner to Mollie who shook her head. Jack shrugged and tossed back on the floor. "So, enough tears. Everything will work out. Men are pigs. We already knew that. We just need to have verification every now and then. It's his loss. He's the fool, not you."

Mollie nodded weakly, then lay back down on her pillow.

"I mean it. And Mollie?" Jack took a deep breath and promised, "You'll always be important in my life. You really are the best person I know. Anytime you need me, I'll be there. No matter what. Promise me? You'll call if you ever need me?"

"Of course. But only if you promise me not to sabotage things with Ron. I won't be here to keep an eye on you."

Jack gave her a look of confusion.

"You know what I'm talking about. Whenever a guy gets too close, you cheat on him and ruin it. I've seen you do it too often."

"I do not."

"Yes. You. Do. Shall I name names?"

"No." Jack blurted and then sighed, her shoulders slumped. "Do you think I have a male gene? Or maybe it was my formative years with my dad. I thought only men feared commitment as much as I do."

Mollie pulled the blankets tight under her chin and took a deep breath. "You need to learn to trust."

Jack rolled her eyes. "I trust that most people are completely self-serving like that little f—."

"Jack!" Mollie scolded.

"I'll be good. I promise."

Mollie gave her a smile, and then changed the subject, "I'm going to go home, but I'll be back. And when I do, you'd better be prepared to serve me the best dinner west of the Allegheny."

"You'll come back? Even after…?"

"Of course. No loser like Craig Coulter will keep me from my best friend."

"So, you're going to be all right?"

"Of course. I told you, I'm stronger than anyone gives me credit."

"One day, Molls. The right guy's out there somewhere."

"Speaking of good guys. Why don't you let me sleep and you go hang out with Ron?"

"Trying to get rid of me?"

"Yep. I can't sleep knowing you're hovering and feeling sorry for me. I feel the pity oozing from your every pore. And Craig might be a despicable human being, but he sure knows how to tucker a girl out."

"For God's sake, don't say that! You must say, for the official record, he's got a tiny stick and a short swing. It's girl code. Never say anything they can brag about."

Mollie laughed. "Shall I complain to his hate club?"

"Nope. Walk away and never look back."

"Agreed. Now, go find Ron."

"Can't. I have to go to the bar. A handy man's coming to begin work and I need to decide what needs done."

Mollie opened an eye. "I'd go help you, but I'm beat."

"I understand. You rest. When I get back, we'll go somewhere for lunch."

Mollie nodded and closed her eyes. Jack scooped up her keys and headed for the door. She paused for a moment, and said, "Someday, Molls."

"Most certainly." Her optimistic tone was good enough to fool Jack, but as her friend closed the door, Mollie buried her head in her pillow and cried.

****

Jack used the key Ron gave her to unlock the back door to the bar. The deadbolt slid out of the way easily. However the wooden door sat crooked on its hinges and did not want to swing open. Jack put her shoulder in it and hit it hard. It gave way with a crack and a groan, and then dumped her into the bar's storeroom. She twisted on the bare bulb hanging in front of her and looked around. Crates and shelves of alcohol and soda lined the walls. The place was dusty, but pretty well organized. Jack nodded in approval. "Not bad, Ron. For a man."

The door in front of her opened to the bar. Jack looked it over. "We'll need more tables." Jack made a note on a napkin she picked up from a table. "And it needs to be brightened up somehow. Needs more character." Jack chewed her lip. "I'll ask Mollie. She'll know how to turn a bar into a comfy place to eat."

She turned her attention to the kitchen, which was off to the right of the stock room. "Strange setup. Quite a haul to get food to the dining room." Jack scribbled a note on the napkin about adding a door directly to the dining area. Jack stopped in the kitchen doorway and groaned. "Good Lord, Ron. What a mess." Jack stepped into the room, her head shook back and forth. "Hell, any budget I have will have to be dumped here. Kitchens should sparkle."

During her inspection, Jack opened cabinets and drawers. They were stocked full of utensils. Whoever Ron bought the place from didn't bother to clean it out. Just walked away from it all, including the 1995 calendar on the wall. Jack flipped through the calendar with a grin. "My senior year of high school. That a good sign?" Jack shrugged and sighed. She looked around the mess of a kitchen. "Never dreamed in 1995 that I'd be in a two bit town ready to open my own place."

"If it's only worth two bits, why bother to stick around?"

Craig Coulter. Just the man she wanted to see.

"Sure as hell isn't for your charming company."

"I never claimed to be charming. I have other skills that make me popular."

Jack's body felt immediately warm, and she shook from head to toe.

Chapter 15

Mollie cried into her pillow until it was wet and itchy against her cheek. She rolled onto her back and stared at the ceiling. She was fresh out of tears and ashamed of herself for sulking over a guy she barely knew. A guy who flat out warned her he wasn't the relationship type. She could now be the four hundredth member of the Craig Coulter hate club. She covered her eyes and groaned. How could she have been so stupid?

Mollie dragged her body out of bed. Score one for the player. Next time, she'd be wiser.

She dug through her purse for a tissue and blew her nose. She took a deep breath and rolled the tension from her neck. She needed to make arrangements to head home. Windham had lost its charm, and she wanted out as soon as possible. She called information and got the number for the airport. The airline was kind enough to charge her an exorbitant price for a one way emergency ticket. She flipped her phone closed and tossed it on the bed. "Thanks for cutting me some slack, assholes."

Her phone rang and she grabbed it. It was Justin. She thought about hitting ignore, but then figured she may as well keep the crappy streak going. She flipped it open.

"Mollie." He sounded relieved.

"Yeah?"

"I've been calling you like ten times a day."

"I've been busy."

"Or avoiding me?"

"Ya think?"

"Yeah, but I don't blame you. Look Mollie…" He paused, and then asked quietly, "What happened with us? This break up is killing me, and I know it's mostly my fault and I need to tell you how sorry I am. I can't tell you why I did what I did. I guess I was just scared."

"It's all right. I forgive you."

He breathed a sigh of relief. "Good. My mom was about to kill me. People have been saying I dumped you because you have cancer again. They think I'm a real shit."

Mollie squeezed her eyes closed and bit her lip. Her temper flared. What was wrong with men?

"Look, Justin, bottom line is you *are* a shit. You could have ended it when I asked you the night before the wedding. You could have called me that morning. Hell, you could have told me at the church! You didn't have to make me look like a fool in front of every God-blessed person I know. You're not just a shit, you're an evil little shit."

"Mollie, I've never heard you…be so mean."

"Mean? Am I being mean? Did I hurt your feelings? Did I dump you at the altar? Am I the mean one, Justin? Am I hurting your wittle feelings?"

"Well yeah, I mean no. I guess I'm saying I deserve it. You're right about everything, but you've got to believe me. I didn't think about not marrying you until we were standing there in front of everyone. I got scared, but I should have manned up; calmed down. I don't know, something, but I didn't. I screwed everything up, and I'm sorry."

"And you were plugging Joanie, why?"

"I…I was upset."

"Seriously, that's your excuse?"

"I'm a man. She offered. I accepted."

"So, you have absolutely no self-control?"

"Hardly any man says no when it's thrown at him. That doesn't mean I have any feelings for her."

It felt like a punch to her gut. Justin's words explained it all. She threw herself at Craig, and he took her offer. Tears rolled down her cheeks and suddenly her breath came in labored gasps.

"Mollie, Mollie! Calm down. Breathe. God, I'm sorry. I didn't mean to do this to you. I even had myself convinced you wanted me to dump you. I swear, I'm sorry."

Mollie tried to gain her composure. "It's all right. It really is. I um…I can't talk now."

"Don't hang up. Talk to me."

"There's really nothing more to say."

"There's lots that needs said. When will you be home?"

"I have a flight tonight. My dad called last night. My test results are back and he wants me home. As a matter of fact, I need to call and tell him."

"He doesn't know?"

"Not yet."

"Well, then, don't. Let me pick you up. That way we can talk."

"I really don't…."

"Mollie…I did get punched in the face by a chick and called enough names to make Reverend Lowry speechless."

"That was funny."

Justin laughed. "For you."

"And for Jack, my other friends, and my family."

"Mine too. Even my mother sent the YouTube link to everyone on her email."

"I suppose that makes up for it, somewhat." Mollie sat on the bed and relaxed her shoulders.

"I'm a dick, and I'm sorry. My mother hates me, my sisters hate me, and my brother says I'm a fool."

"Ha, serves you right!" Mollie laughed into the phone. "And for the record, you are a fool. I was one hell of a catch."

"Yes, you are. Give me another chance?"

"Not on your life."

"At least can we be friends? If you forgive me, and let everyone know I'm not a complete and total dick, then maybe at least my mom will like me again?"

"I'll put in a good word for you, okay?"

"And you'll tell her I tried to get you back? But you turned me down?"

"Sure, I'll tell her I'm just sick to death of men."

"And Mollie, it wasn't because you have cancer. I just…hell…I was just scared. I mean forever? That's a long time."

"It sure is." Mollie spoke the words quietly. "I better go."

"What time do I pick you up?"

"You sure? My flight comes in at 3:00 a.m.?"

"That's fine, just text me the details."

Mollie hung up and sent the text.

One problem solved.

Now, how did she get from here to the airport in Great Falls?

She supposed she'd ask Jack if Ron would take her. Mollie kicked dirty clothes out of her way as she headed to the bathroom to dress and find Jack.

"Joanie, you selfish, self-centered, unthinking, unfeeling bitch. How could you just take the car?" Mollie complained out loud.

She plucked jeans and a tee-shirt from her suitcase, stripped off her jammies, and pulled on her clothes. She splashed cold water on her face and brushed her hair and latched it in a clasp.

Leaving the hotel, her stride was quick and tense. At the bar, she pulled on the front door, but it was locked. She knocked, but Jack didn't answer. She went around to the back door and came to a dead stop.

A state police car was parked in the gravel lot.

Her heart thudded painfully. She wasn't ready to face Craig, and she assumed the car was his. She sidled up to a window and rubbed away the grime for a better look. It was Craig. She couldn't hear what he was talking to Jack about, but she nearly fainted when she saw Jack grab him by the waist of his pants and yank him close. They stood, bodies inches apart, noses brushing. Mollie turned away and covered her eyes. She couldn't watch. They looked like they were about to kiss, and Mollie was certain she didn't want to see that. Justin's words filled her ears about guys taking whatever is thrown their way.

But Jack?

Mollie brushed away the tears with cold, trembling hands and stumbled back to the hotel.

She packed her bags in a frenzy, stuffing belongings in at random, she pushed and poked unfolded clothes, trying to get them in well enough to zip the bag. It kept catching, so she gave up, leaving it half zipped, clothes sticking out of the top of the bag. She found the book Craig bought her on the table. She grabbed it, and in a fit, she tried to rip it down the spine, but she couldn't. Tearing it apart one page at a time had to do. She flushed the flowers down the toilet and scooped all of her cosmetics from the counter and dumped them into a grocery bag.

She was ready to go.

But she still needed a ride. She looked through the phone book, searching for a cab. Nothing. She phoned the lady at the IGA. She said there were no cabs, but…Mollie quickly told her she had a ride, and was just checking to avoid having to bother a friend. Mollie hung up the phone and thought of her options. As she debated how far it was to walk, the phone rang.

It was Ron, looking for Jack.

"She's at the bar," Mollie told him.

"Anxious, is she?" Ron laughed.

"Yeah, I suppose."

"I think this will be good. Don't you?"

"Look, Ron, I don't mean to be rude, but I was in the middle of something when you called."

"Something wrong?"

"No, I just need to get home." Mollie's voice cracked, though she tried to sound carefree.

"Something is wrong. You want me to call Craig?"

"God no. I just need to hunt down Joanie and find out when she can get here with the car so I can get home."

"Is someone in your family sick?"

Mollie paused a moment. "Yeah. Someone may be in real trouble. I need to get home to find out for myself."

"Well, Mitch hasn't called, so I doubt they're back. How 'bout I give you a ride?"

"I couldn't ask you...."

"You're not asking, I'm offering. Jack could—"

"No. Don't mention it to Jack. She's so...um...happy. If she knew I was skipping town because of a possible crisis, she'd go ballistic and insist she come with me."

Ron was quiet a second, then he said, "You're right. And you don't want me to tell Craig?"

"No. I doubt he'll even notice I'm gone."

"I don't know about that."

"Well, I do."

"Did he screw you over, Mollie?"

"I suppose that's one way to put it."

"Son of a bitch." Ron sighed hard. "I'm sorry. I really thought...well, I just thought he felt something for you. Don't take it personally. He just doesn't connect well with women."

"I'll be fine. I just want to get home."

"I can do that much for you, and I'll keep it on the down low. Just tell me when."

"I'm ready anytime you are."

"Well, I suppose we could leave now."

"I'm packed and ready."

"I'll be there in ten."

Mollie hung up the phone. Grabbing her bags and purse, she went out to the parking lot to wait for Ron.

Chapter 16

Mollie thanked Ron for the ride and tried to leave him in the parking lot, but he insisted, escorting her into the airport, and up to the ticket counter. Mollie gave the woman her name and her credit card and was issued her ticket with an, "Oh, my! Aren't you early?"

Mollie frowned at the woman and stuffed the ticket in her purse. She turned to Ron and gave him a sad smile. "Thanks again. You're seriously a life saver. Please, take some gas money?"

"What time's your plane leaving?" Ron asked.

"In a bit. I have a book to read."

"Well, how 'bout I let you buy me a sandwich? We can eat some lunch, then you can read your book and wait on your plane, which evidently leaves a bit later than 'in a bit'."

Mollie hesitated. She didn't want to be Ron's problem, but then she loathed the idea of being alone for the next eleven hours before her plane took off.

"I skipped breakfast," Ron added with a grin.

"All right. You sure you don't have anything else you need to do?"

"Nope, and I am starved."

"Seriously?"

"Girl, I don't lie."

Mollie smiled a little brighter. "Well, then, since you're *starved*, you pick the restaurant."

"My pleasure." Ron looked around the tiny airport. It was void of anyplace to eat; there wasn't even a Panera stand. They'd be lucky if they could find vending machines. He shook his head. "We got enough time to leave and come back?"

Mollie nodded her head. "I've got a couple of hours."

"Good, 'Cause I hate food wrapped in paper, much less from a vending machine."

They drove to a local restaurant owned by Crow Indians. Ron was familiar with the owners, already had a favorite seat, and knew what he wanted to order before the waitress arrived with a menu. Mollie ordered a BLT, fries, and a chocolate shake. Fortunately for her, mental and emotional anguish never killed her appetite.

They ate and talked about their lives and their families. Mollie couldn't help but laugh at Ron's stories. Couldn't help but feel just a little better with a full stomach and a few giggles. Ron went for the car as she paid the check. Outside the swinging glass door, a little girl in braids and a Pretty Kitty tee-shirt offered Mollie a crocheted bracelet. Mollie gave the girl a five dollar bill and a smile.

She put the bracelet in her pocket until she said good-bye to Ron at the airport gate. She handed it to him, a bit embarrassed, but needing to thank him with more than lunch. "The little girl at the restaurant was selling these, and I wanted to just give you something to thank you. You're a really nice guy, and…well, I hope things turn out…." Mollie thought of Jack and Craig at the restaurant. Mollie felt the tears sting her eyes, and she wondered if Ron, too, was headed for a heart break. *Oh, Jackie*, she thought, *don't blow this. You could be throwing away the best guy.* Mollie cupped his hand in hers and took a deep breath, "Look, Ron, promise me something."

"Yeah?"

"Jack does stupid things when she's scared, but she really does have feelings for you." She looked up at Ron, who brushed away a tear for her. Mollie said, "So forgive her, all right?"

Ron gave her a bear hug and kissed the top of her head. "Don't you worry about Jack, Mollie. I think I know how to handle her."

"Good." Mollie's tears flowed unchecked. "Because no matter what she does, she's still the best, you know. And she will need someone, with me gone, and all."

"You'll only be a phone call away," Ron assured.

"True." Mollie couldn't spit out the word without some hesitation.

"And Mollie, I'm sorry about Craig."

"It's all right." Mollie gave Ron a squeeze and a quick kiss on his cheek. "Thanks again."

"Busy day and night, Mollie?" Mollie jumped at the sound of Craig's voice. All color drained from her face as she faced the last person on earth she wanted to see right now.

"Hey, Craig...." Ron held out his hand for a knuckle bump, but Craig sneered. "Go home, Ron." He then turned to Mollie, "Does Jack know you're hanging out with her boyfriend? Or does she still think you're sweet and pure?"

"Screw you," Mollie shot back. "Why don't you tell me what Jack knows?"

"I know she's fooled by you, but I'm not."

"Come on, Craig." Ron tried to pull Craig back, but Craig shoved him, causing him to stumble.

"I told you to go home, Ron."

"I can't leave Mollie with you acting like this. Come on, man. Calm down. We're friends. Since when don't you trust me?"

"It's not you I don't trust." He glared at Mollie.

Mollie took a sharp breath. "Me? What have I done?"

"If you wanted to screw my friend, Mollie, the least you could do is get a hotel instead of making out with him in airport lobbies."

Mollie felt her anger rise from the very tips of her toes. Her temperature and her ire lifted beyond sustainable levels. She lunged at Craig, punching him in the chin. Ron grabbed her around the waist and pulled her back. He held her in one arm and used the other to keep Craig at a distance.

"You're a pig," Mollie hissed.

"Tell me something I haven't heard before." Craig laughed. He looked at Mollie and grinned. "I guess this gives a whole new meaning to the phrase *lay over*, huh?"

"Go to hell." Mollie spat.

"Also uncreative. I expected more out of you, being an educated bitch and all." Craig took a step back and addressed Ron. "Watch yourself, buddy."

With that, he headed to the door.

Mollie's body shook. Ron let go of her, his face full of sympathy. "You going to be all right?"

Mollie's world spun, but her mouth opened, and she calmly answered. "I'll be fine. I just need to go home."

Mollie picked up her bag and headed for the gate. Ron called to her, and she turned. He asked. "What would Craig know about Jack?"

Mollie's shoulders sagged as she debated what to say. Jack was her friend, and even if she had fallen to Craig's temptation, she still was the best friend Mollie ever had. "It's just crazy talk. Be good to her."

Ron looked relieved, looked over his shoulder at Craig's disappearing form. He seemed anxious to end the conversation with Mollie, yet hesitant to leave her.

Mollie looked in Craig's direction, then to Ron. "I'd better get going. Thanks for keeping me company."

"I'm sure I'll see you around, right? You'll come see Jack?"

Mollie shrugged and bit her lip. She couldn't start blubbering now. She gathered up her bags. "We'll see. I really better go."

Ron nodded. "Have a good flight…and I hope you meet a good man one day."

"That's the least of my worries." She waved good-bye and headed for the gate, only pausing long enough to watch Ron jog through the terminal and grab Craig by the arm. She ducked behind a potted plant and watched them talk. Craig still seemed mad. Both looked in the direction she should've headed. Craig said something to Ron; Ron shook his head; and then Ron gave Craig a shoulder bump, and they walked away.

The miserable hollow in her gut brought abstraction to the world. They had each other. The whole world had somebody, but she had nothing.

People passed her by, but they seemed surreal, their voices an echo in a tunnel, their laughter a foreign language. She didn't even recognize her own name until someone pulled on her elbow. "Mollie, are you ignoring me?"

Joanie. It figured. Mollie sighed and dropped herself into a plastic seat. Joanie sat next to her.

"You on the ten o'clock flight too?" Joanie asked.

"You?" Mollie asked.

"Yeah."

"Where's Mitch?"

Joanie dropped her bag on the floor and leaned back in her seat. An exaggerated moan escaped from under the hands she used to cover her face. "I had to get away from him. He was smothering me. He wanted to go everywhere I went. He even followed me to the pharmacy. I can't live like that. I need space, some room to breathe."

"Did you tell him that?"

Her shrug told Mollie no.

"You have to tell him what's bothering you. How else will he know?" Mollie asked.

"I don't want to hurt his feelings."

"So then, what excuse did you give him?"

"I sort of said nothing. I just left."

"You did what?"

"I left. He went to work, and I came here."

"You're kidding me?"

"No. I'll call him later."

"So, how did you get here?"

"I sort of drove Jack's car."

"You sort of what? Do you realize you abandoned Jack and me in Windham the whole time you were on your little adventure? Where's the car now?"

"In short term parking."

"And how the hell is Jack supposed to get it? Walk to it? Do you ever think about anyone but yourself?"

"I'll reimburse her for a cab. God, Mollie, why are you being such a bitch?"

"Being a bitch? Me? Oh my God, Joanie...you're such a moron. A self-absorbed, egotistical moron. You don't care about anyone. You just do what the hell you want, when the hell you want, with whom the hell you want."

"Is this about Justin?"

"Screw Justin!" Mollie's voice echoed in the terminal, but she was too mad to care. No longer in her seat, she shook a finger at the blond with the trembling lips and wide eyes. "People like you disgust me. You don't put anything or anyone above yourself. You're the bitch. You can call it free spirit, or whatever in the crap you want to dress it up as, but bottom line is you suck. You're a mean, selfish bitch."

A tear slid down Joanie's cheek. Her voice was nearly a whisper. "That really hurts. I expected something like this from Jack, but you?"

"I've forgiven you for a lot of things, but this takes the cake."

"You're this mad over a car?"

"The car? You stupid bimbo! You married a man, a stupid man evidently, but still a human with feelings, and you just ran away without saying a thing to him. Who does that?"

"Why do you care? You never even met him."

Her body trembled with frustration. "I don't have to know him to know you hurt him. To know he probably blames himself, wonders what he did wrong. It's called empathy. Something you don't understand. Hell, I don't think anyone understands."

With that, she turned and walked away.

Chapter 17

Jack returned to the hotel and found Mollie gone. She checked the bathroom; looked everywhere for a note.

Nothing.

Then she realized her bags were gone. The book Craig gave her was shredded in the trash can. She pulled a few pages out and wadded them into a ball. Hugging them to her chest, she fell back on her bed and cried. "How dare you, Craig?" she asked to the empty room. She sat up and wiped away the tears. She dialed Mollie; the phone on the dresser rang. Jack cursed and hung up. She was about to call Mrs. Hinkle, when a knock at the door made her drop the phone. She looked out the window. It was Ron.

A soul never looked so comforting. Flinging open the door, she pounced on him, wrapping her arms around him in a near death grip. "I'm so glad you're here."

"Really? Now, that's what I've been waiting to hear." He held her tight.

"I think Mollie left." Jack sniffled.

"I know she left. She asked me for a ride to the airport."

Jack shoved away. "She did what? You took her? Why didn't she say good-bye? Why didn't you guys ask me to go with you?"

"She was afraid you'd try to talk her out of leaving. Or that you'd go with her because she was upset. I didn't want that to happen."

"So, she was upset?" Jack looked around the room. "How upset?"

"She'd been crying, but she cheered up…sort of…till she fought with Craig in the airport."

"What?"

"I broke it up, after I let her give him one good punch to the face. He deserved to give him that much."

"She threw punches? Mollie?"

Jack dropped onto the bed, her head shaking back and forth. "She must have been heartbroken. She left here bleeding and broken, and she didn't have a friend to go with her? Of course I would have flown back. She shouldn't be alone right now. How could you take her?"

"I only did what she asked me to do."

"You should've called me."

Ron shrugged. "She made me promise."

"That doesn't matter. You should've known." Jack stood and started packing her bag. "How could you just dump her at the airport alone?"

"I didn't dump her there. I even had lunch with her so she wouldn't be there all day by herself."

"What's that supposed to mean?"

"Well, I drove her up at noon, but her plane doesn't leave until eight, so I kept her company until five…when Craig showed up…then I took him out to dinner to cool him off. I've been dealing with those two all damn day."

"This just makes no sense. Why wouldn't she say good-bye to me, come hang out with me? Unless…Oh, God, no." Jack picked her phone up and dialed a number.

"What is it, Jack?" Ron asked, but Jack put up a hand to silence him.

"Hi, Mrs. Hinkle? This is Jack…I'm good. Thanks. Hey, did anything change with Mollie?…Like…well, was the biopsy bad?…It came?…She won't?…Oh, that must be why she left in such a hurry…Yeah, she's on her way home…." Jack checked her watch. "Her flight will leave in one hour…No, I'm staying here…It's a long story, I'm sure Mollie will fill you in…I don't know why she didn't call…No, she didn't tell me she was leaving…No, she's fine.

Maybe she wants to surprise you…No, I don't know her flight number or anything. I don't even know what airline." Ron wrote Northwest on a piece of the shredded book and handed it to Jack. Jack nodded and said, "Northwest airlines, Mrs. Hinkle. She'll be flying on Northwest…When she gets in, will you please have her call me? I was busy when she left and didn't get to say good-bye…And Mrs. Hinkle, promise me, sincerely promise me…if this biopsy is bad, tell me the truth. Mollie might not need me, but I need to be with her, if it's…." Jack choked on the words. She whispered into the phone, "If it's back, I need to be there with her. I could never forgive myself if…." Jack sat, back bowed, eyes closed, phone gripped in her hand. Ron sat beside her and wrapped an arm around her shoulders. Jack continued to listen and nod. She swallowed hard and said, "I know everything will be all right, Mrs. Hinkle. Thank you…No, I'm the lucky one."

Jack hung up the phone and stared at the wall for several minutes. Then she turned to Ron and burst into tears. He pulled her close as she cried against his chest.

"It'll be all right."

"Like you'd know." Jack pulled away and went to the bathroom where she draped herself over the basin until she felt she had her emotions controlled.

Ron followed her. "You're right. I don't know everything will be fine, but you don't know that everything won't."

"I'm going home." Jack stepped past him and resumed packing her bags.

"Come on, this is crazy."

"No." A shove to his chest didn't move him or even make him flinch. "No, it's not crazy. What's crazy is that one of the world's most perfect people just had her heart broken…*again*…and she took a flight all by herself with the weight of knowing she may have cancer…*again*…and…and…she just needs me."

Ron took the suitcase from her hands. "Settle down. Wait till Mollie gets home, then call her. If she's distraught, I'll buy your plane ticket home. She didn't leave here brokenhearted anyway. She's the one who dumped Craig, not the other way around."

149

"Bullshit. Who told you that? Mollie? She was just trying to spare your feelings."

"Not Mollie. Craig. Craig told me she was running back home to her old boyfriend."

"To Justin? Never in a million years. Mollie might be sweet and nice, but stupid? Never."

"Craig overheard her talking to him on the phone. Told him she was coming back to him. That's why she ran home."

"She's going home, More-Ron, to find out if she has cancer."

"That was low, Jack. I don't see why you have to fight with me. All I'm suggesting is that Mollie may not be the perfect saint you make her out to be. She may just be human."

"I never said she was a saint, but I'd believe her over your skank whore friend."

"You don't even know Craig."

"And I don't want to!"

"I'm just saying Mollie—"

"*GET OUT!* Get the hell out of here. I won't listen to you say a single word about her. You don't know her. You don't know what she's been through. You don't know what pain she's already suffered. And to try and justify Craig to me? That's too much. Why, I have half a mind to go over there right now and knock him over the head with a baseball bat."

"Craig heard her on the—"

"He's lying."

"Craig heard them on the phone this morning. He asked Mollie about it and she lied and said it was you. He checked her caller ID, and it was Justin Scott. Is that the right name?"

"Yes, but."

"How would I know that Jack, unless the guy called?"

Jack shook her head. "That makes no sense." She picked up Mollie's phone and scrolled down through the calls. There were tons of calls from Justin. There was also the text to him with Mollie's flight information. Jack deleted it without mentioning it to Ron. "So what, he's been trying to call her. She didn't go back to him. I just know it."

"Craig heard her."

"Oh, bullshit. I talked to Craig this afternoon. He didn't seem the least bit torn up. He was a caustic ass. Let's go talk to him; I'll prove it to you."

"He's not home."

"Out on a date?"

"No, he flew home to North Carolina. I think Mollie broke his heart."

"Ha!" Jack's laugh was bitter. "That's the funniest thing I've heard all day. Craig Coulter has a heart, the rat bastard. You know what? I hope Mollie did run home to Justin. He may be a creep, but at least he's small enough for me to beat the shit out of. And I hope Craig *is* suffering...Suffering so much he can't see straight. Sad thing is; I know he's not. He looked me in the eye and admitted he just wanted to see if he could score with Mollie. Now get out, Ron. Birds of a feather flock together. You're probably a rat bastard too."

"Well, maybe you're playing games like Mollie."

"So...LEAVE!"

"My pleasure!" Ron slammed the door so hard on his way out it shook the wall. Jack was right behind him in the parking lot screaming, "And I still expect you to buy me a plane ticket tomorrow." With that, she slammed the door. She wasn't strong enough to make the wall shimmer, so she gave it a kick, then squealed in pain and fell on the bed in tears.

****

Mollie's family—her mom, her dad, her twin sisters...and Justin—waited at the airport for her arrival.

Justin leaned forward in his chair, his whole body stiff and nervous. He looked like a younger version of Doug Hinkle, both lean and narrow-bodied with mousey brown hair. "You guys don't have to wait. It'll be after three when the plane comes in. I already told her I'd drive her home."

Doug Hinkle growled. A low rumble that might have been him clearing his throat, but his wife, Vickie, jumped in before he could open his mouth. "That's nice to offer, but we're as eager to see

Mollie as you are. I'm still a little surprised she called you, and not us, for a ride."

"We were going to talk things over."

Doug's eyebrows rose, and his mouth opened, but his wife, an older version of Mollie, patted her husband's thigh and said quickly, "I can see where you two have plenty to discuss. We'll gladly give you two some time and space to talk, when we get to the house."

"Or maybe we should all participate in this *discussion*. I spent over five thousand dollars on that little fiasco that was supposed to be a wedding," Doug said as he stood and paced the waiting area.

"Now, Doug...."

"Don't 'now, Doug' me. Damn it, Vickie. I won't sit and...and pretend we're all happily waiting with this little troglodyte. That we're happy he's here to *work things out*. When the honest truth is, the devil himself might be a better mate for my baby girl."

Doug turned to Justin. "You're callous and cruel. A gentleman would've thought ahead to a girl's feelings. You embarrassed her. In fact, you humiliated her."

Justin sprang to his feet. "Look. I had my own share of humiliation that day."

Doug's eyes narrowed. "You, you dare say that to me? You little...." The two men took a step closer, but Vickie was quickly between the two of them.

"Enough. I swear. You're *both* going to get thrown out by security." Vickie's voice was firm, but quiet. "Either sit, or go outside. I will *not* have this, not tonight. Mollie is coming home, and she *will* be greeted by a happy group; a group that puts their own anger and issues aside and thinks of her." She looked to Doug, then Justin. "Do we understand?"

Doug sat. He grumbled, but added nothing coherent.

Justin ran a hand through his hair. "Just tell Mollie I'll talk to her tomorrow. I don't need this shit."

Vickie had a hand on her husband's shoulder, keeping him in his seat so he couldn't get to his feet and choke the boy before he stormed off.

"Do you see? What a...."

His words were interrupted by the growing clamor of arriving passengers.

****

Mollie recognized the familiar faces instantly and lost what little bit of control she had maintained during the flight. She couldn't see through her tears as she walked toward them, allowing her heart, not her eyes, to be the guide. Doug got to her first. She collapsed against his shoulder and cried. He stroked her hair as he promised. "It's all right, baby. Hinkles can make it through anything."

Her mother burst into tears and grabbed hold of Mollie. She held her daughter close, squeezing her against her as if a hug could make all the pain go away. Vickie pulled away, but never relinquished her grip on Mollie's arm. "Go get her luggage, Doug. Here, sweetie, have a tissue. Meg, Maddie, go get your sister a Coke." Vickie rubbed her back. "It'll be all right. It's the not knowing that rips you apart. Once you know what you're fighting, you'll find the strength."

Mollie nodded at her mother. She stopped crying and smiled. "You're right. It was just a long flight…too much time to think. I'm better now." It was a lie. She couldn't imagine anything being all right at this moment. Her dad and her sisters returned. Meg quietly handed her the cold can, and Mollie held but never opened it.

On the walk to the car, Maddie, a tall blond who was beginning to look less like a cute little girl and more like an attractive young lady—all but the braces and the Mario Party sweatshirt—asked, "Where's Jack? Why didn't she come home?"

"She's staying in Montana and opening a restaurant."

"She told me she was staying when she called. Opening a restaurant? I have to admit, I'm shocked." Vickie said.

"I guess Joanie's staying too." Meg, the other twin, was born three minutes later. She was identical to her older twin, Maddie, however, her dress and style were more mature…as if overcompensating for the lateness of her birth. She turned to her parents and explained. "She married some guy."

"And he's bald and ugly," Maddie declared, pretending to gag herself.

"That's not nice," Vickie scolded. "But how do you know that?"

"Joanie's blog," Meg answered.

"I told you to stay off that," her mother reminded.

"What's not sexy about a balding man?" Doug asked his teen-age daughters.

"Oh, Daddy, you're a dad. You're not supposed to be *sexy*." They both giggled.

"I think you're hot, dear," Vickie offered with a pat on his arm.

Mollie listened to the banter and bit her lip. She didn't want the world on a silver platter; she just wanted a happy family. Just wanted someone to look at her when she was approaching fifty and think she was still *hot*. She blinked back the tears. She turned to her mother. "So, you talked to Jack?"

"Yeah, she called, she seemed really worried, said you took off without saying good-bye. Why'd you do that to her? That wasn't very thoughtful."

"I…ah…it's just that Jack has such a good thing going for her…and I admit I was up all last night thinking about that letter from Dr. Samms, and I was edgy and tired, and I honestly thought if I told her, she would see right through my, 'I'm just fine', and insist on coming home too. She didn't need to do that."

Vickie nodded, though Mollie could see her mother was suspicious of her answer. They loaded into the mini-van and headed home. Mollie watched as the familiar world passed by. The city lights of home offered no comfort, when her heart was left broken and bleeding on the brown plains thousands of miles west. She felt fresh tears spring to her eyes. She looked out the window and let them drop silently from her cheeks. She was grateful for the darkness and her sisters' incessant chatter. No one seemed to notice she couldn't get herself together.

Once home, in the quiet solitude of her childhood bedroom, Mollie snuggled her head into her fluffy pillow. Her mother sat beside her bed and stroked her hair like she was still a child.

"You want to tell me what happened out there?"

"Not really."

"This has nothing to do with Justin or the test results…though that would be enough for most people. I just can't help but wonder…is it something with Jack?"

"No." Mollie closed her eyes. "I'm just worn out. It just never seems to stop."

"But you knew all of this before you left…what changed?"

Mollie closed her eyes and sighed. It was useless to lie to her mother. She opened them, her lip trembled, and her chest hurt. "I met a guy. I thought…well I really liked him."

"A guy? Like a new guy?"

"Yeah. I met him at a party the first night we were in Montana. Then Joanie left us there, so we kind of hung out and…."

"Oh, Mollie, there's reasons I told you to never…it's why you wait."

Mollie turned into her covers and pulled them over her head. "I can't do this." But she knew her mother would never go away now, so she pulled the blanket down and rolled back toward her. "It's not about sex, Mom. I can't explain it. I can't explain it to myself. I don't know why, or how, but I love him. I'm a fool, and I need to get over him, but for right now, I can't. It hurts so damned bad."

"I'm sorry, sweetie."

"Want to know what the worst of it is? He told me from the very beginning that he wasn't the marrying type, wasn't the relationship type. He's thirty and a confirmed bachelor all the way…and what do I do? I fall so hard, I feel crushed."

"Oh, Mollie." Her mom closed her eyes and scowled.

"Bet you wish you'd never asked."

"No, I'd always rather know what's going on, than not. Are you sure he…?"

"He made it quite obvious; cut and dried."

"I'm sorry, baby. I know it doesn't feel like it, but all wounds heal eventually."

"I know." Mollie looked up at her mom. "Please, don't tell Dad?"

"Oh, no, of course I won't."

"Now, I'm going to sleep. I'm so tired."

Vickie tucked the blankets around her daughter like she was twelve again and placed a kiss on her forehead. "Of course, sweetie, you need your rest."

Mollie closed her eyes and listened as her mom switched off the light and pulled the door closed. Thankfully, an exhausted sleep blotted out the pain.

Chapter 18

Pulling into the driveway, he flipped off the lights, but kept the engine running. The house was a total surprise. He expected a large stilted home, with a multitude of decks and levels, not the squat farmhouse that sat sturdily on the ground. Scattered toys cluttered the drive, the furniture was arranged helter skelter on the porch, and drooping flowers adorned the hanging baskets. There was little order. He never expected such chaos from his big brother. The house they grew up in always had order. Even when they ran through it like feral children, command was maintained, but then Babs knew how to crack a whip and keep people in line.

He closed his eyes and imagined a life where kids played freely as parents watched, relaxed and happy. He surprised himself with the mournful sigh. "You're a lucky man, big brother."

"Well, thank you." Tres leaned against the hood and popped his head in the car window and laughed. "Holy shit. I never expected to see you here. You're staying, right? Or are you planning on making an escape and that's why the engine's running?"

"I just got here."

"Well, shut it down and get out here."

Craig got out of the car. Tres grabbed him and gave him a hug. "You came. You son of a bitch." It was the most awkward hug Craig could ever remember, but it felt good.

"I guess we're both sons of a bitch." Craig tried to untangle himself.

"Shh!" Tres ordered with a laugh. "She's sleeping inside, and you know even when she's asleep, she hears everything."

"How could I forget?" Craig smiled. "What are you doing out here? Did I wake you up?"

"No, I've been up. Trying to catch Tanner sneaking back into the house. He's found himself a girl, so now he thinks his curfew is just a suggestion." Tres frowned and looked the yard over. "Tomorrow I'm going to install motion detector lighting all over the place."

"Killjoy."

Tres put his hands on his hips and smiled. "Sure am. He reminds me so much of you it's unbelievable. I guess it's my job to make sure he makes it to adulthood alive and childless. So keeping up with that kid is how I spend most of my days."

"Guy chases girl. Guy gets girl. Guy gets child. Then spends his life chasing the child. Sounds like fun."

"I love it. You ought to try it some time."

Craig shook his head. The lump that rose in his throat was unexpected and unwelcome. He cleared his throat and answered, "I'll leave that to you."

"Still living 'da dream'?"

"Not so much anymore. It all gets boring after a while. Give me my dog and a fishing pole, and I'm good."

Tres walked toward the house. "Fishing? Ah, man, now I'm going to have to come join you. I haven't fished in years. Drink some beers with my brother, fish…damn that sounds good."

"I'd like that," Craig said.

Tres took him to a small den where he flipped on a table lamp, and then pulled down the shades. "Don't want Tanner to see the light." He winked at Craig as he pulled a key out of his pocket and unlocked the liquor cabinet and pulled out a bottle of whiskey. He poured them each a glass. He handed Craig his. Then he motioned him toward the leather wingchair opposite his. "When you called, you said you couldn't come. So what changed your mind?"

Craig shook his head and shrugged his shoulders. He was shocked by how badly he wanted to tell his brother everything, but somehow the words wouldn't come. He opted for a simple, "I guess I was just curious."

Tres nodded. He didn't look convinced, but he didn't press.

"Come on. See my boys."

Even though their steps were silent on the carpet, a woman's voice called into the hallway. "Tres?"

His brother flashed him one minute and stepped into the bedroom. Craig tried to squelch the envy as his brother's wife lifted a heavy head from her pillow and asked, "Is something wrong? The boys' all right?"

"Mmm hmm…you go back to sleep. It's Craig. He came to visit."

"Craig? I should…."

"You sleep, sweetheart. You can see him in the morning."

Her head dropped back on her pillow like a stone. Tres smoothed her hair and then backed out of the room, closing the door quietly behind him. He put a finger to his lips as he led Craig into the nursery.

Two cribs stood side by side. In one a toddler slept on his belly, his hands tucked under his chest. Blond curls topped his head and he made happy sucking sounds every so often. In the next crib, a newborn lay on his back swaddled in a blanket. He slept so peacefully, Craig felt the urge to touch his chest and make sure he was breathing. A monitor on the dresser hummed with a white noise and relayed every sound to a handset by their mother's head.

"The big boy's Sammy. He can really throw a ball. Maybe he'll be a quarterback like his big brother."

"And the new fella is Charles Winston Coulter the fourth. Mom insisted. I refused, but Jenna caved, poor guy. What the hell will we call him? A baby named Charlie?"

"Quatro?"

"Dear lord no. That's almost as bad as Trip." Tres whispered with a laugh.

"Trip. I haven't talked to him in ages."

"He was here till this morning. Too bad he couldn't stay. He'd have loved to see you."

"What's he doing now?"

"Working for Mom, the poor bastard. She put him in a job; hell, I think she even picked his girlfriend."

"Shit. What's that chick like?"

"Perfect. Flawless. A total freaking bitch."

"Is he happy?"

"With Trip, it's hard to tell. He's so easy going; I doubt he'd complain even if he was miserable."

"You should bring him out to Montana. We'll talk some sense into him."

A serene look of peace washed over Tres' face. "I'd like that a lot."

The men slipped out of the room and returned to the den for whiskey and conversation. They talked about fishing, hunting, jobs. The clock ticked toward 3:00 a.m. before they heard a window scrape open. Tres put a finger to his lips and switched off the light. The sound was coming from the room next door. Then there were cautious footsteps coming down the hall. When the source was in front of the open den door, Tres flipped on the light. A shocked, blond haired kid stared back at them. Craig grinned in spite of his mood.

"Tanner…." Tres looked at his watch. "You're three hours past curfew."

"Really? I guess I lost track of time."

"Funny. Your mother says you went to bed at 11:00."

"Yeah, I was, then I remembered…I uh…."

"Needed to help Christy with homework? Forgot to kiss her goodnight? Left your shoes on the beach? Make it a good one."

"Look, Dad, I…."

"Be honest, and I might not tell your mother, who I can assure you will make a call to Christy's mom first thing in the morning. I wonder how long she would ground her daughter for sneaking out to meet up with the likes of you?"

Tanner's eyes popped open. "Mom wouldn't do that."

Tres raised an eyebrow. Tanner fell into a seat. "Please don't tell her. I'll do anything…."

"Then the truth?"

"I was with Christy, but it's not like you think. We weren't alone. She was at a sleep over with a bunch of girls and Jimmy needed me to go to it with him because he cheated on his girlfriend and he wanted to talk to her because he heard she found out. *And* we were only there for fifteen minutes, because she lives up in Rodanthe and it took us over an hour to walk there and an hour to walk back."

"What happened to Jimmy's car?"

"Come on, Dad, we're not stupid enough to sneak out *and* take a car."

Tres shook his head. Craig snickered. Tanner looked at him, his eyes squinted with curiosity. Craig could tell he wanted to ask who he was, but figured the kid was smart enough not to change the subject while his dad threatened full exposure and certain banishment from his princess's kingdom.

"The sneaking out will stop. Do we understand each other?"

"Yes, sir."

"And since I can't ground you without explaining things to your mother, you will offer to paint the outside of her art studio and repair the loose boards on the dock, and I think you'll want to stay home tomorrow since we have family visiting."

Tanner swallowed hard, licked his lips, but said nothing.

Tres smiled and asked, "Aren't you curious who this is?" He pointed to Craig.

Tanner nodded.

Tres said with a smile, "Tanner, I'd like for you to meet your Uncle Craig."

****

Craig woke the next morning to the sounds and smells of his brother's house. Coffee brewed, pans clanked, and hushed voices filtered through his door. Craig tucked his arms behind his head and listened. The domesticity was both comforting and unsettling. Rising, he rubbed his head. It was time to venture out and face the whole family, to make amends in whatever way he could for causing them heartache. But then if last night was any indication, maybe it wouldn't be so bad.

Tres forgave him. Tanner said the whole story was a "trip and a chick magnet." He even offered to let Craig buy him a Mustang if it'd make him feel less guilty.

Two down. One to go. Getting forgiveness from Jenna would be the hardest. *Man up,* he thought. *Can't run away forever.* He picked his pants up off the floor and was about to dress when the doorknob turned. He tried to yank them on before the intruder made it in the room. Craig pictured Jenna storming in and tossing him out of her house. He nearly pulled a muscle as he tried to get the twisted denim up over his calves.

Instead of an irate sister-in-law, in walked his mother. She was only five feet tall and weighed no more than a hundred pounds, but she had a spine forged from steel and her perfectly coiffed hair never seemed to be ruffled. She was dressed in a pink linen shirt and white pants. She almost looked demure, until she opened her mouth. "The prodigal son returns."

"Mom," Craig choked and held the pants over his naked legs.

"Oh, I've seen it all before."

Craig sighed and sat on the bed. "Ever heard of knocking?"

"I didn't want to wake you. Tres said you were up late. Just wanted to see for myself that you really were here."

"Well, you've seen. Now can I get dressed?"

She nodded. "Hurry, breakfast is done."

"I'm not hungry."

"Maureen cooked all morning; you'll get hungry."

"Maureen?"

"Privett, Jenna's stepmom. Married to Pastor Privett? Do you pay attention to anything that's been happening in your family?"

"Evidently not."

"Well, they're all here, and they're waiting on you, so hustle it up."

"What the hell was I thinking?" Craig mumbled as he pulled on his pants.

"What's that?"

"Nothing, give me a minute, and I'll be out."

Barbara hesitated at the door, but finally gave a curt nod and left.

Craig went to the adjoining bathroom and washed up. He looked like hell and he didn't feel much better. Pastor Privett was here too. This was a mistake, but he couldn't get out of it now.

The chatter in the room stopped when he entered the dining room. Tres stood, grabbed his arm and guided him to a seat. "Maureen's been fattening us up since Jenna got out of the hospital."

The rounded Maureen nodded, smiled, and approached Craig. "Well, I'll be. You do look like your brother. I was sorry not to meet you at the wedding. But you're here now." Then much to Craig's shock, she hugged him. "Why, you're a big boy. You better watch Tres, your little brother might just be able to lick ya'."

"He's always been bigger, but that doesn't mean he's better. I've always been smarter," Tres said.

"That's true," Craig admitted as he peeled away from Maureen and took a chair.

The food was served, and the conversation in the room was stilted and broken as if no one could think of a safe subject they could all share. Sam Privett kept glancing at Craig. It was as if he was trying not to stare but couldn't help himself. Thoughts of Angel squirmed through Craig's memory, making him restless and even more eager to leave. He knew the man wanted answers; wanted to know why. But what could he say? "I'm sorry your daughter was crazy"?

As if reading his mind, his mother said, "Craig, do you have anything you'd like to say to Pastor Privett?"

Nearly choking on a bite of scrambled egg, Craig coughed and reached for a napkin. Once he could speak, he said, "I'm sorry for your loss…sir."

Sam answered with a very brief, "Thank you."

"Craig, that's all you have to say? His daughter is gone and all you say is sorry." Barbara's voice rose, but remained steady.

"What do you want me to say, *Mother*?"

"That you're sorry for the pain you caused her. Sorry for the pain you caused her family."

Craig pushed himself away from the table. "This was a mistake. I didn't come here to fight or cause trouble, but it seems my being here's uncomfortable for everyone."

"Craig, please." Tres made the first plea and stood to block the door.

"It's all right, Tres. You enjoy your family, your new baby. Don't worry, we'll get together. I'll call."

Tres nodded and moved. Craig was almost out of the house when his mother grabbed his arm. "You will not run away from this again."

"Run away? I don't *run away;* I just don't have the answers you want. I don't know why Angel killed herself."

"It seems it had a lot to do with you."

"You know what, Mom, that's bullshit, complete and total bullshit. You have no idea what happened with Angel. She claimed I was abusive, and you sent me away. Not one time did you ever ask me my side of the story."

"Fine then, what excuse do you have?"

"Go to hell."

"You don't talk to me like that, young man. You will have respect."

"Fine, what do you want to know, *Mother*? That Angel was my first lay; that she was the first one to talk me into a line of coke; the first person to talk me into stealing a car? That what started out as fun ended up being a psychotic game of relationship roulette? That slut made my life a living hell. Is that what you want to know? Yeah, I broke up with her. I did it nicely, but you know what? She wouldn't listen. She wouldn't go away. So I told her I was done. I wanted nothing to do with her, not then, not ever. You want me to admit that she said she'd kill herself? That I told her I didn't give a damn…is that what you want to know?"

A tear rolled down Sam Privett's cheek as he stood in the door and quietly listened. Craig closed his eyes and shut his mouth.

"I am truly sorry she's gone. If I'd had any idea she really would try it, I'd have done something. I had no clue she was serious. Hell, she threatened and then she started dating that Jake guy. I thought everything was fine. How was I to know she'd mistake Tres for me and think Jenna and I were dating and go off the deep end? As long as she wasn't bothering me, I didn't give a damn what she was doing, and if that makes me to blame, then I'm sorry. I honest to God truly wish I had never met her." Craig took a step toward Sam. "Sir, I don't know if it helps…but I apologize for what happened all those years ago, and I apologize for what I've said today. Angel wasn't all bad. When she wasn't consumed with jealousy, she was a pretty nice girl, but she was obsessed with…" Craig stopped himself. He looked at Jenna, who nodded as if she knew what he was thinking. She didn't need to be told her sister hated her, was obsessed with hurting her, even if it meant swallowing a bottle of pills and laying the blame at her sister's feet. He'd said enough, so he added a simple, "She had issues."

With that, he was gone.

The room was so quiet, the hum of the refrigerator sounded like a jet.

****

Craig waited in line to get his airline ticket, though the last thing he wanted to do was go home. He blamed Jack. Her presence ruined the place. She reminded him of Mollie, and thoughts of her made him feel like his guts were about to fall out.

"OMG…Craig Coulter?"

By the sound of the voice, he guessed two-toned hair, too much make-up, and fake nails. He turned to face a woman with blonde hair with chunks of burgundy highlights, heavy eyeliner, and blood red nails that could double as weapons. He was correct.

"It's me! Violet! I *cannot* believe I ran into you here. Nobody's heard from you in, like, years."

"Yeah, I moved out west."

"Cool. So, what brings you back east?"

"Not much. Just a visit."

"You snuck into town and didn't even call? Come on, we've had sooo much fun together."

"Crazy." *And I'm sure we have, just too damn bad I don't remember any of it.*

"Do you have to leave tonight? I mean it's Friday and I just got off work...blah...Daddy cut my allowance, so I'm an airport waitress. A waitress! Can you imagine that?"

"Not at all."

"I know. It sucks. But I'm happy now, 'cause you're here! And I won't let you go without a night out." She grabbed his arm and gave it a tug.

Craig thought of all his choices and said, "Sure, it's the best offer I've had today."

Chapter 19

"So, you'll go with me?"

Mollie sighed and sat back on her heels. The sun was warm on her back and reminded her she could still feel. The sweat poured down her spine, though the occasional gust of wind offered some relief. The heat and humidity of Pennsylvania was extremely different from the Montana summer, where the air was dry and the winds never stopped.

Pulling off her gardening gloves, she nodded slowly. "I guess."

"And you'll come talk to my mom after the dance? Explain to her what happened between us?"

Her eyes squinted, partly from sun, partly from confusion. What did happen? Justin dumped her. Craig dumped her. And it seems Jack betrayed her. Now, somehow it was up to her to salvage Justin's reputation and relations with his family. She should tell him to go to hell, but her mealy-mouth opened and said, "Sure."

"Thanks Mollie. You're the best." He grabbed her by the shoulders and planted a kiss on her forehead and was gone.

Resuming her work in the little vegetable garden, she tugged at weeds and flipped soil with a vengeance. The smell of ripening tomatoes and fresh cut grass filled the air. A mosquito buzzed in her ear. She slapped at it and managed to make her own ear ring and swiped dirt across her cheek. Then the buzzing returned. Smacking at it again and again until frustration brought tears to her eyes. One slid down her cheek, and she brushed it away and took a deep breath. There was no way she could cry now, not with her parents

167

watching her like a hawk from the kitchen window. She didn't have to turn to see them; she could feel them.

She wouldn't add to their worry by sobbing over pests, especially when she refused to open the doctor's letter this morning. It wasn't fair of her to make them wait, but she just couldn't bring herself to break that seal. She was a regular, healthy young person until she was informed otherwise. As soon as she knew she had cancer, then she was a patient.

She sighed and sat down in the grass. She pulled off her gardening gloves and turned her hands over palms up. She looked at the veins that lead down her arms to the fingers. She squeezed her hands into a fist then opened them. She felt so normal, but was her body hiding a secret fragility? It was hard to imagine that she wasn't made to last forever. That this skin would fade to dust. It was just a matter of when. Now or later.

Her mood slid from bad to black. She had to shake it off, and think of the family. They loved her and needed her to be strong. Wallowing in pity wasn't an option, when they were petrified. Her death scared them to their very core. She knew that. She felt a strange ambivalence about it. She would never admit it to them, but she had no fear of dying. Her only fear was a life absorbed by hospitals and treatments; a life that slowly wasted away until she had to make a conscious good-bye. That gave her nightmares.

She would not think of that now.

She plucked several plump tomatoes from the vines and carried them to the house, cradled in her tee-shirt. Fresh tomatoes, warmed by the sun were one of the good things in life. Rolling them onto the counter, she flashed a smile over her shoulder at her parents. "Don't these look absolutely delicious? I've been craving these as soon as I walked outside. Nothing says summer like the smell of ripe tomatoes. I just love it."

"I prefer the smell of freshly cut grass. It says beginning of summer. Tomatoes are at the end, so they make me just a little sad," Vickie answered.

Mollie frowned. "I never thought of that. I guess fall is good too; a new school year. Maybe I'll go to the mall and buy a bunch of new clothes. Like when I was a kid, start out the year in crisp new everything."

"So, you've decided to renew your contract?"

"Yeah, it's a good job, and I'm not going to let avoidance of Justin dictate my life. He's trying to be a sport. I guess I can too. Heck, I could move back here and walk to work."

"Give up your apartment?"

Mollie rubbed her tomatoes with a towel till they shined. "It won't be the same without Jack."

Vickie nodded and drank her tea. "That would be fine. Or you could get a puppy."

Brutus. Craig was afraid of losing his dog. Her, he could let go.

She turned quickly, so her mom couldn't see her tears. "Still reading that same page, Dad? Must be an interesting one, you've been on it since I went outside."

"Hmm?" Her father laid the paper on the table. "Well, to be honest, Mollie, I just ran over here and grabbed the paper so you wouldn't think I was nib nosing out the window, but I was, and I have to ask, why was Justin here?"

"Oh, that."

Mollie pulled out the cutting board, "He asked me to go with him to the dance tonight. As friends, and as teachers at a school function that desperately needs extra chaperones." Mollie began slicing the tomatoes.

"Mollie, I don't know about this. I don't trust him," Vickie said.

"Don't think? Hell, Vickie, I know you can't trust the little—"

"Little ears," Vickie interrupted.

"I hear what you're both saying," Mollie said hoping to quell a spat between her mom and dad. "You have to trust me. I know how to deal with him."

Mollie finished slicing her tomatoes and got out bread and salad dressing. She assembled her sandwich and joined her parents at the table.

"I'm not so sure. He can be slick, and you just got home. You have so much on your plate already."

"I don't have anything on my plate, Mom."

Vickie looked across the room at the envelope on the counter. Mollie followed her gaze and reached out and patted her hand. "Monday, I promise."

"Well, there's also Jack. I talked to her again last night. She said you still haven't called."

Mollie sliced her sandwich into two triangles and avoided her mother's gaze. "Jack needs to worry more about getting her life together. She has a great chance in front of her. She doesn't need to mess it up by babysitting me."

"All the more reason you should call her."

"And I will, soon." And she would, as soon as she could talk to her without accusing her of being a cheat and a rotten friend. As soon as she could pretend none of it ever happened. Craig might have robbed her of her good sense and self-respect, but he'd not steal her best friend too. She would forgive Jack. She just needed more time.

"Good. I hate to have her worry. So, what does Jack think of this man you met out there?" Vickie asked. Her father gave her a surprised look. "She met a guy out there, Doug. No biggie, now you know." She answered Mollie's wide-eyed stare. "You didn't say having a date with a guy was a secret."

"I don't think I like having daughters who date. Goodness, Mollie, after all the trouble with Justin, you don't need the complications of another relationship."

"Oh, pooh. I fell for you *while* in a relationship. You can't time things like when you meet the right guy." She reminded him and then turned back to Mollie, "So, what does Jack think?"

"I'd say her feelings are mixed," Mollie answered honestly.

"Maybe Jack could explain…" Vickie wondered aloud.

"Mom, stop. It was a date. Like you said, no biggie." Mollie's voice was becoming shrill.

"It's not sounding like a 'no biggie.' I want to know what the hell is going on."

"There is nothing going on, and unless you want me to call Justin for a rescue from this silly conversation, I suggest we drop it."

Her parents were suddenly silent. Mollie sighed. "Stop worrying. I'll call Jack this afternoon. I'll open the letter on Monday. I'll chaperone the dance tonight and be sociable to my miserable ex. Who I'll surely get brownie points in Heaven for forgiving. And...I think I'll take Meg and Maddie to the mall to do a bit of shopping. Life continues. Now, please may I eat?"

"Of course." Her mother rubbed her hand. "I'm sorry. I only mentioned your *date* because Jack is still out there...she might know something...that might make you...."

"It's over." Mollie's words were sharp. "Time to get back to reality."

Mollie regretted snipping at her mother; she looked like she was about to cry. Mollie didn't think she was strong enough to take her mother's tears right now, but thankfully, shuffling footsteps came from the hallway as her sisters emerged from bed. Mollie was delighted to see them. They were still young enough not to worry, and that lack of concern was a comfort.

"You guys going to the dance tonight?" Mollie asked.

They both nodded, rubbing the sleep from their eyes.

"Good then. How about a mall run? I'd really like to look my best." They stared at her with blank faces. "I'm going to chaperone."

"Justin will be there." Meg warned her big sister.

"He's the one who asked me," Mollie said.

Maddie landed in the seat next to Mollie and took half of her sandwich off her plate. She took a bite and frowned. "Too much salt."

"How thoughtless of me not to make *my* sandwich to your liking." Mollie grinned at her sister.

"I like mine with salt." Meg scooped a half from over Mollie's shoulder and took a bite. "Perfect. Thanks, Molls."

"You're welcome, I suppose." Mollie picked up the plate. "You want the other half too?"

"Thanks." She took the plate and joined them at the table. "You know, Mollie, I know he's acting all nice and all, but Justin has been an absolute jerk about the break up."

"I expected nothing less from him." Mollie went to the counter to make herself another sandwich.

"No," Maddie added, "more of a jerk than usual."

Repeating the process all the way down to the triangular slicing of the bread, Mollie carried two plates to the table and placed one in front of Maddie. "There. No salt." Then she sat, setting her own plate before her and taking a bite.

"Thanks, Mollie. You're the best big sister."

"I'm your only big sister."

"See, Meg, you're lucky enough to get two big sisters," Maddie said with a grin.

"You're only three minutes older, like that counts."

"What exactly has Justin done?" their mother asked. Her mom was like a dog on a trail, Mollie thought with a frown.

"He hasn't exactly *done* anything. He's just been telling everyone that the break up was all Mollie's fault. Says he tried to get her back, but she's being cruel to him."

"I told you he'd not be decent in any way," Doug shook his head.

"Oh, well, I refuse to worry about, think about, or give one iota of thought to any of it. I should just be thankful that I dodged a bullet. Imagine a whole life with a guy as selfish as him."

"You could've divorced him in Tijuana," Meg said.

"Tijuana? What in the world gave you that idea?" Vickie asked.

"Joanie, in her blog. You know that guy she married from Montana? She divorced him in Tijuana."

"Yeah, then she said Mollie told her she was mean to marry and run, so she offered him a divorce and some French thing," Maddie informed them.

Meg interrupted. "She said she told him she'd fulfill his craziest wish, and the French thing was at the top. Maddie says it's like a scarf, but who puts a scarf on a wish list? Especially a man. You might be older, but you're also dumber."

"Well, then what is it?" Maddie challenged.

"It's like a blackberry, but leave it to Joanie to buy a french one, like a men-age a troise is somehow better than an iPod."

Vickie's brow rose as she asked, "A ménage a trois?"

"Is that how you say it? What is it Mom, a scarf or an iPod?" Maddie asked.

"It is…well…it means that I am saying this for the last time…stay off Joanie's blog!" Vickie pounded the table with her fist.

Doug dropped his paper and shook his head back and forth. "You're the one who demanded they have internet and their own laptops. I recall saying—"

"Hush, Doug!"

"But she's funny," Meg whined.

"Real hilarious," Vickie said, shaking her head. "Playing with someone's feelings and cheapening the sanctity of marriage. It's all rather disgusting if you ask me."

"She's all right. Isn't she, Mollie?"

"Stay off her site. Joanie's increasingly out of control and self-centered. You guys don't want to be like her."

"It's just that, she's soo funny."

"Listen to your sister," Vickie ordered, her voice brittle.

"Eat guys," Mollie changed the subject, "so we can get to the mall. I want this to be a fun day."

Maddie and Meg shrugged, checked the clock on the wall, and then took off to dress.

Mollie set her plate in the dishwasher. "You want to come, Mom?"

Vickie gave it some thought, then nodded. "I think I might. I might even buy us lunch somewhere with a waiter."

"Ooh, fancy. No wrappers or cardboard? Are you sure we can afford it, dear?" Doug laughed.

"I'm going to splurge." Vickie kissed her husband's head.

"Well, you ladies have fun. I'm going to slop around in some sweat pants and watch sport's center all day long."

Mollie watched as her mother rubbed her father's shoulders and teased him about his idea of fun. Mollie thought of her time with Craig. No matter how cruel he was to her, she still missed him. It wasn't fair that he felt so right. How could she have been so wrong? She grimaced and scooted from the room so her parent's couldn't see the coming tears. Mollie called jokingly over her shoulder, "You two are getting too old to make out in front of your kids."

"Too old," Doug shouted. "Brat! We're like fine wine." To prove his point, he pulled his wife into his lap. Mollie heard her mother squeal. Mollie smiled for them, but couldn't stop the tears from falling once she was safely behind a closed door.

Chapter 20

"Ron hasn't heard from him. Says he hasn't talked to him since he left. Told me the girl he met jilted him. How was I supposed to know?" Barbara paced the living room floor. "He never tells me anything."

Jenna rocked the baby. Tres stacked blocks on top of blocks with Sammy.

"I should call the police." Barbara reached for the phone.

"No police." Tres' words were firm.

"He could be in danger." Barbara's voice was almost shrill. Jenna tucked the baby tighter and rocked a little quicker.

"Mom, he's a grown man. It's not like he's been kidnapped or anything. He's probably on his way home. Maybe he's driving. It'll be days before he gets there."

"I shouldn't have yelled at him."

"No, you shouldn't have, but you did. When he calls, apologize."

Barbara nodded. She rubbed her forehead. "He's too much like me. That's the problem. Hot headed. Judgmental. It's no wonder we don't get along."

The phone rang on the table. Barbara jerked away from it like it was a coiled snake. Tres grabbed it. His face contorted with worry as he listened; then he simply said, "Be right there." He laid the phone on the table. "Well, we found him."

"Where is he?"

"Jail."

"What?" Barbara nearly collapsed in the chair next to her. "Oh, dear lord, why?"

"Public intox. All I have to do is pick him up. No big deal."

"I'll go with you," said Barbara.

"No. Last thing we need is another fight. I'll go…alone…and you'll practice accepting him, warts and all."

"Fine," she agreed with her arms crossed over her chest.

Tres kissed his wife good-bye and left.

****

He was able to spring his brother with nothing more than a promise that he'd be taken straight out of Norfolk and not return. Tres walked him to the car and was headed down the road before he asked, "Fun night?"

"Not exactly."

"Well, was it exciting at least?"

"I'm tired of it all." Craig blotted dried blood from his lip with his shirt collar. "And I freaking hate to get hit. It pisses me off."

"You start it?"

"Nah, sucker punch. Totally blindsided, and the hell of it was I was on my way out when the asshole hit me."

"Way out?"

"Long story."

"It's a long drive."

"True. Sorry 'bout that, and I'm sorry I ruined your family gathering."

"It's all right. Angel's death was the elephant in the room. It had to come up eventually."

"Ya think?"

"Definitely. You weren't exactly eloquent, but that was stuff Mom needed to hear."

"Sam didn't."

"Sam knows. He forgave Maureen's son, Jake…and hell, Jake was the one with her when she died."

"But I'm the one she pointed the finger at. Not Jake."

The car was quiet. Craig shifted in his seat and leaned against the door. They turned off the I-64 to VA-186 toward the Outer

Banks. Craig took a deep breath and said, "You can just drop me off in Chesapeake. I can catch a flight home tomorrow."

"Don't think so. For my troubles, you promised to tell me what happened tonight."

"Met a girl, she had a boyfriend, and I got punched."

"Hmm…Cliff Notes version isn't acceptable."

"Man, are you parenting me?"

Tres laughed. He flipped on the defroster. "Are you sweating? Steaming up my car?"

"Kiss my ass."

"So, what happened?"

"I met up with a girl I used to know, and she invited me to go to a few clubs. We went out, had a few drinks, and then we went back to her place. I stayed there a while, got bored, and was leaving when her boyfriend comes through the front door and freaking decks me before I even knew who the hell he was."

"Got bored? What the hell does that mean?"

"It means I was ready to go find myself a hotel and go to bed."

"So, how did the police get involved?"

"Violet called them. Said she was afraid I'd kill her boyfriend."

"You beat him pretty bad? Think he'll file charges?"

"He didn't tonight; don't know about tomorrow."

Tres gripped the steering wheel. "A battery charge could lose you your job."

Craig rubbed his eyes. He knew he should be worried, but he wasn't. Tired, that was all he felt. But Tres looked concerned, so he said, "He threw the first punch. I was only defending myself."

Tres nodded. "Good. That's good. I'd hate to see you lose your job. You seem to really like it."

"It's a paycheck. If I lose it, I'll just do something else."

"Really, it's that simple?"

"Yep."

Tres took a deep breath. "I'm not starting a fight, but I have to ask…do you have anything you care about?"

Craig laughed. "My dog; unlike women, he's loyal and predictable."

****

Barbara met the car as it pulled into the drive way. Legs barely out of the car, Craig was approached by his mother. "I'm sorry. I was wrong."

"Babs? You feel all right?" Craig asked as he got out.

"I shouldn't have said those things, and I should have asked you years ago about your side of the story. I never should have…" Her voice cracked, and the breath caught in her throat. Before she could say another word, Craig dragged her to him and crushed her with a hug. Barbara buried her face against his chest and gripped him tightly.

"It's all right," he said.

Pulling back, Barbara dabbed at her eyes with her finger tips. They walked arm and arm into the house, where Jenna met them in the living room with a pot of coffee. Craig sat on the couch and stretched his long legs out in front of him. Tres sat in the recliner next to them. Barbara patted his knee. "I've taken care of the situation. There are no further charges. I spoke with Ron, and I want to know a little about this jezebel I spoke with on the phone."

"Mollie isn't a jezebel. She's just smart."

"Smart?" Barbara sounded shocked.

"I'm not exactly a knight in shining armor."

Jenna seated herself on the arm of Tres' chair. She bit her lip before asking, "What happened?"

Craig told the story as he saw it while they all listened. When he finished, he turned to his mother and said, "Oh well, Babs, you always said I deserved to have a woman chew me up and spit me out. Looks like it's your dream come true."

Barbara, frustrated when powerless, and protective of her child even though she had nearly daily threatened Craig that he deserved a good heartbreak spat, "Don't be a fool. Evidently the little bitch doesn't deserve you."

"No, Mom, I don't deserve her."

"You can't possibly mean that." Jenna's quiet voice was filled with sympathy.

"You're a saint to say that, Jenna. Especially after everything I did to you."

"Oh, Craig." She twisted her hands in her lap. "You have to forget about the mess with Angel." Jenna looked toward the door, then back at Craig. "Angel was insane. She was cruel to me as a little girl. She and her mother drove me to the brink. They blamed me for everything and anything that went wrong. I ended up," her cheeks flamed and her voice dropped to a low whisper, "trying to commit suicide. I know better than anyone who my sister was. I don't say it often because I know Dad loves her, but deep down, he knows, and none of us blame you."

Craig's eyes filled with tears, but he shook them off. "That means a lot to me. You're kind to say that."

"It's the truth. I've wanted to tell you that for a long time." Jenna's cheeks reddened and she added cautiously, "Can I ask you a question?"

Craig nodded.

Jenna licked her lips and swallowed hard. "Did this girl leave you or did you run her off?"

Mollie's crestfallen look the morning after flashed through his mind. "I…," he began, but stopped. His words hurt her, but she was leaving him. She'd lied to him.

Jenna didn't wait for him to answer before adding, "I let Tres slip through my fingers because I thought I wasn't good enough for him. I let my own insecurity stop me from fighting for what I knew, in my heart, was real. I knew," she patted her chest, "in here, that he loved me, but I let my cluttered brain rule. Are you sure you aren't doing the same?"

"The hell with her, there's other fish in the sea." Barbara's face looked pinched and furious.

Jenna smiled at Barbara and shook her head. "Don't make my mistake, Craig. Don't give up until *she* tells you to go away."

"She left me. For her ex-boyfriend."

"You *think* she left you for him. Did you ask her?"

Craig shook his head.

"See," Jenna said, "and I thought Tres left me. I saw you with the girls at the pool and drew all of my own conclusions. I walked away and licked my wounds instead of fighting. Is that really what you want to do?"

Craig shrugged.

"You can't be serious," Jenna prodded. "You can't plan to just give up."

Craig rubbed his eyes, "You don't know me, Jenna. You're kind, but you have no idea what I've done in my life. This sort of thing was bound to happen."

"Cosmic justice for years of being a hedonistic abuser of women?" Barbara asked.

"Yeah, something like that." Craig agreed staring into his coffee.

"Balderdash." Barbara stood. "I can't listen to this. What's with you? I never taught you sit around and pine over a bad hand. Grab life by the throat and fix it." Barbara pressed a well-manicured hand to her cheek. "Oh, Lord, you're making my blood pressure rise."

"Do you love this girl, Craig?" Tres asked.

"Love?" Craig shrugged. "I don't think I'd go that far."

"So, what would you call it?" Tres asked.

"I like her."

Tres laughed, his head thrown back as the laughter moved its way from his chest to his throat. "Liking a girl smacks you on your ass like this?"

Craig shrugged, grinning despite his horrible mood.

"Hope you never fall in love. It might kill you."

Craig rubbed his hands roughly across his chin, his whiskers scraping the palm of his hand. "Maybe I do more than like her, but it doesn't really matter. She went back to her fiancée."

"Then make her tell you why," Jenna prodded.

Craig's laugh was hollow and mocking.

"I'm serious."

"Go tell her boyfriend she cheated on him." Tanner appeared and grabbed a cookie from the plate on the table. The adults stared up at him in shock. He took a seat, throwing his legs over the arm of the chair. He swallowed the cookie in one bite. "That's what I'd do."

"Don't you have somewhere to go?" Tres asked.

Tanner grinned. "We have family visiting. Thought I'd stick around the house."

Tres groaned.

"I appreciate the advice, Tanner, but I think I'll just let Mollie be happy. Honestly? She deserves to be happy."

Jenna's eyes were suddenly misty. "Oh, you do love her. You have to tell her! What's the worst she could say? That she doesn't love you? Big deal. Then you can come back here, just like now, brokenhearted, and looking to heal."

"I'll think about it." Craig stood. "Now, if you guys wouldn't mind, I need a minute to think."

He stood and walked out the back door. Barbara followed barely a step behind.

She caught up with him on the porch and linked her arm in his as they followed the path toward the dock.

"I've missed you." It wasn't exactly an emotional statement. She may as well have said, "I had eggs for breakfast."

Craig didn't know what to say, so he mumbled, "I…uh…missed you too."

Barbara laughed and patted his hand. "The hell you did. But that's all right. I'm your mother. I understand. I've been worried about you."

"I'm fine."

"Getting arrested isn't fine."

"You fixed it."

"Because I started it."

He looked at her wide eyed.

"I should've known you didn't come here to see the baby. I should've known you needed your family." He didn't argue. "So, what really happened with the girl?"

Craig shrugged. He made it a habit to never share his business, but part of him needed more than anything to show his mom his wounds and have her promise they would heal like a child with a skinned knee.

"It's hard to explain."

"I've never been accused of being stupid."

"No, Babs, you're not stupid."

She gave his cheek a pat. "You know, I look at you, and I still see my baby boy. I may not be the best mom, but I am the only one the lord gave you." Her smile was soft, sympathetic. "So, this girl, she wasn't the typical Craig sort of girl was she?"

"No, she was smart, sweet, beautiful…with just enough sass to keep me on my toes." Craig laughed. "She punched me in the airport. Not a slap. She punched me. You've got to give her credit for not taking my crap."

"Why would you give her crap if you like her?"

"Because I knew she was going back home to her fiancée, and I was pissed."

Barbara shook her head. "Oh, darling, never get involved with people in relationships. Did the lesbian teach you nothing?"

"You heard about that?"

"Trust me, everyone who knew you heard about that."

"Well, I guess some lessons bear repeating."

She wrapped an arm around his. "So, this relationship she's in, is it solid?"

"Not at all, or at least, not from what she told me. He left her at the altar once. I'd think that was a deal breaker. But then, I'm not…."

"For the love of God, do not say it again. You deserving to get your heart broken is hogwash. I never meant it. I only said it to try to make you behave."

He looked at her aghast, she grinned. "Mark it on your calendar. *Babs* said she lied." She sighed and added, "Darling, you *are* a good man. You deserve to be happy. If this girl can't see your worth, well then she wasn't so smart after all. There are other, smarter girls out there."

"I suppose."

Barbara gave his arm a squeeze. "Come home, darling. You've been away too long. I can get you a job. Max can get you into his grandson's security business, or I could get you a job at any level of law enforcement…being a senator does hold some clout you know."

"Tres told me you had a boyfriend. Who is this Max?"

"Oh, that's right, you've been avoiding me. You haven't met Max. He's my friend."

"Babs has a boyfriend?"

Barbara laughed. "Why, of course. I'm still a hot tamale to a sixty-something man."

"Unbelievable."

"Watch it, son."

"It's not that. You are, I guess, not without merit." She laughed and patted his arm with her free hand. Craig added quietly, "I just never thought you'd want another man."

Barbara smiled, her eyes misted with tears. "No man will ever be to me what your father was. I still feel his presence. I even talk to him in my head. Can't say as though he answers back, but I feel like he's with me. And believe me, I would give anything to have him here, but until I'm called to the big rotunda in the sky, I'm stuck alone. And I've found I enjoy spending time with Max. He's clever, and he's willful, a real match for my domineering personality."

"Do you love him?"

Barbara shrugged. "I'm comfortable with him."

"So, you what about Dad?"

She shook her head as she looked out across the moon on the water. "Ahh, Charlie Coulter was different. He was a better man than this woman deserved. Oh, how I loved him, and always will love him. But lightning only strikes once."

"You really think that? Do you think if you hadn't married Dad, you'd have missed the opportunity to find love? Real love?"

"I don't know. I suppose I would've married somebody, been one of the countless numbers of couples who try to escape their spouse. No, a love like ours was rare. He was everything that was the best for me. And there was and always will be only one

Charlie." She wiped away a single tear. "But I suppose I would never have known the difference…had I never met him."

"But if you knew him and he left you…of his free will, then is it real lightning or just heat lightning?"

"Heat lightning's real, darling, it's just farther away."

"I was just using it as an example."

"Sweetie, what *really* happened with this girl? Do you think she's your lightning?"

"Two days ago I would have said yes. Today, I don't know." Craig shook his head.

"Did you tell her you loved her?"

"I only knew her a week."

"I met your father at a festival some friends of mine dragged me to, and I agreed to marry him by the end of the week. Like I said, lightning is rare. It's quick and unpredictable and it happens oh, so fast."

"And sometimes only one person gets hit?"

"Well, sometimes some people try to run from the coming storm. I sure did. I was such a bitch to your dad. I knew he was getting to me; I knew I couldn't control how I felt about him, so I wanted to distance myself from him. Maybe this girl got scared? She sure defended you like a lioness on the phone. She didn't seem phony. You need to talk to her. That's the only way you'll ever know."

"What if she…."

"Then Jenna's right. You'll be right back here where you started, but with all your questions answered. Don't let pride be your downfall. Tell her you love her. Tell her you want her."

He didn't look convinced.

"I mean it. Call her, right now." She handed Craig her cell phone. She kissed his cheek, ruffled his hair like he was twelve, and walked away.

Craig dialed her number. Jack answered and he winced. "Jack? Can I talk to Mollie?"

Jack started to bitch him out, then there was arguing, and a good bit of cursing. Then Ron got on the phone. "Buddy! I've been trying to call you." Ron covered the phone, but Craig could hear him say to Jack, "Craig has a right to know, dammit."

Then he was back on the line. "Look, buddy, first of all, you need a damn cell phone. I've been trying to hunt you down all day, and I didn't know what number to call you at, and 411 was no help cause I couldn't remember Tres' real name, and the bitch wouldn't just give me the number of every Coulter living on an island in North Carolina…Did you know there was more than one island?"

"What about Mollie, Ron?" Craig said, trying to remain patient.

"Craig, she didn't leave for the boyfriend…she left 'cause she has cancer again. Remember when I told you she might? Well, she does and that's why she took off."

"But I heard her, on the phone."

"Not sure what that's all about. I do know she's at home with her parents, and her mom told Jack it's not a boyfriend issue."

"Are you sure?"

"I told you, Jack talked to her mom."

Craig thanked him, and then closed the phone. He didn't know how long he sat there, looking out over the water. He felt like the world had stopped and all truths in the universe were turned on their ear.

Every promise of good winning over evil was a lie.

Chapter 21

Mollie waved good-bye to her sisters as they disappeared around the corner of the school. They tried to make excuses to skip the bonfire, but Mollie insisted. She fondly remembered her days in high school, and she didn't want her sisters to miss out on memories because they felt the need to babysit their incredibly pathetic big sister. Justin had invited her tonight, then called and suggested she meet him at the gym. She knew he feared facing her parents again, but still, way to man up. She was going in alone and not crying about it.

Until the gymnasium loomed in front of her. Swallowing the lump in her throat, she moved boldly ahead on heavy legs. How many dances had she attended here? Even the smell of the place was ingrained in her soul. The freshly painted walls and new varnish on the gym floor sparked a dozen bittersweet thoughts. She was transported back to an age of crushes and BFFs. To a time when dreams were fresh and finding true love wasn't fantasy, it was a promise. She suddenly missed that magical time when everything was possible, when her body was healed and invincible, and her hopes impenetrable to rejection and pain. She was so certain of happily ever after that she never asked herself if, only when.

Now she simply hoped her body and her heart were able to mend without too many scars. She sighed hard and looked around for something to do. A table to move, a decoration to hang, but everything was done. The streamers were hung, the tables were

187

covered. Even the long buffet table was prepared, laid out with snacks and punch in the corner of the gym.

Mollie passed a few parents who were helping with the food. They said hello and told her she looked pretty. Mollie thanked them and took the cup of punch offered to her. Mollie did feel pretty. Not drop dead, knock out gorgeous, but pretty. Her soul may be bruised and battered, her body possibly being invaded by damnable little cancer cells, but she looked good. Her sisters and her mother had worked hard to accomplish what they had decided was "smokin'." Her eyes were outlined in smoky grey, her hair curled to absolute perfection, her clothes chosen to accentuate her very best features, at least what her sisters called her "apple bottom." Mollie grinned at the memory of her father's look of disapproval. "Justin will surely notice her; what are you guys thinking?" This was his complaint, as though if Justin saw her, and if he wanted her back, Mollie would fall head over heels for him. *Silly, Dad,* Mollie thought. *It's not the guy I dated for four years that would cause me to flip, but the guy I only knew for a week.* But then she supposed no one of any reasonable thinking would imagine her thoughts were filled with a man she barely knew. Mollie closed her eyes a moment, and he was there. She could virtually see him, feel him, and remember the smell of him. He was so real to her mind's eye that she could almost feel his touch against her skin.

Someone knocked over a folding chair. The bang jolted her from her daydreams. She frowned at the hold Craig had over her, even after acting like an ass at the airport, she couldn't hate him enough to rid her mind of him. She wished she would have just asked him why he was being so hateful.

Wished she knew why Jack had betrayed her.

She looked at the phone she borrowed from her mom. She had eighteen missed calls.

All from Jack.

She should let her explain. Mollie rubbed the side of her phone with her thumb, thoughts of what Jack could say to explain herself floating through her mind. She would probably say she was protecting her. That Craig was sleazy, which was probably right.

That she was trying to stop him from hurting her by proving to her he was bad. Or maybe she'd simply say she couldn't help herself, as Joanie had done. Mollie bit her lip and shut off the phone. She wasn't ready to deal with this right now. It was hard enough to deal with the hurt, but to admit that she never saw it coming made her feel like a total fool. Just hours ago, Mollie honestly thought life couldn't get any sweeter. Now she was out one best friend and had been duped by the worst kind of player—one who had warned her that he was a single-minded mutt.

But it was done, and she would think of it no more. If she kept this train of thought, she couldn't trust herself not to break into tears. If she cried, everyone would assume it was over Justin, and she did have enough dignity to refuse to allow that; not tonight in front of everyone, not ever.

Mollie filled a plate with food and munched on a potato chip.

Casey Smith, fellow teacher, profuse gossip, and staff trouble maker made eye contact with Mollie and made a bee line for her. Mollie's radar caught the blip, but she was unable to maneuver out of the line of fire as she was flanked from the right by Casey's cohort, Lynn Martin.

"Mollie," Lynn called, greeting with her arms outstretched for a hug which Mollie did dodge. "Two-minute warning, doll. We just came in from the bonfire."

"Justin will be coming. I'm sure he plans to give his 'headed to State' victory speech," Casey informed her rather gleefully.

"I know. We've talked. If you'll excuse me…" Mollie said quickly searching the room for an ally, any ally. The closest person to her was Ms. Hardy, a fifty-year-old spinster, who most of the staff knew very little about. She did her work and offered zero input to the gossip or discussions in the teacher's lounge, but Mollie knew her well enough to know she was far more trustworthy than the vipers that were scenting the air with their flickering tongues.

"Really? That's good, I guess. I mean it's a shame that it didn't work out between you guys." Lynn sighed. "He's such a great guy."

Mollie said nothing intelligible, though she mumbled something about things always happening for a reason. It didn't matter that her words were too low and too disjointed for anyone to make out; they weren't really interested in listening. They seemed happy enough to be first to stir the pot. Mollie excused herself, saying, "I'd better go. I need to talk to Sue. I hear she went to Rome. And I thought it'd be interesting to hear about her trip."

Lynn and Casey nodded. They shared broad, knowing grins and asked Mollie as she walked away, "Trouble in paradise for you and Jack?"

Mollie paused a second, but never turned. She continued her trek across the floor with their eyes and their giggles following her. How did they know about Jack? Surely Jack wasn't bragging about her…about whatever went on between her and Craig?

Sue gave her a bit of quiet allegiance in her simple welcome. "They're bitches, Mollie Hinkle. Always have been, always will be. And your old boyfriend belongs right with their ilk."

"So you've heard about my unfortunate nuptials too?"

"I'm ashamed to admit it, but yes, I've heard. You, of all people, deserve better. But, if it's any consolation, I'm glad you're free of him. I never did like him. He's so self-centered and a bit on the stupid side, if you ask me. You'd have grown bored of him in no time."

"Trust me. I realize that and more now. I just wish everyone didn't feel sorry for me. It makes me feel a little pathetic."

"Well." She frowned at Mollie. "It's hard to have a heart and not to feel bad for you. It's one thing to break up. It's another thing to do it with everyone paying attention, and…" Sue picked at her Styrofoam cup and chewed her lip as if debating whether or not to say any more.

"I'm healthy. I'll be fine. I know it."

"I'm glad to hear that," Sue said quietly. "I really am…it doesn't make me feel quite so bad to tell you…and I only say this because I feel you should know…Justin has been spreading rumors."

"Like what?"

"Like the reason the wedding fell through was because of your, um, very close relationship with Jack."

"You've got to be joking?" Mollie could tell by the pained look on Sue's face she was telling the truth. "How could Jack come between us? That's just absurd."

"Let's just say, he's insinuating that you're closer to Jack than anyone. Especially after your friend's blog got him teased."

"We are best friends, but I don't see…."

"Mollie, dear…he's saying you're *significantly* closer to Jack," Sue explained with wide eyes.

Mollie thought a moment, then it dawned on her. Her own eyes popped open and her chin hit her chest. "You've got to be joking."

"I wish I was."

"Oh, lord, what a pig. And people believe him?"

"It used to be that you had to be over forty and single to be gay. Now I suppose if you're single at any age and have a close friend, then you're suspect. I've had to live with it since I transferred here."

"Holy crap. I'm glad I haven't signed my contract yet. Oh, why did I come here?"

Mollie felt her eyes sting. Sue sighed and patted Mollie's forearm. She looked Mollie in the eye and said, "Look, you'll learn to either let them flatten you or live your life however you want in spite of them. People like Justin and those two bitches over there aren't worth the carbon their made of."

Mollie nodded. "But everyone thinks I'm a lesbian?"

"It's just juicy gossip. There will be something new to talk about by mid-fall."

Mollie groaned. "I didn't think my life could get much worse."

"I'm sorry, kiddo."

Mollie sighed and wished it was all over.

Chapter 22

Craig stood in line at the Pittsburgh International Airport and waited to rent a car. He kept looking at his watch; it was already after 9:00 p.m., and he was anxious to be on his way. He felt strengthened by his family, in their words of encouragement and in the ultimate freedom of their forgiveness. Whenever he felt like he was on an insane mission, he had their words of strength and promises of hope to fortify him. Even Pastor Privett and his wife, Maureen, had hugged him and prayed for him. Craig couldn't believe he had waited so long to mend fences with them. Jenna, who he expected to throw him out; had been the deciding voice in his plan to just go to Mollie immediately. "No phone calls," she said to him with tears in her eyes. "Never believe you don't deserve the person you love. Make her look you in the eye and say it's over. You'll regret it forever if you don't."

Craig felt, for the first time since he could remember, optimistic. And eager. He was eager to reach Mollie before the magic wore off.

Process done, keys in hand, he nearly sprinted to the lot where he found the only available car left, a bright yellow Aveo. He slid his tall frame behind the wheel of what he decided had to be a clown car in a former life and took off.

The streets of the city were narrow, flanked on each side by high rises. He assumed they'd been at the height of modern architecture a hundred years ago when steel was king and the Carnegie's and Mellon's ruled. The city had grown on top of itself like a Picasso painting—disturbing and unruly to some and a work of art to others.

Craig wound his car up a steep hill and stopped at the apartment building listed on the address. Craig took a deep breath and went to the lobby. He pushed the call button and waited nervously. There was no answer. He pressed the buzzer again and again to no avail. He went back outside to his car and phoned Jack, who was suddenly his accomplice after he admitted to her "I love her, Jack, and as bad as I am, I've got to be better for her than the guy who left her at the altar."

"She's not home," he groaned impatiently as soon as Jack picked up on the other end.

"Try her parent's house. I probably should've thought of that first."

"Where's that?" Jack gave him the directions, Craig wrote them down, and then hung up the phone.

He put the tiny car in gear and headed to the next location.

Craig arrived at the brownstone cottage that sat on a quiet drive in the suburbs of Pittsburgh. The lawn was neatly cut and the hedges trimmed to box like perfection. A wooden sign on the front door proudly announced: The Hinkles: Doug, Vickie, Mollie, Megan and Madison.

This was the right house. Craig took a deep breath and approached the door. He gave the frame two quick raps and waited. A dog barked. A tiny dog, which someone on the other side of the door picked up before swinging it open. Craig stood face to face with the woman who had to be Mollie's mother. Craig instantly saw the resemblance. Same build as Mollie, only a little heavier, same chocolate brown eyes, same broad smile that spread to her eyes. "Hello?" she answered in greeting as she cradled the squirming, yipping dog.

"Ma'am, I'm looking for your daughter, Mollie?"

"Oh," she said, her voice suddenly more serious. "Mollie isn't here right now, she's out."

Craig felt his heart hit the floor. He should have known. "Well. Thank you, Ma'am." He turned to leave when Vickie stopped him. "Did you come all the way from Montana?"

Craig felt hope. Mollie must have said something to her mother, made some reference to meeting him on her vacation. Why else would she assume he was from Montana? "Yes, Ma'am. I came hoping to see her, but if she's not here." Craig shook his head. "Would it be all right if I just left my phone number for her?"

"Of course you may!" Vickie handed him a pad of paper and a pen. Craig took it and wrote a simple plea, *please call me*, added his cell phone number, and handed the pad back to Vickie. "I'm not sure yet where I'll be staying, but I can't leave until I talk to her. Tell her I really need to talk to her, Ma'am."

Vickie Hinkle took the number and nodded when a voice behind her erupted like a gun shot in the room. "Why the hell should my little girl call you?"

Doug Hinkle stood eye to eye with Craig, and though Craig outweighed him by an easy 70 pounds, Doug Hinkle's irritation made him a bold adversary. Doug snatched the piece of paper from his wife's hand and crumbled it. "I think my daughter has enough to worry about without having to be bothered by the kind of complications dating brings. I want you to leave her alone."

"I can't," Craig answered. "I love her."

"Love," Doug spat." "You boys don't know what love is. To young men like you, it's transient and based more on hormones than brain cells. I love my daughter. I held her when she was born, I held her when she had her first battle with cancer. I even held her when that little miscreant left her at the altar, but you know what?" Doug closed the distance between them, squared off nose to nose, and poked him in the chest. "None of that hurt me so much as when my little girl came off that plane with her spirit broken. Now, I have to assume that was caused by you."

"Doug," Vickie scolded.

"Let me speak. I knew she wasn't crying at the gate over Justin or any test result. I know my daughter better than that."

Before Vickie could argue, Craig spoke up, "I never meant to hurt her. There has to have been some sort of misunderstanding. I do love her." Craig turned his gaze at Vickie as he explained. "Mollie left me, and she never explained why. She made her flight plans without mentioning it to me. I assumed she left me for Justin, so I came to convince her that he doesn't care for her like I do."

Doug Hinkle took a step back, though he wasn't at all won over. "She'll date Justin over my dead body. She doesn't need you to stop that."

Craig argued his case. "Sir, I guess I'm just chasing a dream. Maybe I've finally gone off the deep end, but I won't walk away until Mollie tells me she doesn't have any feelings for me."

"Mollie told me she met someone, but it hadn't panned out. It broke her heart, but you say it was a misunderstanding?" Vickie's voice was full of excitement, hope lighting up her countenance.

"Slow down, Vickie," Doug cautioned his wife. He looked Craig over and pulled an envelope from his back pocket. He handed it to Craig. "You say you love her." He sounded snide and condescending. "Let's be honest with each other. Inside that envelope are the results of her biopsy. There should also be the results of a genetic marker screening for breast cancer. Did she tell you about that?"

"She told me she had cancer as a child. Jack told me she came home because she had cancer again."

"We pray it's not that." Vickie breathed and hugged her dog tighter.

Doug cleared his throat and adjusted his glasses. "We don't know where we stand. Mollie refuses to open the envelope. We've had that for three days. I called her while she was in Montana, and she said wait till she got home. I gave it to her when she got home, and she said wait until Monday. I think she's just worn out from so much going wrong in her life. She doesn't need any more pain."

Craig nodded. "I want to help her. I want to spend the rest of my life with her."

Doug's eyes narrowed. "You've known her a week. You look old enough to know better."

"I am. I plan to ask her to marry me. I have my mother's blessing, and I'd like to have yours."

"Are you insane? You barely know her. And have you given a single thought to what a life with her may mean? Do you realize this may be the beginning of an economic hardship, a time-consuming treatment that doesn't have any concern whatsoever for your calendar, or for holidays or anything? Do you love her enough to stand by her in the worst of sicknesses? Don't accept something you're not willing to see through to the end. Because my baby's been through too much. Don't make her promises you can't keep. Imagine life with my daughter at its worst and be sure that's what you want. If you have any doubts, walk away. Let her mother and I care for her."

Craig considered Doug Hinkle's words. He imagined his life being the same as Doug Hinkle's. Remembered the stories of him selling all he possessed to pay medical bills and sacrificing professional status by taking time off work for her care. Craig understood that Doug knew what true love was about. It wasn't just that head-dizzying feeling when bodies touched, or the warmth that spread through him when her smile was directed at him. It was the willingness, the commitment to hold on even when it was easier to walk away. Craig didn't answer immediately. He owed Mollie and this man the dignity of a well-considered response. Was he, commitment leery as he was, ready to make this leap?

Impatient, Vickie Hinkle squeezed Craig's hand. "Well. Do you? Do you love my daughter?"

Chapter 23

"Sir," Craig answered in a voice both quiet and reverent. "I have never been a trustworthy, noble person. In fact, I don't deserve a woman like your daughter at all." Craig looked down at the envelope he held in his hands, his thumb rubbed the smooth paper. "But I do love her."

Craig took a deep breath. He looked Doug Hinkle eye to eye and revealed more honesty to this stranger than he would ever thought possible twenty-four hours before. The confession caused him surprisingly little pain. He had nothing to lose. Nothing could hurt as bad as the thought of losing Mollie without putting up any fight. "I know it sounds insane, and I've told myself over and over again that I might possibly be crazy. I've tried to be reasonable. I've tried to walk away, to talk myself out of loving her, out of needing her, but no matter how rational I try to be, I come back to the same place. I can't lose her. Especially not to some…some guy who doesn't even recognize her value. I'm not a kid. I've had plenty of opportunity to meet my share of women." Craig paused to stay his emotions. "And I know for certain there are no other women like Mollie. She is the one human being on earth that makes me feel…." Craig thought a moment then answered, "Calm. When I'm with her, I feel things are just right."

"A completeness?" Vickie answered, her eyes glowing. Doug scowled at her, but she shrugged and allowed her grin to spread.

Craig nodded his head at Vickie and lifted the envelope and turned his gaze to Doug. "And this, sir? This just clarifies it for me.

It urges me not to over-analyze this, because I can't waste a single precious minute. If Mollie will have me, then I can help her. I have resources and connections. I may be able to help her beat this."

Craig rubbed away the burn behind his eyes. "And if she doesn't feel the same, and she wants to stay with her old boyfriend, I still want to help her. I owe her that much. Mollie made me realize there is more to this world...more to life...than I ever imagined possible. Now, if you would give her the message that I'm in town, I'd appreciate it. I won't leave until I see her. If she refuses to call, I'll just keep coming back until I talk to her."

Vickie Hinkle shook her head. "No need for that. I can tell you exactly where she is. You go," she clutched Craig's arm. "Go make my daughter the happiest woman on earth." Tears fell from Vickie's eyes, and she hastily wiped at them while smiling at Craig. "My baby loves you, and she does need you, whether you offer her anything other than a hand to hold. I don't know where you get the crazy idea she'd ever have Justin in her life again, but that's a matter you two can work out." She led him to the front door. "Mollie is at the high school chaperoning a dance. It's just straight down the road a couple of miles. It's easy to find. You go there and tell her what you told us."

"I don't think this is such a good idea, Vickie," Mr. Hinkle complained. "She'll be home around midnight. Then, he can talk to her in private."

"Oh, pooh, Doug. You think like an economics professor."

Doug Hinkle shook his head. "It's rational thinking."

"Rational, maybe," she agreed, "but not exactly romantic."

"She doesn't need to suffer any more embarrassment."

"A dream come true is not an embarrassment." Vickie waved a hand at her husband and then turned her attention back to Craig. "The gymnasium doors are right off of the main parking lot. Go there, and you'll find her. Tell her you love her. Sweep my little girl off her feet, all right? She so deserves to be happy."

"Yes, Mrs. Hinkle, I believe she does." Craig turned his attention to Doug. "Sir?"

"Vickie, how can you be so certain, *she* loves *him*?"

"A mother knows. I could see it in her eyes, a pain that wasn't there when she left, so I knew it wasn't Justin or the biopsy. All of that happened *before* she left, and she was fine then. And besides, Jack can't ever keep anything from me. This will make her so happy."

"I will only do so with your blessing, Mr. Hinkle."

Doug sighed, "I suppose my wife knows best. Go, get going if you're certain."

"I've never been more certain of anything in my entire life."

****

Mollie questioned her sanity. She never should have come here. She should have stayed home with her mother and father. She was still too edgy to deal with the rumors and the long glances that turned to stares after Justin and the rest of the coaching staff entered the gym. Justin had taken the stage to brag about the upcoming season and thank his team. Mollie tried to disappear in a corner shadow, but still, she felt all eyes on her. Meg and Maddie had appeared from the crowd and brought her a drink and piece of cake. Mollie accepted and hugged them both then shooed them off to return to their friends. They seemed hesitant, but wandered off slowly. When they turned back, checking Mollie for worry, she smiled broadly and waved them off. Once they melted back into the crowd, Mollie turned her attention to Justin.

He was handsome, that she couldn't deny. He was a blond, handsome idol for all the teenage girls, but as Mollie looked him over, she realized he was smaller than she remembered. He was only what five eight, five nine? Maybe that explained his big attitude. He was nothing like Craig. Craig was taller, broader shouldered. Craig's eyes had depth. There was more going on behind his rugged face than what kind of hair gel to use. Mollie felt her eyes sting, and she quickly wiped at the corners.

She refused to cry. Everyone watching would assume she was suffering under the presence of the boy toy chattering away on the stage. No one knew her heart was breaking for another man she thought was thousands of miles away.

Not a thousand feet.

201

****

Craig slipped quietly into the gym. All eyes were on the stage as the coach discussed the goals for the season. Craig approached a young man whose attention was on the buffet table.

"Excuse me." The boy turned his round, youthful face to Craig. Craig asked, "I'm looking for Mollie Hinkle?"

"Miss Hinkle?" the young man asked. Craig nodded.

"Ask Miss Sheldon." The boy pointed to a middle-aged woman at the end of the buffet.

Craig thanked the boy and moved on to the woman at the end of the buffet. "Miss Sheldon?"

The woman turned to him, her brown eyes tired and worn, but friendly. Craig asked the woman, "I'm looking for Mollie Hinkle."

"Oh?" Sue Sheldon answered. "I'll take you to her." she offered, but didn't move. She looked to the stage then to the man in front of her. She looked him over from the top of his coal black hair to the very tips of his size-eleven shoes. He was the kind of man who haunted a woman's dreams. His shoulders were broad and fit perfectly into his suit jacket. The dark skin of his neck and the hollow of his throat accentuated by corded muscles. Sue could have taken a surreptitious route around the crowd, instead she cut straight across the gym floor disrupting the crowd and gathering stares as the handsome stranger passed through like the pied piper. As they moved on, they accumulated more and more attention. Soon, the droning of Justin's words was slowly drowned out as the cumulative whispers rose to a uniform buzz.

Mollie didn't notice the buzz, didn't notice the kids all turning in her direction, but she did notice the feel of familiar eyes on her. She felt him before she saw him. His presence caused her heart to beat rapidly in her chest and made her mouth suddenly dry.

As he came closer, all else drifted away. All Mollie noticed was the man who had stolen her heart and soul. She was frozen to her spot, her heart nearly stopped from the exhaustive pounding. He stopped in front of her, took her hand in his, then caressed her chin with his thumb. "Ahh, Mollie," he said, his voice a low rumble.

"Craig," she answered, nearly faint from her erratic breathing.

"I've missed you."

Mollie nodded, unable to speak if she had to. She could not believe this was real.

Craig took a deep breath. "I have to be honest with you."

Mollie licked her lips nervously and nodded.

"I never wanted to love you. I never wanted to need you. And I sure as hell didn't want you to rip out my heart and take it with you when you left. I wanted to hate you for it, to blame you and demand you give it back, but I've decided I never want it back. I believe it's safer in your hands." He kissed her hand. "Please, Mollie, I was hard and cruel. I hated you for still loving him…for saying you'd come home to him. I should've told you that morning how I felt…that you were making a mistake. He'll only hurt you more and you deserve so much better. I can't say I'm a good man, but no man could love you more than I do. I'd never intentionally hurt you. And I know you may not feel the same, but I'm asking you to give me the chance to make you love me. I can assure you I feel more for you after one week than he will in a lifetime. Give me a chance, Mollie? Let me prove to you I am the man who will make you happy?"

Mollie couldn't speak. Her head was spinning. Yesterday he was so rude. And why did he think she was back with Justin? But the questions began to fade from her mind as she felt the solid warmth of his hand. It was real. He was real. He was right here in the flesh. Her heart soared, her smile was broad, and her cheeks were pink. She tried to take a breath, but she was too excited.

Craig dropped to one knee still holding Mollie's hand in his own. As his mouth opened to say the magic words, a voice behind him interrupted the moment.

"What the hell." Justin stepped out of the crowd and addressed Mollie. "So, this explains why all the sudden you had cold feet; why you were questioning whether or not getting married was a mistake?"

She couldn't take it all in. All eyes were on her. Craig was here, holding her hand, on a bended knee…and then there was a red-faced Justin bitching her out.

Craig's jaw twitched, and he glanced back at the carping ex. Craig stood and turned. Justin took an instant step back as if trying to escape even being in the shadow of the towering man. "You got a problem?" Craig asked.

Justin shook his head and disappeared into the growing crowd of teenage girls.

Craig turned back to Mollie and took her hands in his. "Now, where was I?"

You were going insane...evidently lost your mind in the flight from Montana to here. Or maybe she lost her mind? Maybe it was a delusion? Or maybe she died and went to Heaven?

Mollie brought her fingertips to her lips nervously. Her body was charged with electricity; her mind swirled with the surreal quality of the moment. This had to be a dream, but as she looked around at the familiar place, looked at the multitude of gaping faces, saw her sisters' wide eyes and nodding heads as they seemed be trying to tell her to go for it. She looked back at Craig. His rough hand held hers, his eyes locked on hers. He was so close, she could smell his aftershave.

"Mollie Hinkle," Craig began, "I can't live without you. When you left I thought my heart would break. I need you. I love you and I want you with me for the rest of my life." Craig's eyes were glassy, his emotions were raw as he opened his heart and soul and made himself as vulnerable as he had ever been in his entire life. "Marry me, Mollie."

Mollie said nothing. She looked around the room as if this was some sort of dream, then she looked back at Craig. He repeated his question, ready to beg if he had to. "Please, Mollie. I need you. I love you enough for both of us. Just say you'll marry me, and I swear you'll never want for anything. I'll love you every day of your life."

Mollie felt the tears roll down her cheeks. "Oh, Craig." She smiled through her tears. "You don't know what you're asking."

"Yes, I do. I know everything. I'm ready for sickness as well as health. It doesn't matter. I love you for better or for worse, no matter what. I don't care if I have to take you to every hospital on the east coast. I don't care if it means we never have children. All I want is you. Can't you understand how badly I need you?"

"No," Mollie said honestly. Craig's stricken face was white as the blood poured from it as it drained from his heart. Mollie gripped his hand in both of hers. "But I understand that I do need you. I love you, Craig. I love you in ways I never knew existed. I may not deserve you either, but I do want you. I do love you." Mollie brushed away the tears and smiled a glorious, glowing smile, "I love you." It felt so good to say those words.

"So, you'll marry me?"

"Yes," Mollie said quietly, then finding her voice she repeated with exuberance, "Yes, Craig Coulter, yes. I will marry you."

Craig let out a whoop and leaped to his feet. He wrapped his arms around Mollie's waist, lifted her from her feet, and spun her around. He kissed her; his hand twisted into her hair and held her lips to his. She wrapped her arms around his neck and held him close, kissing him back, slowly returning to reality as the rallying cheers and whistles broke into her dream world. Mollie blushed as she began to make sense of the shouts and cheers. She recognized plenty of "you go, Ms. Hinkle's" and other cat calls.

Mollie blushed and pulled back. Craig placed her feet on the floor, but kept a hand at the small of her back. Sue, grinning from ear to ear, suggested Mollie head home. Justin and the rest of the coaches could monitor the dance. Mollie and Craig, hand in hand, snuck out the side door. Mollie felt as giddy as the multitude of teenage girls she left behind.

Chapter 24

Mollie felt like she floated from the gym to the parking lot. Once outside in the balmy summer air, she pulled back on Craig's hand and brought him to a stop. "Wait a minute. My head's just spinning, and I think I need to pinch myself."

Craig pulled her close "How about this?" He kissed her, his hands spread across the small of her back pressing her body into his. He didn't pull back until her body was fluid, her knees incapable of holding her up. Bracing herself against his body, she allowed her head to lean against his chest. She couldn't believe he was here, warm and solid against her cheek.

"I just can't believe you're here." Mollie breathed, finally able to think straight. "You're really here. You were so mean. I thought for sure you hated me."

"I'm sorry, Mollie. I was…." He kissed the top of her head. "I should've just talked to you; asked you why you lied to me."

"Lied?"

"The other night, the night we were together? I heard you on the phone…you said it was Jack."

Biting her lip, she stepped back and looked up at him. "It wasn't Jack."

"I figured that out on my own. It was the ex, right? I heard you tell him you loved him; that you were coming home to him."

Mollie hugged him close. "I'm so sorry, Craig."

"It's all right, Mollie. I figured I was crazy to think I was in love with you and that you could love me. I'd only been with you

207

for a few days, and he'd had you for years. It made sense to me that you'd return to him, but it didn't make me very happy to lose. I couldn't talk to you about it. I didn't want to hear you say you didn't want me. It was easier to pretend I got smart and walked away."

"So, you think I came home for Justin?"

Craig took a deep breath and nodded.

"So, why are you here?" Mollie asked.

"Because I don't lose. I want you. I figure I just have to make you see it my way."

A grin spread slowly across her face.

"Even with all the shit I've done, I'm still the better man. A guy who ditches you at the altar because you have cancer doesn't deserve you. You belong with a man who loves you no matter what and will stand by you no matter what."

"Oh, Craig, you crazy, silly man." Mollie touched his cheek as tears rolled down her own. "I never left you for him. That was my dad on the phone the other night. I should've just said that, but it just felt so weird at that moment. I just never thought…."

"Your dad? Are you serious? It was your dad?" Craig's laugh was robust, full of relief. He tucked her in so tight she could barely breathe. "I was mad as hell to hear you say, 'I love you,' to someone else. If I knew what the guy looked like, and had him close by, I would've punched him."

"It was stupid of me."

"I should've just called you on it, let you explain. I was rude to you. God, I wanted to hurt you so bad. Then after I did; that look of pain on your face? It didn't help. It didn't make me feel any better. The look on your face at the airport has haunted me."

Mollie nodded. "That did hurt." She smiled and hugged him to her. "It's hard for me to believe, but you're right here! It feels so good to touch you. Oh, how stupid I was, I shouldn't have lied. I made you doubt me when truly, there is no one in this world I want to be with other than you. I do love you, Craig. It's crazy. I may be crazy, but I love you."

"I love you too. I guess we're just crazy together."

He kissed her again then escorted her to his car. "Should I take you home? Grab a bite to eat?"

Mollie grinned. "Definitely not home. My parents have had enough shock."

"I've already talked to them."

"Really?"

"Of course, how do you think I found you?"

"You are brave. Did Dad give you the third degree?"

"Pretty much, but I don't blame him."

"So, you won them over?"

"I hope, maybe a little. I'm sure more grilling will be coming, especially if I convince you to marry me sooner, rather than later."

"So, you're serious about that?"

Craig smiled and cupped her cheek. "It's the only solution to our predicament that I'll accept. I want you with me forever, and I don't want to wait years. Life's too short for that."

Mollie closed her eyes and sighed, she didn't want to talk about cancer, but she knew what he meant. They had to discuss it, but not now. She put a finger to his lips to silence any further talk of lifetimes. "I'm not hungry. I don't want to go to my parents. We can go to my apartment, and I want you to hold me. I want to feel your skin." She kissed his cheek and whispered in his ear, "I want to taste your sweat then I'll know this is real. That all right?"

Craig looked to the stars and declared, "Thank you, God. My baby's perfect."

Mollie couldn't stop the squeals of laughter. He lifted her off her feet and spun her round and round. She giggled and sighed in his ear, "I do love you."

"Say it again," he ordered.

"I love you."

He carried her to the passenger-side door and dropped her in the seat. Grabbing him, she pulled him in for a kiss and ordered, "Let's get out of here."

He buckled her in and shut the door. He slid across the front of the car and took his seat beside her. He held her hand like a frightened child grips a trusted adult as she pointed out the turns that lead them back to her apartment building. Craig parked the car on the street. Mollie got out and dug through her purse for coins for the meter. Craig rounded the car and scooped her up, tossing her over his shoulder. "Damn the meter. I'll pay the damn ticket. You're coming with me."

Mollie squealed as he goosed her bottom on the way to the building. "I might like this side of you better, Mollie dear."

"Ahh," Mollie giggled, "you're a bad man, Craig Coulter."

"And you're stuck with me, baby. You had your chance to be rid of me, now you're stuck. I warned you. I told you to run, but you didn't. Now I'll never let you go."

He set her down in front of her door. She kissed his nose. "I guess I'm good with that."

"You better be. Now find the key, woman."

She dug through her purse methodically. Craig groaned and took it from her and dumped its contents on the floor. Mollie laughed and plucked the key from the pile. Craig gathered the contents and stuffed them back in her bag.

"Not very patient, are you?"

"After that little speech by the car? Baby, you better get that door open, or I'll rip it off its hinges."

Mollie swung the door open, and Craig lifted her off her feet. She held him tightly; her hands locked behind his neck as she directed him through the small apartment to her bedroom. He nudged the door open with his foot and tossed Mollie on the bed. She broke out in giggles and scooted to the top of the mattress and hugged her knees to her chest. "Oh, no," she teased. "The rogue returns."

"Where are you going?" He pulled her to him by grabbing her ankles and straightening her body. He pinned her under him, but she wiggled and squirmed. "Be still, woman. How am I supposed to ravish you if you won't hold still?"

Mollie giggled louder, enjoying her newfound advantage. "I changed my mind. I think we should talk."

"We'll talk in a minute when I can think straight."

"A minute? What are you saying?" Mollie laughed so hard her eyes were watering.

"I'm admitting," he said, kissing her throat, trailing fiery nips from her ear to her collar bone as his hands deftly unbuttoned buttons and stripped away her clothes, "that I may not be much use to you...this time...but it will be most enjoyable for myself." He looked down at her, his lids heavy with passion. "You, sweet little morsel, are absolutely driving me insane."

"Really?" Mollie relaxed her body and allowed him to finish disrobing her as she mused, "I've never thought of myself as irresistible."

"I would gladly chew off my leg like a wolf in a trap in order to get to you."

Mollie unbuttoned his shirt and spread her hands across his chest and enjoyed the growl her touch brought.

ELIZABETH SECKMAN

212

Chapter 25

"I thought you said you wouldn't be any good for me?" Mollie whispered, her breaths ragged, her heart still pounding.

Craig rolled onto his back and dragged Mollie with him. "It took every ounce of control I own. You'd think I was a teenager again."

Mollie laughed and ran her fingers through the black hair on his chest. He stroked her hair and sighed, content as a well-fed cat.

Mollie looked up at him, his eyes were closed and his breathing relaxed. "Are you asleep?"

"No, I'm just daydreaming and planning my next assault. Though I may need to make a store run. I didn't come prepared for you to take such advantage of me so quickly…and so frequently."

"I never said there'd be any kind of frequency." Mollie smiled against his chest.

"I'm pretty sure you did."

"No. I think I'd remember saying that."

"Maybe it was when I read your mind."

"You can read my mind?"

"Of course."

"So, what am I thinking right now?"

"Hmm." he wrapped a curl around his finger. "You're thinking you'd prefer to marry me as soon as possible."

Mollie looked up at him trying to read his face, judge his resolve. "You're serious."

"Of course I am. I may not leave this town until you're married to me."

"Why the big hurry?"

Craig shrugged and thought a minute. "I guess I just don't want to risk letting you go. And...." He grinned down at her. "I doubt your father will let me put you on a plane and take you back with me unmarried. He doesn't seem like the kind of guy who would let his baby girl live in sin."

Mollie laughed. "You got that right. So, you plan to take me back with you?"

"Damn straight."

"Hmm. I'll have to think about that. That's a long way to go." She leaned up on her elbows and grinned down at him. She traced the contours of his face with her finger, stopping when she reached his mouth. "What happened? How'd you bust your lip?"

He took a sharp breath. "It's nothing."

"Nothing, it looks like it was split."

He closed his eyes and gripped her body tight against him. "You want the truth?"

"Of course I want the truth, unless it will break my heart."

He opened his eyes and looked in her eyes. "I'll never lie to you, and I'll never break your heart. It really was nothing. I did a stupid thing. I ran into a woman I used to know at the airport, after a horrible fight with my mother. I was mad and in no mood to fly back to Montana, to a house that seemed as welcoming as a tomb. So she asked me to grab a few drinks, and I did. Then she asked me to go home with her, and I did. When I got there; it felt so damn wrong, I told her I had to get home. On my way out her door, I got punched by her boyfriend."

"Oh." Mollie's body tensed. "Did you?"

"Have sex with her?"

Mollie nodded, resting her chin on his chest.

"No. She wasn't you, and I only want you."

"Did she try?"

"She tried all sorts of persuasion. Is that what you're asking?"

"Yes. She offered and you said no?"

"Of course I said no, I love you. That's how her boyfriend got the first shot in. I hadn't done anything, so I wasn't expecting it."

"Really?"

He pulled her up next to him and kissed her. "I love you so much. I want you in my life forever. I want a home, kids, dog, cat…you name it. I want it."

Tears welled in her eyes. When she blinked, one rolled down her cheek. "Craig, this future…have you considered all the things that need to be considered?"

"Like what?"

The phone on Mollie's night stand rang. She ignored it, but the machine picked up the call. *"Mollie, I just want to say…this is bullshit. You made everyone hate me…blame me for being the bad guy when the whole time you were slutting around…."*

Mollie lunged for the phone and grabbed it. "Justin," she said, wary eyes glancing at a furious Craig. "Are you drunk? You sound drunk. You go sober up and we'll discuss this later."

"There's nothing to discuss," Craig growled as he reached for the phone.

Mollie ducked and gripped the phone tighter. "I'll send a cab for you; where are you? Have you lost your mind?"

Mollie jumped off the bed and grabbed her robe. She was tying the belt when the pounding on her door started. "Craig, stay here. I'll get rid of him."

Craig had his pants on in lightning speed. "No, you stay here, hang up the damn phone, and I'll get rid of him…for good."

"Craig, I don't think…." She stopped mid-sentence. He loved her, and he'd protect her, no matter what. Cradling his face in the palms of her hands, she planted a kiss on his lips. "I love you, and I love that you would hurt anyone who would hurt me, but…"

"You're asking me to let him get away with this?"

She hugged him close and rubbed her cheek against his chest. "I'm telling you what you can and can't do. I trust you."

Craig kissed the top of her head.

"But Craig?" Mollie looked up at him. "He's such a little man, so if you kill him…I'll be your alibi."

Craig grinned and brushed the hair from her eyes. "It won't come to that…but this…" His head tipped toward the sounds of the pounding "This ends tonight."

Mollie kissed him as he pulled away. She waited until he was gone before she snuck to a dark corner of the living room to watch and pray that Justin got some sense and would simply go back home.

Craig pulled the door open so quickly the drunken Justin toppled into the living room. He lay on the floor looking up at Craig, his eyes blinking as if he couldn't focus.

"What the hell?" Justin sputtered. "Why are you here? Mollie!" he yelled into the room. Mollie shook her head and ignored him.

"Mollie!" Justin yelled again.

Craig grabbed him by the shirt collar and pulled him to his feet. When he let go of him, Justin stumbled and fell into the door jamb, clutching the painted trim with the ferocity of a drowning sailor gripping a life vest.

"I want to talk to Mollie."

"She's done with you, understand?"

"She owes me…"

Craig took a quick step forward, Justin flinched, let go of his grip, and fell on his ass in the hallway. Craig looked down at him and said, his voice echoing in the empty corridor, "Mollie doesn't owe you a goddamn thing, you understand? You had your chance, and you blew it. You only have yourself to blame, you little piece of shit." Craig kneeled beside him as Justin tried to slither toward the elevator and said, "Listen closely…you think the beating Jack gave you was humiliating, I swear to you, you ever talk to Mollie again, ever call her anything but a friggin' saint, and I will beat your ass so bad your mother won't recognize you. You understand me?"

"Mollie! You going to let him do this to me?"

Mollie stepped out of the shadows and looked down at Justin, her head shaking. "Craig is a man of his own mind, Justin. You should have let me call you a cab when you had the chance."

"Mollie!" His plea was desperate.

She turned and left the situation in capable hands.

****

Craig returned less than ten minutes later. Mollie was sitting cross legged on her bed. Craig crawled up beside her, lying on his side, his head resting on her bent leg. He planted a kiss on her exposed knee and said, "You're beautiful, you know that, right?"

"Hmm, so you say." Her fingers played with the curls on his head. "So," she asked, "you going to need that alibi?"

Craig shook his head. "I didn't put a scratch on him. I took his phone out of his pocket and called his mom. She sent a cab and I carried his drunk ass to the curb to meet it."

"I'm sorry he ruined our fun."

Craig laughed as his fingers traced lazy lines up her calf. "I thought that was fun."

"Seriously?"

"No, I'd rather have beaten him, but I couldn't."

"Because he was so drunk?"

"No, because he's an idiot...an idiot who will spend the rest of his life missing you, and I will spend the rest of my life with you. Seems to me, that's a heavier price to pay than a few bruises."

"That's so sweet, but Craig...this talk of lifetimes...I think there are things you haven't considered. Things you should think seriously about before making the decision to marry me."

"You're kidding me, right? Does this have anything to do...."

Mollie put a finger to his lips. "Shh, don't even say it. I'm talking about things like...kids. I know you say it doesn't matter, but seriously, what if there are no kids?"

"That doesn't matter, my offer stands. I want you. I don't care about anything beyond that."

"You say that now..."

"I say that forever. Mollie, I love you. And when the time is right, we'll adopt. Till then, we have Brutus. He's a big baby."

Mollie smiled and Craig wiped away her tears. "It'll be all right. We'll get through anything. Infertility isn't a problem."

"Well, infertility isn't a sure thing. They just don't know for certain. My parents were very careful during my treatment to do all they could to ensure me the possibility of children in the future.

They had me undergo ovarian transposition and had the chemo monitored very carefully."

"Ovarian what?"

"Transposition. They surgically moved the ovaries out of the way, so they were better protected from the radiation, and they say I have a better chance of healthy eggs because I hadn't hit puberty yet, and they hope that immature eggs are less susceptible to the effects of chemo."

"Well, then we'll get you good doctors and go from there."

"But all that's expensive."

"I can take care of it."

"But I don't want to…"

"Shush, Mollie. I love you. That's all that matters. The rest is details." He kissed her deeply and pulled her body close to his, nearly suffocating her with the bear hug. "It breaks my heart to think of you as a little girl going through all of that. I'm so sorry, baby. I'm going to make sure you get everything. Tell me what you want, and I'll get it."

Mollie wiggled loose until she could look up at him. She laid a hand across his cheek. He looked so sincere, so heartbroken for her. "I've got what I want." She kissed him lightly. "And it wasn't all so terrible. I only remember bits and pieces. It was probably harder on my parents. I remember going bald…I still despise needles…and I remember getting toys from everyone. Even strangers would hand me things. I just thought we lived in a generous world where strangers handed little kids gifts and candy. I didn't realize my bald head and sunken cheeks gave me away as a cancer fighter." Mollie grinned. "And of course, I had Jack. What a crazy best friend she was."

"I have to agree."

Mollie took a sharp breath. She pulled herself up on her elbows. "Be honest with me, Craig." She looked him right in the eye to judge his honesty. "You and Jack? That day in the restaurant? The day I left?"

Craig looked confused. Mollie sat erect and crossed her legs under her.

"I saw you guys through the window. Day before yesterday. You guys were…quite close. She had her hands…well, it looked bad."

Craig's face lit up with awareness. "Ahh, yes, the meeting between Jack and me. Someone in town called the police, thinking she broke in, and I went to check it out."

"And?" Mollie took a big swallow.

"And…and you've got to remember, Mollie, I was mad at you. I thought you were still in love with, and still in contact, with your old boyfriend."

"So you two…?"

"Jack asked me how I felt about you, and I told her that I got what I wanted from you, and I was moving on, at least something like that. I don't remember verbatim. Jack did grab me by the pants, but not to hit on me, but to threaten me. When I left, she slammed me in the head with a damned napkin dispenser. I still have the wound. See?" He pulled up the hair to reveal a gash near the temple. "She's loyal to you, Mollie. She even broke up with Ron and threatened to come back here because he took my side of this argument."

"They broke their arrangement?"

"I think they're all right. It was Jack who helped me find you. Once I humbled myself enough to tell her I loved you, and had to talk to you, she lightened up on Ron."

Mollie breathed a sigh of relief. "How stupid could I be to think Jack would do anything like that? Gosh, I'm glad I didn't accuse her. It would break her heart to know I doubted her."

"It'll be our secret." He rubbed her back, trailing his fingertips down her spine to her bottom. "But be warned, I've been a scumbag most of my life, so to be certain of my silence you'll have to bribe me…often."

"Mmm." Mollie enjoyed the feel of his hands. "What would that take?"

"All I ask is that you do whatever I ask…you know?" He winked and leered at her, his eyes scanning her up and down.

Mollie broke into laughter, her head tipped back. She looked down at Craig and shook her head. "Is that all?"

"All? I've got quite an imagination." His teeth grazed her kneecap. "But I promise you'll enjoy it."

Mollie snuggled herself into his body, relishing in the warmth and hardness of him. She nibbled on his neck, then his ear, where she whispered, "I suppose I'm flexible enough to make that deal."

Craig propped himself up by his arm and looked down on her. "You're the most beautiful woman I've ever seen."

Mollie laughed, a bit nervous by the intensity of his scrutiny. He looked so intent, as if he was looking over every inch of her. It was a strange feeling for Mollie, whose first instinct was to pull the covers over her naked body. Craig ran his fingertips down her arm, across the curve of her hip, slowing to a stop at her breast. He cupped it in his hand and flicked it with his thumb. "You're so perfect." He kissed the smooth skin above her collar bone as he worked his way to the second breast. His perusal stopped cold at the scar at the top of her breast. Mollie quickly covered it with her hand.

"I know it's ugly. I'm hoping it heals lighter."

"It's not ugly. Oh, Mollie." He pulled her close, cradling her head against his chest. "I'm such a prick. I can't believe I ever hurt you. With all you're dealing with, and I had to act like that. How will you forgive me?"

"It's all right. I should've been honest with you. It's just that…when my dad called, he was pressuring me to come home because the biopsy was in, and he wanted to know what it said. I didn't know how to say that to you. I felt like I was living a beautiful dream, and I didn't want reality to ruin it. It felt so good to just be feeling. I was having so much fun with you; I just didn't want it to end."

"And it won't. Mollie, we'll get you every treatment available. We'll beat this."

Mollie nodded and sighed. "I'd rather not have anything to beat. I pray that biopsy is clear."

"Why don't we check?"

"Not tonight. Kiss me. Let's just enjoy right now." Mollie tried to hold him to her, but he pulled away. He rummaged through the pile of clothes until he found his jacket. He dipped his hand in the breast pocket and pulled out the letter.

Mollie sat up and took a deep breath. She shook her head. "Where did you get that?"

"Your parents."

"They gave it to you?"

"Your mother suggested you might want to open it once you knew you weren't jinxed."

"I'd just as soon leave it till Monday."

"Why?"

"I just don't want to know. I'm happy right now."

"Whatever it says, you'll never lose me. We're in this together. I know you think that as long as you don't know, then you don't have to think about it. But it's on your mind, whether you think it's worrying you or not. It's not just your battle anymore—it's ours. And I like to know all the facts and plan my game. I say we open it, but..." He put the letter back in his pocket. "I respect your need to wait."

"No." Mollie closed her eyes and took a deep breath. "You open it, but if it's bad, I don't promise not to cry."

"No matter what—together. Forever."

She closed her eyes and waited. Her heart sped up as she listened to the paper tear. Her breath stopped in her throat as she heard him pull the letter free. There was a long pause. Mollie opened her eyes to look at Craig's face. He brushed away a tear. Mollie felt her heart stop. The nightmares of childhood that had dulled in her memory came flooding back with extreme vividness. She didn't want to do this. She covered her mouth with her hand and told herself to just stay calm. Craig closed the letter and looked at her. "Thank you, God. Baby, you're just fine. Biopsy was negative, genetic marker for future breast cancer...also negative."

Moving across the bed on her knees, she held out her hand for the paper, reading it, she let out a sound that was half cry, half laugh. "It really says I'm fine. I'm fine!"

"Ah Mollie." He joined her on the bed, wrapping her up in his arms, showering her cheeks and lips with kisses. He laid her back gently, slowly. He kissed her long and deep. His breath was hot against her ear. "It's good to know I have all the time in the world to savor you."

Chapter 26

Mollie pulled on her shoes and sighed. "Too bad we're here and not two thousand miles away. I don't want to leave. I want to snuggle up with you all night."

"Don't tempt me, or I'll kidnap you, and your father will hate me forever."

Mollie grabbed him around the waist and hugged him, resting her head on his chest. She groaned. "You know I won't be able to sneak away too much. My dad will watch us like a hawk. I can guarantee you…even if you stay in a hotel, I'll be staying at home. So, I suppose I'll just offer you my apartment, and I'll plan to stay at my mom and dad's."

"Whatever makes you happy."

"That would be to stay here with you, never leaving, attempting to absorb the fact that this is happening."

"I doubt your dad would care for that."

"Never."

"That's why you'll marry me quickly. As a matter of fact, I plan to ask your dad tonight, again."

Mollie looked up at him, a grin lit up her face. "Seriously? Isn't that a bit…hoaky?"

"Hoaky or not, I think it's the smart thing to do. Your dad is about as excited about me as having a leper at a hug convention."

"A hug convention?" Mollie laughed.

"Well, whatever analogy you use, he isn't thrilled by my presence, and he's probably wondering where you are right now."

Mollie glanced at the clock on the wall. She squeezed him even tighter. "You're right. Meg and Maddie will be home by now. We were talking at the river, all right?"

"Sneaky little wench. I'm almost jealous seeing how well practiced you are at hiding your affairs."

Mollie looked up at him. The hurt was visible on her face. Craig touched her cheek gently. "I'm teasing, Mollie. I love you." He kissed her lips, then the tip of her nose. "You were made for me; no one else." He framed her face with his hands. "This is our future. Ours, not mine, not yours, but ours. I've never—not once—thought I'd ever feel this way. Mollie, I'm not good with words, and I'm sure I'm going to say stupid things. I've spent most of my life offending people and pissing off most everyone I know. Be patient with me. Love me even when I'm a fool."

Mollie fixed his collar and buttoned a loosened button. "I know you were teasing. I guess I just feel guilty. I don't want you to think you're not first in my heart...."

"Shh. I trust you. I trust you with my life, my heart, even my dog, who already likes you better than me."

"He has good taste."

He kissed her until her world spun and her legs were wobbly. Then he pulled away. "Now, let's get on with this. I want a ring on your finger and tag you with the Coulter name. That says you're mine."

"You are a caveman." Mollie laughed as he dragged her out the door and down the fire escape to his car.

"And you've agreed to marry me. A whole lifetime, that's what you promised, and I'm going to hold you to it."

Mollie let out a squeal that caused neighborhood dogs to bark. She covered her mouth and turned bright red with embarrassment. Craig winked at her and squeezed her hand. Mollie breathed the night air, not remembering a time when the air in Pittsburgh smelled sweet or how the street lights twinkled off the steel and glass buildings. She had never taken the time to notice just how perfect the world was.

****

Mollie was accurate in her assumption that her dad would exert some control over where they slept in an effort to stop any premarital liaisons. Craig got the apartment; she got her childhood bedroom. Craig was also right in thinking that Mr. Hinkle would be hesitant to sanction a hasty marriage. He wasn't a believer in love at first sight or soul mates, at least not until the souls had the proper amount of time to become acquainted. Even Vickie Hinkle, the believer in whimsy and romance, was not thrilled with the idea of a wedding taking place so soon. But both were elated their daughter was cancer free.

Vickie brewed a pot of tea while the couple sat at the kitchen table, hands clutched together, looking as happy and naïve as a young couple could. She allowed her husband to take the reins and try to steer them away from matrimony. Doug Hinkle shook his head as he removed his glasses and rubbed them till they sparkled. He returned them to his face and looked to Mollie. "I think you're enjoying a surge of excitement from the good medical news…and the heady feeling of chemistry from a new relationship, but this is not a stable foundation of a lifetime commitment."

"I dated Justin for four-and-a-half years, and that didn't make it a sure thing," Mollie argued.

"And the closet is still full of unopened gifts," Vickie pointed out.

Mollie bit her cheek and looked to Craig. He rubbed her hand.

"Well, I don't say that to be crude…or to be a killjoy." Vickie brought the tea pot to the table along with a tray of mugs, sugar, and creamer. "You just have to consider that you may be on the rebound."

"It's not that, Mom. I know how I feel about Craig. My situation with Justin hasn't muddied my thinking; it's clarified it. It's like night and day. I promise you, it's not the heady feeling that makes me think I love Craig. It's the feeling of calm. He makes me feel like even if those tests had been bad, that even on my worst day, I could still count the day as a blessing because I have Craig with me."

Vickie's eyes misted and she reached for a napkin. Doug shook his head. "You're very eloquent, Mollie, but it doesn't change the facts."

Mollie felt her temper rise. Her father was being ridiculous. She pushed her chair form the table. "Well, I am an adult…."

Craig squeezed her knee. "Your father's right."

Mollie's mind raced to the possibility that Craig might change his mind, maybe her dad talked him out of wanting her…maybe even out of loving her. Mollie's heart slowed. Craig faced her dad and explained, "I won't marry her without your blessing, sir. I know how I feel…and I know how she feels…and I have no doubt that it's real, but it will still be real one month or one year from now. I want to do it now, but I won't do it against your will."

"That's so sweet," Vickie sobbed. "I know you two will be so happy together."

"Hold yourself together, dear. We're thinking clearly for our daughter, remember?"

"Well, you and I only dated—"

"We're not talking about us. Mollie has had a devastating month. The dust needs to settle before she decides which road to take."

"Mollie says you like to fish, Mr. Hinkle. Maybe you and I could spend a day where I promise to answer any question you want to throw at me…political affiliation, religion, you ask it, I'll answer it."

"Well, I think I will take you up on that offer," Doug said with a somber nod.

Mollie sighed. Vickie smiled at her daughter and took a sip of tea.

****

A day of fishing evolved into a week of camping and bicycling along Lake Erie. Mollie missed Craig and was a bit jealous that her father had spirited him away. She never worried though because she was certain he'd win her father over. And when she didn't think it was possible to love him an ounce more, she did. The reverence he showed for her parent's values made her want to squeeze him until he couldn't breathe. When they returned from their *man trip*, Doug Hinkle still dominated Craig's time. He took him to his office at the college, to the Steelers' training camp, and even to a special gathering of poker buddies. Mollie was beginning to worry that Craig would have to return to Montana before she'd even have a chance to spend an evening with him.

Craig didn't seem to mind at all. He'd even offered to host her father and his poker buddies for a week of elk hunting in Montana. Mollie was ready to wail "what about me?" when her father admitted with a laugh, "Well, Vickie, the young man has worn me down. I need a couple days' rest, some ibuprofen, and the funds to pay for another wedding."

"Seriously, Daddy?" Mollie squealed, jumping up and down in spite of her maturity.

"He's a good man. I like him. So, without any hesitation, except for the expense, he will gladly receive my blessing tonight on the nuptials."

Mollie kissed her dad then hugged her mother. "And don't worry, Dad. I don't need a big wedding. Gosh, I'd be fine with eloping if it would help."

"We'll work something out," Doug promised. "When things are right, they have a way of working out."

Mollie kissed her dad again and ran to her bedroom where she flung herself on the bed and dialed her apartment to ask Craig to come over as soon as he could. Then she called Jack. She'd need her maid of honor to come home for the wedding, which she was certain would be soon.

Chapter 27

When Craig said he wanted the wedding sooner rather than later, Mollie had no idea how fast things would happen. Before the sun set on her father's blessing, Mrs. Coulter, along with a man Mollie first mistook for Secret Service, arrived in a surprise wedding planning attack.

As Craig and Doug dallied on the golf course, Mollie and Vickie carried boxes they packed up from the apartment to store in the family's garage. A cab stopped in front of the house and a sharply dressed man adorned with blue tooth and sunglasses held the door for a tiny woman. She smoothed her unwrinkled clothes as she stood on the sidewalk and looked over the house.

Vickie dropped her box in the drive way. "Hello? May I help you?"

"I'm looking for Mollie Hinkle?"

"I'm Mollie." She stepped past her mom.

"Good, good to meet you. I'm Barb Coulter. We spoke on the phone?"

Mollie's cheeks turned red at the memory. She wished she wore something nicer than cutoff jeans and sweat soaked tee-shirt.

"Sorry for dropping in. I was on my way to New York when Craig called with the news. I just had to stop. I can't tell you how excited I am, and I know it's hasty and normally I would caution against haste, but I saw how badly he hurt when he thought he'd lost you, so I know it's the genuine article. To show my support, I brought Gary. He's my party planner and I'd like to offer his services. Craig said you two were thinking small affair?"

Mollie nodded.

"Very classy, I like that."

"Uh, thanks." Mollie turned to her mom for a rescue.

Vickie rubbed her sweaty, dirty palms on her jeans then extended a hand to Barbara. "I'm Vickie Hinkle, Mollie's mom, nice to meet you Mrs. Coulter."

"Barb. I mean, we are about to become family. In which case, there are a few things to consider…could we go inside and talk?"

"Oh, certainly!" Vickie gushed as she led the group inside. They settled at the dining room table.

"Can I get you drinks?"

"Scotch?" Barbara asked.

"Iced tea?" Vickie offered.

"Sounds delicious. Gary?" Barbara said.

"Unsweetened?" Gary asked.

"I can make some." Vickie offered.

"Leave the sugar in mine. I'm a Southern girl through and through." Barbara placed her purse on the table and stretched out her legs. "Now, Mollie, how can I help with this wedding? You know it would be my pleasure. I have all boys, so I have never gotten the opportunity to look at even a prom gown, much less a wedding gown." Mollie smiled and nodded. Barbara continued, "I'm imagining a wedding in the evening, outdoors…timed so that the sun will set as you are announced man and wife; the close of the old life, the dawn of a new life just hours away."

"That sounds marvelous," Vickie said as she carried the glasses to the table. "I like it, Mollie. Don't you?"

"I think it sounds perfect," Mollie agreed, though she would agree to a wedding at 7-11 if it meant marrying Craig.

"Good." Barbara gave Mollie's hand a squeeze. "If you wouldn't mind traveling; I know the perfect place…our home in Virginia. We have a little hill that makes you feel as if you're on top of the world."

"I guess that's up to Mom." Mollie looked to her mother.

"Well, I'd have to talk to your father, though when we were discussing the guest list, we only came up with what twelve people we were going to invite."

"If you all will let me take care of this, I'll gladly arrange all the travel and lodging expenses. It's worth that and more to me. When I was pregnant with Craig, I was certain he was a girl, and I had the whole thing planned. But he was a boy…and then so was Trip, so I gave up the dream. When Craig told me your, um, situation, I thought I might be able to nudge you in my direction."

"If it means that much to you; I am just so overwhelmed," Mollie said, looking to her mother who shrugged and nodded.

"Good. Good." Barbara knocked back her tea, checked her watch, and announced, "I have a plane to catch. I'm leaving Gary here, with his help, we'll have you saying, 'I do,' next weekend."

With that, she was gone.

Gary opened his briefcase and pulled out a binder filled to overflowing with sketches, pictures, and samples. "Dress: classic or conventional?"

"I kind of like the classic."

"Good choice. How about some bare shoulders? It's still summer and hot as hell in Virginia, which leans us toward silk. It breathes, and you're thin enough to pull it off. They sell the full body slimming wear, but…" He looked her over critically, before surmising, "you don't need it. Naked flesh will be more of a tactile pleasure. Nothing between you and your groom but the softest silk! Craig can thank me later." Gary winked and Mollie blushed.

"Veil? Or tiara?"

Mollie shrugged. "I guess…."

"Both, we'll go with both. I like the mystery of the veiled bride. Very romantic. Flowers? Roses or hydrangeas?" Gary opened the page to flower arrangements galore. As she scooted closer to look, he tapped his finger against a page and raised his brow at her.

Mollie took the hint. "The pink hydrangeas?"

"Smart girl! We'll fill pots and pots of them. Throw in some green and some white, and purple…hang them from baskets and put in some old timey lamp posts...it will be the most beautiful thing anyone has ever seen."

"It sounds lovely...and...extravagant," Vickie said as she took her seat at the table.

"Barbara prefers things done right as opposed to done cheap," George said.

"But we wouldn't feel comfortable...." Vickie rubbed her hands together.

"Leave the guilt darling...Senator Coulter will get at least a two point bounce from this little affair. I can assure you of that. Heck, if you're worried over the cost, I can leak a few pictures to the right people in the press and recoup most of it."

"Seriously?"

"Honey...you're about to become Cinderella...didn't anyone tell you that?"

****

Mollie sealed the last box with tape. She slid it into place with the others and breathed a sigh of relief. "Ahh, it's good to be done."

Jack stacked her last box on top of Mollie's and gave it a pat. "Your whole life, neatly stashed in cardboard."

"Are you sure you have enough room to store all of this, Mom?"

Vickie nodded. "Of course we do. Your dad just cleaned out the garage."

Mollie laughed. "So he could buy a boat."

Vickie shrugged. "If he ever decides on a boat, I'll put all of this in the basement. Goodness, he's been looking at boats for ten years. You'd think he'd just choose one and buy it."

"I still can't believe Mr. Hinkle gave Craig the thumbs up after two weeks." Jack said, pouring Mollie, Vickie, and herself a plastic cup of soda.

"Shocking, I know. He seems to have really taken to Craig. Maybe years of being surrounded by women just made him desperate for male companionship." Vickie took a sip of her soda and shrugged.

"Justin was a male...sort of." Jack laughed.

"Doug never really liked him."

"He didn't?" Mollie was shocked.

"Not especially. There was always something about Justin that was…well, never endearing. I'm so glad you've got Craig. I only wish it wasn't so far away, but I'm thrilled beyond rational thought to know my baby will be so happy. True love is just so rare, and I'm just so…." She started to cry. She dug through her purse for a tissue. She found one and blotted her eyes and nose. "Well, it's just rare, and precious."

Mollie hugged her mom. "You and Dad were great role models."

Vickie nodded her head and blew her nose. "Your dad's a special guy. I'm a very lucky woman."

Jack sat crossed legged on the floor. She studied her cup as she asked, "Mrs. Hinkle, how did you know Mr. Hinkle was the right guy for you? I mean, I know Molls here was just struck by lightning and never had a single doubt…this time around…but how can a rational person know when it's right? I mean, what if Mollie had married Justin? She never would've met Craig. She would've settled, and maybe regretted it years later."

"True," Vickie answered slowly. "I'll be honest with you, Jack. There is no foolproof way to decide on love. I think it's the one condition that we have to surrender ourselves to. It's not a rational choice, and if we are quiet, we can hear the truth. Plug your ears, Mollie. I need to be honest with Jack."

"Hah. I get to listen too," Mollie warned.

"Doug was only a friend all through high school. I dated his cousin."

"Which cousin?" Mollie gasped, her mouth dropping open.

"Denver."

"Denver the dork?" Mollie blurted. "Ooh, Mom, he's fat and…and gross."

"He used to be handsome. At least I thought so. Well, anyhow, I thought I liked him. Doug was just my buddy. I never thought of him as a boyfriend."

"Seriously, Mom? The Dork?"

"Mollie, if you can't plug your ears, then please quiet your lips. This is embarrassing to admit. I mean, honestly, I'd rather be saying I loved your dad forever since I was twelve, but that isn't the story. Now, don't you ever tell your dad I told you this, he gets very jealous when he thinks of the dork, I mean Denver. Anyhow, Doug was my friend. Probably the best friend I ever had. I was graduating high school and everyone assumed I would marry Denver and have kids, etcetera. Rumor had it he had bought me a ring as a graduation gift. Well, your dad would go fishing every Saturday morning...even then, he was as predictable as the sunrise...so every Saturday, I went and kept him company, filling his ear with my incessant chatter. Then, that Saturday before graduation, he said...." Vickie's eyes filled with tears, but she smiled. "He said, 'when you marry Denver, I'll miss this the most. I love to hear your voice. It's the perfect tone, perfect volume. You could read me the phone book, and I'd enjoy it.' Well, I was shocked, so I asked him why I wouldn't be able to come and talk to him. He looked at me, and I swear, it was like I saw him for the first time. I never realized how blue his eyes were, or how honest and handsome his face was. He shrugged and said simply, 'It just wouldn't be right for you to hang out with me and be married to him.' I was shocked. I never thought about the reality of marrying anyone. Then he said simply, 'He's a lucky guy, and I know it's wrong, but I envy him. I'd give anything to know I got to spend a lifetime with you.'"

"So, what did you do?" Mollie asked like she didn't know the end of the story.

"I left. I was in shock. I went home and called Denver. I listened to him talk, but I wasn't listening, you know? I just kept thinking of Doug. So, then I asked Denver, what's your favorite thing about me? And he said, 'Huh? What are you talking about?' It was like a different sort of lightning strike. This was *not* the right guy. I was suddenly filled with this image of a happy home, a happy life...and that life was with Doug. I broke up with Denver and went to Doug and told him he had to marry me. I didn't give him a choice...very precocious of me, right? Anyhow, we eloped...which your grandmother has never forgiven...and lived in this studio apartment eating mac and cheese and peanut butter until we got our degrees…and lived happily ever after."

"You guys eloped?"

Vickie nodded.

"Why didn't I ever know that?" Mollie asked

"Your father never brags about his impetuous behavior."

"But you have a wedding photo."

"We had a ceremony because your Grandma Hinkle insisted. Lord, how she hated me. She was just certain I was pregnant and trapping her baby boy into marriage. What an awkward little gathering that was. Denver's people boycotted, the rest just showed up to see if they could see if a train wreck was about to happen."

"I was born after college, right?"

"Yes, Mollie. Your dad and I were married six years before you were born, though I think your grandmother still thought that was too soon."

Mollie laughed and shook her head. "Denver the dork. Man, Mom, here I thought I dodged a bullet."

"So, Mrs. Hinkle, you got that lightning strike too?" Jack asked.

"No. It wasn't lightning. It was an epiphany. I realized I could not imagine a life with Doug *not* in it. And I couldn't imagine a life…a real life of bill paying and grocery shopping…with Denver. Doug and I can be unclogging a toilet, and I still enjoy being with him. Do you understand what I'm saying?"

Jack nodded.

"You feel that way about your guy?" Vickie asked.

"I don't know. I mean I do like him, and I can honestly say, with the exception of Mollie, he is the only person who knows me and still thinks I'm all right."

"And what do you think of him?"

"I think he's an idiot. He could do far better than me."

Vickie smiled and gave Jack's shoulder a squeeze. "I think you already know your answer."

"A double wedding, Jack?" Mollie laughed.

"No way. I'll leave the flurry of nuptials to you Hinkle women. I'll take it slow. Besides, Ron has Emily to think of. She doesn't need another change in her life. If—*if* we ever get married, it will be only when Emily is good with the idea. Probably not until after she goes to college."

"You guys have talked about it?" Mollie asked.

"It's come up."

"I'm so happy for you, Jackie. Look at us. We're like fairy tales. I'm going to just nail you with my bouquet. Don't try to dodge it. I'm going to tell Maddie and Megan to let you have it. And I'm pretty sure they'll be the only single women there."

"Craig's mother," Vickie reminded.

"Nope, Craig told me she got engaged to some guy he's never met. How weird would that be? Anyhow, I guess Mrs. Coulter's *man friend* is originally from Pittsburgh, and he said since we're fellow Steeler fans, he's arranging our transportation to Virginia."

"And speaking of planes...." Jack checked her watch. "We better get going. We need to get cleaned up and get to the airport."

"Yes. We can't be late for that. I still can't believe Mrs. Coulter came to our house and practically begged to host the wedding, and I'm even more shocked your father agreed to it."

"He was probably afraid of Mrs. Coulter. She can be a little intimidating," Mollie said.

"Well, it's not every day a US Senator visits. It was more than a bit unnerving, and I did feel bad for her. I mean she does have all boys, and it was fun to plan your wedding, even if it did end in a Youtube greatest hits."

"Thanks, Mom."

"Well, last I heard, it had over a million hits."

"Ron watches it every night. I could just kill him. I mean I am so sick of watching myself hurdle that pew in that horrible purple taffeta, but on the bright side? That bell skirt was much easier to move in than those A-line dresses you first looked at. I'd had to have pulled that SOB up over my knees to have caught the little bastard. Now, that would have been humiliating."

Vickie grabbed Jack and gave her a bear hug. "I love you, crazy girl. When you get married, you will let me help, right? You're just like a daughter to me."

Humble red bloomed across Jack's cheeks. "Of course, I couldn't imagine doing it without you." She quickly turned wet eyes to Mollie. "Wow. Just think, only forty-eight hours to go, and you'll be Mollie Coulter."

Mollie squealed and rolled onto her back and kicked her legs in the air. "It just doesn't seem real. Someone pinch me."

"Let's grab these boxes and get you ready to go." Vickie gave her daughter a hand, pulling her up from the floor. "I'm so happy for you, sweetie. God bless you, and keep you this happy always."

"I just can't imagine life getting any better than this. I mean what could be better?"

Chapter 28

When Barbara Coulter's friend promised he'd take care of their flight to Virginia; Mollie never doubted him, but she never gave him enough credit either. He hadn't just scheduled them a flight; he had arranged a private jet. The inside of the jet was filled with vases of flowers. A bottle of champagne was chilling in a silver bucket of ice, a matching silver tray loaded with hors d'oeuvres sparkled next to the crystal champagne glasses, and a velvet box of chocolates had a note to Mollie attached. Mollie opened it and read the typed message, "You're sweeter. Love, Craig." Mollie smiled and held the note to her lips.

Her father rubbed a leather seat, tracing the emblem with his finger. "Steel Eagle, do you know whose company this is?"

Mollie shook her head.

"It's Max O'Leary's."

Mollie's sisters and Jack dug into the food. An attendant offered sodas and sandwiches. They ignored Doug Hinkle's lesson. He turned his attention to Mollie and Vickie. "Max O'Leary is Pittsburgh's own. He grew up right here in our downtown."

"And I see he's done well." Vickie admitted looking around at the fine leather and high gloss wood.

"Done well?" Doug laughed, "He could own this town. He is a financial genius. Every business he touches turns to gold."

"And I've never heard of him?" Vickie shook her head.

"He is the guy who finances companies. You wouldn't know him because he isn't the face of any industry. His power isn't in the physical building."

"So, he's a banker?" Vickie surmised.

"No. He's not a banker; he's a genius."

"Well, that's nice dear." Vickie patted her husband's arm and turned to Mollie. Doug looked around the jet's cabin as if he was cast into a trance. Vickie touched her daughter's arm. "You said Craig was a police officer?"

"Yeah." Mollie shrugged.

Vickie pulled Mollie close to whisper in her ear. "I know I told Mrs. Coulter she could take care of the wedding arrangements, but your dad and I only did that with the thinking that once it was all done, we'd reimburse her for the expenses."

"I don't think she expects...."

"It's our responsibility."

"So, what's wrong then?"

"What's wrong?" Vickie waved her arms pointing out the luxury that surrounded them. "What's wrong?" she sighed. "These people evidently live a much different lifestyle than we're accustomed to."

"Mr. O'Leary is his mom's boyfriend. Craig lives very simply. I've seen his house. It's really tiny and rather bare. This is an exception. Mrs. Coulter is excited." The leather seat was soft and pliable under her hand. Her face was pale. "I'm sure that's it."

"But, Mollie, this is so luxurious, my head is spinning. I think their idea of a simple affair, and our idea of simple affair, are night and day."

"Well, it's a little late to worry about it now. I mean, what do I do? Maybe his mom does have money, or maybe she's just got a lot of clout. I don't know. All I know is that tomorrow night, I'll be married to Craig, and I don't care if it's a ten dollar or ten million dollar wedding."

Vickie took a seat and fanned herself. "Oh, lord," she mumbled. Mollie poured her a glass of champagne. Her mother tipped it back and chugged it. She tried to stifle a belch, but failed. The hiccoughs

240

that followed made her giggle and relax. Doug took her hand and shook his head. Mollie joined her sisters and Jack as they buckled up, ready for take-off.

"Here I thought Ron, with his million dollar trust fund, was loaded. Looks like you might have hit the mother lode, Molls."

Mollie bit her cheek and looked out the window. Maybe Craig was just trying to impress her. It bothered her that he may be a totally different person than who she fell in love with. She suddenly wondered if she knew him well enough; if she was crazy to be marrying a complete stranger.

****

The plane touched down at the Hampton Roads Executive Airport. Waiting on the tarmac was a limousine. Leaning against the limo was Craig. His arms were crossed over his chest, and he looked perfectly at ease in this private world of luxury. Mollie swallowed her fears and smiled at her family. It was just jitters. So his family knew people. It didn't change who she knew, in her heart, Craig was.

But then, who was he? She knew he was cop from Montana, who grew up in Virginia. She knew he had a dog. She knew he graduated from college, though she didn't know where. She had to admit she didn't even know his middle name.

She took a big swallow and gripped the back of the seat. Jack squeezed her arm. "Finally realizing you're crazy?" she whispered. Mollie turned to her friend and her face said it all.

Her family was preoccupied with the search of the plane for Megan's iPod, which she was certain she left on the armrest. Mollie took the moment to ask her friend. "Am I making a mistake, Jack?"

Jack shrugged. "You seem happiest when you're with him."

"But all of this." Mollie's eyes scanned the plane.

Jack whistled low. "Sure is impressive. Lucky girl."

Mollie gripped Jack's arm' "It's not that, Jack. It proves I don't know him."

"Come on, Mollie, be honest with yourself. Him and Ron met in a private school, and Ron tells me his mother just got elected to the US Senate. The US Senate, Mollie. People like this aren't

241

working fast food. He never said he was poor. You made the assumption. I don't see why it's such a big deal."

"How will I talk to them? How will I get along with them? I mean, they may not be the fast food type, but I am. What if I'm expected to know what fork to use?"

"Just do what I do. Anywhere you go, just be cool and wait to see how other people do it. Then do what they do. I mean, hell, Mollie, if you're fast food, my family eats out of the can. Don't ever let anyone tell you you're not good enough. Understood?"

"Yeah, I guess."

"No guesses. Know it. Now get on out there. Be honest with him and tell him how you feel right now. I'm sure he'll whisper sweet nothings in your ear and make you feel better. One thing I can promise you—he does love you."

Mollie nodded and looked out the window. Craig's eyes were squinted as he tried to look into the windows of the plane. He probably wondered what was taking so long. Mollie felt a thrill run through her. She grabbed her bag and stepped past her parents and sisters and headed for the exit.

Mollie waved at him from the top of the steps. He was at the bottom in two strides lifting her from the steps as she hurried down them. He spun her round and round, his arms gripping her as if she was in a vice. He set her on the ground and kissed her, his hands cradling her face, his thumbs stroking her cheeks. "I've missed you," Craig breathed, his eyes tender, his mouth lifting in a grin.

"I missed you too. I can't believe it was only a week since I saw you. It felt like years."

"Two days, then we'll be married. Are you ready?"

Mollie nodded, her eyes glistening with tears, and her heart burning with excitement. All thoughts of not knowing him faded as she held him. His presence in her life was so natural, his touch so familiar that she couldn't believe she ever had a single doubt.

Her family joined them. Craig shook her dad's hand, nodded to her sisters, and was pulled into a hug by her mother. He then turned to Jack who he punched playfully, and admonished, "And you...a very lonely Ron will be arriving at eight tonight. I plan to send you in the limo to surprise him."

"Gee, that was…" Jack said with a blush, "…thoughtful of you."

"Hell, I'm just getting you out from under my feet for a few hours."

"Ha, ha," Jack snarled at him.

"Mr. Hinkle, if you wouldn't mind, I left my car in the lot. You guys can take the limo, but I was hoping to have a minute alone with Mollie on the drive to the house. There's a couple of things I'd like to talk to her about and I know once we get to the house, there will be no peace. I will warn you all right now, there was a surprise engagement party being prepared as I left. My mother thinks she's sneaky, but she's got nothing on this master of deception. Since Mollie and I wanted a private wedding, this is Mom's big to do. I just thought I'd warn you."

Her mother and her sisters erupted in worry for their hair, their clothes, and their make-up. Craig and Doug assured them they looked great, but they still chose to visit the private bath before leaving the airport.

Craig took Mollie's hand and led her to the car. He opened her door, but before she could get in, he pulled her close for a kiss. He held her tight, his fingers threading through her hair. "I've missed you, so much." He kissed her again. "I was going to take you today and let you pick out a ring, but I couldn't get you off my mind, so I went shopping."

"For cold cuts?" Mollie laughed.

"No, not cold cuts…for ice. And…." He fished a box out of his pocket. "My little brother, the romantic, swore all things Tiffany are perfect, so we drove up to Fairfax, and I bought you this." He took her hand and slid the diamond on her finger. Mollie admired her hand. It was a single diamond on a band of white gold.

Craig shifted nervously. "They had bigger ones, but your hands are so little. They also had fancier ones, but the jeweler promised me this stone is one carat of perfection. A flawless diamond.

Flawless, perfect, classic. That just sounded like you. But if you want...."

Craig didn't get to finish his sentence as Mollie wrapped herself around him and kissed him. "You couldn't have done any better." She started to cry.

"Well, you can still look around. I don't mind if you want to pick out your own."

"No. No." Mollie squeezed him and pressed her cheek into his chest. "I was just on the plane thinking: how well do you know me? How well do I know you?"

Craig took a sharp breath. "If you have doubts...." His eyes were clouded.

Mollie looked up at him and smiled a broad, ecstatic smile. "You know me better than any human ever has...even if it has only been six weeks. It's not logical...it's love."

Craig didn't look convinced, a muscle twitched in his jaw. Mollie smoothed it with her fingers. "I'm sorry. I didn't mean to make you worry. It was the plane, and Gary saying I'd be Cinderella and giving me a crash course in dealing with the press. I started to wonder just how much money and power your family has."

"And if they do...that would be a problem?"

Mollie shrugged and looked at her ring. "I just wondered how well I'd fit in."

Craig tipped her chin until she looked at him. "You're a perfect fit. But if it makes you feel better, I'm not rich; comfortable, but not rich. Now, Mom's friend Max? From what I hear, he's well off. My family? Yes, my mother is in politics, but no, you won't be hounded by the press. My mother has maintaining privacy down to a science. And just so you know everything, I'm going to give you a quick Coulter family history lesson. Then, you can decide if you want to swim in the gene pool."

Mollie let him take a step back as he spoke, but she held his hands in hers. He kissed her forehead as he explained, "The Coulter line first came to America with some of the first settlers, shortly after the Mayflower group. They sailed over on a ship full of men looking to make their fortunes. They tried to come ashore in the

Norfolk area and ended up, according to family lore, heading up the James River. They ran aground and ended up carrying their boat up the river into the Hampton Roads area. Evidently, they were stubborn too. Coulters have been in the area ever since, and yes, they had money."

Mollie nodded, ashamed to wonder just how wealthy. Two forks at dinner wealthy? Or just never worrying about paying the cable bill wealthy?

"But then my dad lost his share. He was a wonderful man, but a horrible businessman. He had a law firm, which was deeply in debt when he died."

"I'm so sorry, Craig. I can't believe I—"

"After Dad died, Mom took over and turned the business around, and it is now worth more than my dad ever dreamed."

"Oh. That's good."

"But that's her money. I have a savings, and I have the advantage of a well-connected family. We aren't rich, but I promise you—"

"I don't need to be rich, Craig."

"I know you don't. That's why I love you." He kissed her forehead. "But I do want to offer you everything you deserve, and that's why I wanted to talk to you. I've been made an offer, one we have to consider."

Mollie nodded, her face was solemn, but her heart soared. They were making their first *we* decision. "What is it?"

"My mother is planning to move to DC. She'll keep an apartment in Richmond, which leaves the family homestead unoccupied. She would like us to take it, live in it. I think your parents would be happy to have you on the east coast, but I wasn't sure how you felt about leaving Jack. In addition, I've also been offered the opportunity to be partners in a security business. My mother's friend has a contact who's looking for people for his business. Ever since 9-11, private security is a pretty lucrative venture."

"Would you like it?"

ELIZABETH SECKMAN

Craig thought a minute then nodded. "I think I'd like the challenge, and I'd like the opportunity to prove to myself I can be an adult."

"You're an adult."

"I've lived like a spoiled child till I was twenty-nine. I want to be proud of who I am. I want you to be proud of me."

Mollie frowned. "That's the silliest thing I've ever heard. I think you're the best. But if you want to try a business, try it. If you don't, then don't. As far as where we live, I don't care about that either, but my parents would be happier to have me close. I think your family would like it if you were around more. You could get to know your nephews better…I know I'd enjoy that."

"I would too."

"Then we agree. We'll live here. Any jobs for teachers?"

"I'm sure there are."

Mollie smiled and gave him a peck on the lips. "Looks like we have a plan."

Craig opened her door and gestured her inside. "Shall I show you your new home, my dear?"

"Of course."

As they drove, Craig told her about the security job. They would work by contract with companies and individuals to provide security for homes, offices, even electronic data.

Mollie listened, but she couldn't help but wonder about this house that would now be her home. The family homestead. Sounded quaint. Mollie waited until Craig finished his explanation of his proposed business then she asked, "So, how old is your family homestead?"

Craig thought a minute. "The foundation under the kitchen is over three hundred years old. It was burned to the ground once, then rebuilt. So, the main structure is about two hundred years, though parts have been added on over the years. It started out as a two room cabin and morphed into something a little more comfortable."

Mollie nodded and set her mind to imagining. She pictured an old house sagging on its foundation. Saw the crooked windows and amateurish add-ons sticking out from a rectangular middle. It would

246

be their home. She smiled at Craig, and he squeezed her knee then flipped on a blinker. "Well, we're here."

Mollie sat up straighter in her seat. The paved road wound up a rolling hill. They passed fields of corn and alfalfa.

"We lease the land to local farmers."

"So, all of this is yours?"

"Ours. All of it is ours. My mother bought all the adjacent land she could get her hands on. We'll have about two hundred acres and the house. Each of my brothers will get three hundred acres."

"That's a lot of land."

"This close to Norfolk, it's a gold mine. Mom bought most of it in the eighties, when it was greatly undervalued."

"Smart lady."

"That she is, but she mostly bought the land because she hates to be bothered by people."

"And she's a Senator? And plans to live in DC?"

"Ironic, huh? She'll be building herself a place on the Coulter grounds, but don't worry, it'll be at the back of the property. You'll never know when she's there. My grams will live there and hold down the fort for her between stays. You'll like Grams, she sweet and perky like you. I don't know where my mother came from."

"Sweet and perky? Oh, lord, I like to think I'm mysterious and volatile."

"Only when you're naked."

Mollie blushed and bit her lip. Craig gave her a knowing grin that made her skin heat up. "Well, we're here."

Mollie forgot her tingles as the homestead appeared. It sat like a crown at the top of the rolling hill. It was immense. The two-story plantation house was regal, though its simplicity was obvious. It was painted an immaculate white with starkly contrasting hunter green shutters and wide green double front doors. A large cut glass light hung down from the second story over the porch. Tall corrugated pillars ran across the wide front porch. Two wings branched off the main house. Mollie assumed they were the add-ons, though they looked seamlessly attached. As Craig parked the car on the circular drive in front of the house, Mollie was awed by the immaculate lawn, the concrete planters with perfectly shaped orbs of mums. Geese flapped and waddled to a pond that flanked the west side of the house. "Wow. How will we keep it all mowed?"

Craig never got to answer Mollie's question. They were both distracted by the raised voices coming from the limousine that had arrived ahead of them. Mollie heard her mother order her father to put his head between his knees. Mollie thought instantly of the worst. A heart attack? Her father was having a heart attack. Mollie took off, all thoughts of the house set aside. She brushed past Mrs. Coulter and her new boyfriend.

As Craig approached, Barbara explained to him, "Max and I wanted to greet the car. Mr. Hinkle recognized Max, and when Max told him he had read Mr. Hinkle's articles in Economics Weekly about tax cuts, and suggested he consider joining his advisory team, the man just collapsed."

Craig stood behind Mollie, allowing her space to deal with her father.

"Are you all right, Dad?" Mollie felt the panic rise in her.

"All right?" Mr. Hinkle gasped. "I'm more than all right," he whispered to Mollie, his eyes glancing quickly at Max then to his daughter. "That's Max O'Leary," Doug Hinkle said as if the elusive billionaire was a house hold name. Mollie remained unmoved. Doug grabbed his daughter by the shoulders and shook her gently as he explained, "He's a freaking billionaire, Mollie! And he's read my work."

That Mollie understood. She looked at Jack, who shrugged and wore a smile so broad, it looked painful. "Looks like you won't ever have to clip coupons."

Mollie turned and stared at Craig, her face white, and her mind reeling. Craig grabbed her by the hands and pulled her close. "I'm sorry, Mollie, I should've been more specific."

"No, no," Mollie answered. "I'm fine. I guess when you said restored farm house, I thought of a crooked building with weathered siding. When you said your mother's friend was well off, I just never imagined just how well off that could honestly be. So, just what do you mean by comfortable?"

Craig laughed, his head tipped back in the warmth of the southern September sun. "Let's just say we have enough to hire the lawn care done. I think I can come up with much better ways to keep you busy."

Epilogue

Mollie and Craig met Jack and Ron at the door. Mollie hugged her friend as if she hadn't seen her for two decades instead of two years. She didn't let go as she jumped right to the heart of the visit. "Come. Let's go look over the area by the pond. It'll be a lovely place for a wedding. You just don't know how thrilled I am to have you guys' wedding here." Mollie took her out the side door to the pond. "See, the veranda over here will be a beautiful spot for a small wedding. I would've picked this spot, but Barb had so many people on the guest list for our *small affair*, it just made more sense to have the ceremony at the cathedral in town. I'm still amazed she got that together so quickly."

"Did your dad ever get over the chest pains of the wedding bill?"

"Working for Max, he has plenty of money to reimburse Barb, but she still won't take it."

"Couldn't have happened to a better guy."

"And he said he will be insulted if you don't let him invest in your restaurant."

"I haven't even found a location yet."

"Anywhere within twenty minutes of me is fine. I've missed you!"

"I've missed you too." She touched Mollie's arm. "Is everything okay? You look tired and a little thin."

Mollie ignored her and turned her attention to the pond. "If we string twinkly lights from the trees."

"Mollie, what's wrong...what are you hiding?"

"I'm not hiding anything."

"Mollie."

"It's nothing. We'll discuss it after the wedding."

Tears welled in Jack's eyes. "Oh. No. Don't tell me...."

Mollie grabbed Jack's arm and gave it a squeeze. "No, no. It's not what you think. Fine I'll tell you. I wasn't going to say anything because this is your time to shine. But...." Mollie grinned and rubbed her tummy. "I'm pregnant, and you know all that crap about glowing and blooming? All lies. It's vomiting and nausea. Acne and dry skin at the same time. But I'm not complaining...I'm going to be a mommy!"

Jack squealed and grabbed her friend for a hug. "You bad girl, keeping me in the dark."

"We wanted to be sure everything was all right."

"Well, is it?"

Mollie nodded. "We just got the amnio results last week. They're healthy and growing just fine."

"*They?*"

Mollie nodded. "They. Twins. Two little girls. Craig is so thrilled...and scared. He's going to have girls. He swears he's going to lock them in their rooms until they're thirty."

"Oh, I'm soo happy for you."

"Me too, I'm thrilled for me! Now you and Ron will be living in the neighborhood, and you'll be able to help me. Well, when you can. I know you'll be busy with the new restaurant."

"I'm never too busy to hang out with my best friend...and my new nieces."

"Nieces?" Craig came up behind Mollie and kissed her neck. "I'll have to run a security check on you before I let you near my babies. It's going to be the normal protocol for anyone within twenty yards of them."

Mollie patted his cheek and looked back at him. "You're insane, my love."

"Babies?" Ron asked with a grin. Jack nodded. "See buddy? See? You know, you never thanked me for throwing you that birthday party. I do believe the only thanks I ever got was an ass chewin'."

Craig rested his chin on Mollie's shoulder. "Thank you, Ron."

"Now, might I suggest Roni is a lovely little girl's name?"

Their laughter rolled off the fertile hills, moving softly into the sultry summer air like fireflies sparking in the darkening sky.

About the Author

Elizabeth divides her time between her beach cottage and her scrupulously clean house in the hills of West Virginia. Ooops. That's fantasy Elizabeth. The real Elizabeth spends her days schlepping after her four boys (five if you count their father) and the assortment of pets they swore they'd take care of.

She does live in West Virginia; the house is clean when the mother-in-law visits; and she does have serious dreams of living at the beach.

Elizabeth is a Marshall University graduate with a degree in counseling. This has proven very beneficial when dealing with the make-believe friends she hangs out with all day (she calls this 'writing').

Follow her blog at: http://www.eseckman.blogspot.com

Before You Go...

Share your voice and help guide other readers to these wonderful books. Even if it's only a line or two your reviews help readers discover the author's books so they can continue creating stories that you'll love. Login and leave a review.